THE LONG WEEKEND

New York, 1961. A group of old friends, who knew each other during the war, are reunited. They are all, in their different ways, involved in the arts. But when the Hollywood big-shot turns up, full of his success, the others start to ponder what they've accomplished – or haven't. Ultimately they come to the realization that you can never give up on your dreams. Without dreams, nothing is left...

Julie Ellis titles available from
Severn House Large Print

Desperate Journey
Somers v. Somers
On the Outside Looking In
A New Day Dawning
Silent Rage
Dark Legacy
A Turn in the Road
When Tomorrow Comes

THE LONG WEEKEND

Julie Ellis

Severn House Large Print
London & New York

This first large print edition published 2010
in Great Britain and the USA by
SEVERN HOUSE PUBLISHERS LTD of
9-15 High Street, Sutton, Surrey, SM1 1DF.
First world regular print edition published 2008 by
Severn House Publishers Ltd., London and New York.

British Library Cataloguing in Publication Data

Ellis, Julie, 1933-
  The long weekend.
  1. Success--Fiction. 2. Reunions--New York (State)--New
  York--Fiction. 3. Large type books.
  I. Title
  813.5'4-dc22

ISBN-13: 978-0-7278-7900-4

Except where actual historical events and characters are being
described for the storyline of this novel, all situations in this
publication are fictitious and any resemblance to living persons is
purely coincidental.

Severn House Publishers support The Forest Stewardship Council
[FSC], the leading international forest certification organisation. All
our titles that are printed on Greenpeace-approved FSC-certified paper
carry the FSC logo.

Mixed Sources
Product group from well-managed
forests and other controlled sources
www.fsc.org Cert no. SA COC 1565
© 1996 Forest Stewardship Council

Printed and bound in Great Britain by the
MPG Books Group, Bodmin, Cornwall.

One

New York City.
Friday, October 20, 1961

Holly stirred without opening her eyes. Short dark hair fanned about the pillow, her small, slender frame in the fetal position. Morning sounds trickled in around her. Buses and truck traffic rumbled along eighteen floors below – on Second Avenue. The eerie siren of a police emergency car wailed ominously on a trek downtown.

In the corridor outside the Rogers' apartment a tenant shut the incinerator with a discordant, morning-angry thud. Cans rattled down the dark tunnel to the basement in noisy complaint. Holly winced. Must the idiot do that at seven thirty in the morning?

Holly heard Al moving about in the galley kitchen – a replica of almost all kitchens in Manhattan's so-called 'luxury apartments'. He'd put up coffee. The pungent aroma drifted in to her now on the convertible sofa where she and Al slept.

Don't get up yet. Delicious, these last few minutes under the covers – while the heat hums in the radiators and coffee perks in the kitchen.

Al turned on the kitchen radio. Holly frowned. She wasn't ready yet to hear about more airplane hijackings, more nuclear threats, more American soldiers going to South Vietnam to train troops in counter-guerrilla warfare. In her mind she heard Al's rantings last evening when they'd watched the evening's TV news:

'Hell, that's the first step – sending those guys to South Vietnam. We're going to be dragged into a war that nobody can win! We had to fight in World War II – we were attacked.'

Only quietness from the bedroom, Holly noted. Thank God, Jonny was on a sleeping-late routine again. Four mornings in a row – that established a new pattern.

Damn! The demolition squad across the street was starting up already. Why couldn't they wait at least another half-hour? It was indecent to be jarred into wakefulness this way. But it wouldn't disturb Jonny. Ever since he was born – almost fourteen months ago – a building had been coming down or going up around them.

'Fucking bottle—' Al swore in conjunction with the slamming of Jonny's morning bottle against a side of the sink.

Al was in a bitchy mood. What else should she expect? Why did Ron have to pop into town three days ago? They lived on such a tightrope as it was – always fighting to keep their balance. It hurt to see the anguish on Al's face when he walked into the apartment after running into Ron that way. Naked desperation in his eyes.

He'd paced up and down their assembly-line living-room-dining area that seemed too small to

6

hold him.

'I'm standing there trying to sell a shirt to this nutty broad, and I look up – and there's Ron. He nearly fell on his face – seeing me behind a counter selling shirts in a department store!' Resorting to an air of amusement to masquerade his desiccated pride. 'I hadn't seen him since the last time we were on the Coast.'

'What was he doing in the store?' She'd tried to sound casual – as though she didn't know Al was falling apart inside. She'd never met Ron – yet it was as though she'd known him for years. The others in their tight little circle had a way of bringing him into their conversation at intervals through the years. Ron Andrews, Hollywood screenwriter, was the success symbol among them. Once it had been Al.

'You'd think he'd be too involved with the play to think of shopping in a department store.' Al brought her back to the moment. 'My God, it goes into rehearsal any minute.' Ron's play coming to Broadway. Al's rotted in a desk drawer, along with the outline and half a dozen chapters of the novel that he'd been struggling to find time to write for the last four years.

Al wasn't envious of Ron. He was furious at himself – for striking out time after time. So few people understood Al. They saw the magnetic personality that belonged to a superb con man or a showbiz entrepreneur. Bitterness had blurred the image these last few years.

People – particularly women – still admired his rugged good looks, the firm muscular body that belied his forty-six years. Few recognized the inner sensitivity that hid behind bluster – and sometimes braggadocio. The crusading spirit that ached to put his thoughts into words.

Why couldn't she have found words to answer him last night? She'd felt so helpless. But she had answered in bed. In her he knew he was a man. It was satisfying to realize that after all these years she could arouse more than a mechanical sexual interest in her husband. Al said once that she could have made a mint as a call girl. He took pride in that. Knowing it all belonged to him.

'You're young, Holly. Thirty-five. I'm forty-six!' he'd ranted last night while the roast grew cold on the table. Correction – he'd be forty-six tomorrow, though she wasn't calling this a last-minute birthday party. It was a reunion – with Ron their guest of honor. 'Where am I? What have I got to show for the years? How can a man live this way?' But most of the world lived this way.

It was not enough to say, 'You have a son – we've built a marriage.' Not to a man with Al's creative potential. Deep within she knew it wasn't enough for either of them. Knew, was frightened – and dug her head into the sand of reality.

All right, this was their way of life. For a while it had to suffice. For a *while*. For Jonny they must provide security. Did Al think she enjoyed the deadly monotony of caring for the apart-ment, sitting in the park with the baby, spending hours each day at the typewriter – grabbing them as she could – to knock off a scheduled number of pages a day to meet her deadlines?

In a perverse way Al resented this, too. Because in writing sexy paperbacks she was earning far more than he, and this hurt his pride. Even though he derided the sexy paperbacks that kept them afloat. Without her checks they'd be living in some ghastly slum, fighting to keep food on the table.

Al walked into the dining area now, catapulting her into the present.

'You know, Holly, we're cracked.' His voice wore a lining of tension. 'I should have contacted Ron long ago.' He was digging into the buffet that doubled as a dresser for a shirt. 'With Ron's contacts he could have steered you back into television.'

'Al, don't get on that kick again!' *Doesn't he realize by now how I feel about that era of our lives?*

'Hell, I wish I could write to order.' Al's face tightened. This was much-covered ground. 'I wouldn't tie myself down to penny-ante shit. There're big bucks out there for those who can.'

'I have a steady market,' Holly shot back. Again.

When they'd hit rock bottom and Al seemed not to know where to head next – after twice being on the threshold of a Broadway production – she'd explored writing markets. For a while they'd existed on her sales to the confessions market and the men's magazines – then she'd discovered the paperback sexy romances, aimed for a men's readership. Not pornography, she'd assured Al. Her publisher was canny – he knew just how far they could go with impunity. But she understood Al's alarm – they'd been hard hit by McCarthyism.

And then Al capitulated, went after a sales job in the department store.

They couldn't exist on what he earned – but she wasn't trying to shove the sex-book market down his throat. She knew he couldn't sit down and grind that out. He had to be excited about what he wrote – or he wrote not at all. But her checks came in regularly – and the banks asked no questions.

Like herself, Al had switched from plays to novels – if anyone could call her soft-core porn 'novels', she thought in gentle derision. If Al made it as a novelist, he'd make it big. But now a disquieting realization sprang alive in her. Until now – this minute – it was always 'when Al makes it'. Were doubts breaking through?

Al frowned, fingering the collar of the shirt he'd pulled out of a drawer.

'Bastard laundry's starching the collars again.'

'I'll chew them out,' she promised. No starch. Al needed a scapegoat this morning.

He walked to the bedroom door, peered inside.

'Little monster's still asleep,' he announced with a mixture of relish and regret. 'Likes having the bedroom to himself.'

'I'm glad you finally accepted the inevitable.' She laughed. This was safe ground. 'I told you some night he'd wake up at the wrong moment.'

Al grinned, remembering how Jonny had pounded on the crib rail at the height of their lovemaking. Al swore – but in seconds he was off the bed, sauntering towards the kitchenette to make up the midnight bottle that now was a rarity. Astonishing, that such tenderness could mingle with vexation at being frustrated at the height of their amorous mood. The next morning he'd capitulated. They forsook the double bed in the master bedroom for the convertible sofa in the living room.

Pulling on his shirt, Al headed back for the kitchenette.

'I'll stick a bottle in hot water. Maybe he'll wake before I leave.'

With Jonny sleeping late Al missed the morning hi-jinks with him. Sometimes – even now – it astonished her that Al and she were parents. She'd never suspected that she could be so intensely maternal. Sometimes – looking at Jonny – she could feel her stomach tighten in apprehension. So small, so vulnerable. So much he would need from them.

A thud at the apartment door startled her. The *Times* arriving. When was she going to stop the morbid habit of rushing to read the obituaries? It was neurotic to be concerned about the ages of people who died. Because of Jonny she did this.

Al was coming towards her – a mug of coffee in tow. She looked forward to coffee in bed. A moment of sybaritic luxury before a harried day.

'Sure you want this?' Al joshed. Had he miraculously made peace with himself? No, this was the calm before the hurricane. 'You look wide awake to me. Woke you up last night, didn't I?' He grinned complacently.

'Stop boasting,' she jibed, struggled into a

11

sitting position. 'Coffee, if you expect me to get vertical—' She reached for the mug.

'I might just crawl back into bed with you. You're not bad for an old bat.' He was girding himself for the dinner party tomorrow night. Would the others feel this way, too? 'Screw their three-for-ten-bucks special today.'

Holly grimaced – her mind racing ahead. 'This is going to be a wild day for me—'

'A bastard of a day at the store, too.' Al's attempt at a show of good spirits evaporated. 'I know what I'm going to find this morning. The bums working last night won't have done a thing about the sales tables. All they know is to bitch. Nobody wants to work – they just want to collect salaries.' Al headed back towards the kitchenette. 'Have you rounded up everybody?' He paused en route to scrounge for a tie in the buffet.

'Everybody's set except Eric. I've left messages around town where I thought he might be checking in. I told you about Norm – he has a shortage of help at the store. He can't make it.' Norm – who should have been the next Paul Muni – had given up the fight. He'd married a girl they'd met once years ago – and joined his father-in-law in running an appliance store. Now the store was his – and his dreams long dead. Holly kept her voice low – maybe Jonny would sleep a while longer. Provide a little extra working time for her. 'I have to run over to the stores to see about dishes – unless I borrow them from Betty.'

'Buy them!' Al's voice held an undercurrent of

truculence. 'Over two hundred and a quarter for this crummy dive – you can throw away thirty on dishes!'

Why couldn't Al stop ranting about the rent? Everybody in New York was caught in this rat race. Betty had mentioned what she called her 'dinner-party set' – used once a year. Borrow hers – when would they need a service for twelve again?

How could they seriously consider Al's most recent flight into fantasy? A house in the country, where he could cut himself off from everything except writing.

'You don't have to be in Manhattan to write. You can do it anywhere. Without this crazy rent we could survive on your checks.'

How could he expect her to go along with such impracticality? They were just now getting themselves out of hock. They had some measure of security. As long as they both worked, they had security. And her market might collapse overnight. Al's job was reality.

If he walked out now, where would he get another any less repulsive? Face it – Al was forty-six, with no real job training. With a mental block against adapting to hack writing. At this point in his life he wasn't going to try the agent role again.

He fumbled in a drawer for a cigarette to go with his own coffee. Cigarette in hand, he sat down at the edge of the opened-up sofa. He kept vowing to stop smoking – but this wasn't the time to push for that.

'I have this weird feeling – the clan gathering

13

together this way.' He found a match, lit the cigarette. 'It makes the years smack you right between the eyes.' His face wore a look of baffled frustration. 'You don't have to worry – you're still a kid.' From Al's viewpoint she was a kid.

'How long since you've seen Ron?' In a corner of her mind she remembered Al telling her that just a few minutes ago.

'You know – the last time we were on the Coast. Before that, it must have been ten years. Ron was anxious to meet some broad I knew then – to promote money for a Broadway play. Ron always knew how to promote.'

'So did you,' Holly flashed back. But that belonged to another era.

'No more. I lost it, baby.' He looked tired. Not work tired. Frustration tired. 'You have to give Ron credit – he's got drive.' A flicker of amusement sneaked through. 'Did I ever tell you how he got through college?'

'No.' He'd told her much about Ron – but not that.

'Ron latched on to this middle-aged lawyer with a wife and three kids. The lawyer had a thing for good-looking boys. Ron was nineteen. He met the lawyer at some gay party he went to for kicks. So Ron took care of the lawyer's extramarital sex life, and the lawyer took care of Ron's college expenses. I suppose the lawyer wasn't really middle-aged. It seemed so then.' Al rose, ditched the cigarette. 'The little creep won't see his old man this morning.' He kissed her briskly, returned to poke his head into the

14

bedroom for a final look at Jonny. 'Good-look-ing little bastard,' he said with relish, headed for the foyer closet to collect his jacket. 'I'll call you later.'

Two

Seconds after Al left, the phone rang. Holly hurried to pick it up before Jonny was awakened.

'You're really going ahead with the dinner party?' Claire's voice – with the perpetual tiredness Holly had come to expect.

'Sure we're going ahead. Why wouldn't we?' Holly settled herself in the charcoal club chair. It should be relegated to the Salvation Army, she thought. 'You know we have practically no social life these days.' In lousy moods, Al belly-ached about the time she spent on the phone – but this was her major contact with people.

She listened to Claire with half her mind – the other half concerned with Al. It was going to be tough – tomorrow night – for Al to sit back, listen to the glossy reports of Ron's success. She'd been relieved when Al had dismissed thoughts of a Broadway production – even an Off-Broadway production. He'd insisted he found the switch from plays to novels exhilarat-ing.

15

'With novels you need nobody except your-self,' he'd said with an air of triumph.

'And a publisher,' she'd reminded.

'No producers, no backers, no stars!' he'd shot back. 'How many plays get produced each year? Thousands of novels are published.'

But what time could he salvage for writing, the way he was always grasping for overtime? What place – in a baby-oriented apartment? Not like her book-by-the-numbers output. Al was intent on serious writing. She worked wherever she could set up her typewriter.

'My mother's decided she won't sit for us tomorrow,' Claire reported. 'I may have to come alone. She's on one of her kicks again—"I've raised my kids, now you raise yours." But Mom's great most of the time,' Claire hastened to point out. 'I thank God for every minute she's alive.'

'It'll be a shame if Bernie can't make it.'

Holly's eyes grazed the current issue of the *Village Voice* that lay across an end table. She'd have to stop stalling, place an ad for part-time help. Somebody warm and understanding with kids – and to keep the house in livable condition. Al was impatient sometimes about how the apartment looked – but she couldn't divide herself into twins. Having a woman in wouldn't be depriving Jonny – she'd still be with him most of the time. So she'd squeeze in an extra manuscript at intervals to cover the cost.

'Where are you putting everybody?' Claire demanded. 'I think you're out of your mind – and on such short notice!'

'We'll manage,' Holly insisted, staving off a flutter of panic as she considered the guest list. Al and herself, Wendy and Jerry, Claire and possibly Bernie, Linda and her current boyfriend, Eric if she could locate him, Mitch – and Ron. Ron's wife – the third – was still on the Coast, closing up their house out there. Al said Ron was renting a house in Chappaqua – on the strength of the play's being a hit. God, to have that kind of confidence!

'You know how long it's been since I've seen any of the old group – except you?' Claire asked. 'It scares the hell out of me, the way time passes.'

'Oh, Lord!' Holly recalled with a rush of guilt. 'I forgot to call my mother last night!' That had never happened since her father died eleven years ago.

'So she'll survive,' Claire said drily. 'You'd be surprised what she'd do if she had to.'

'She must have flipped last night.' Holly sighed. 'I can be logical about almost anything except her.'

'You spoil her rotten,' Claire said bluntly.

'What else can I do? She's the way she is.' Jonny's arrival had been a real blow. A wry smile touched her face – Al said with his characteristic candor that her mother resented being replaced.

'It's going to be fabulous to see Ron after all these years.' An electric anticipation colored Claire's voice. 'After this weekend, I swear – I'm going on a real crash diet. I can't stand myself any more.' A new quality came into her

17

voice. 'I ever tell you I had a mad crush on Ron once? At a party he finally made a pass. I nearly flipped. But I was too scared in those days to lift my skirt for anybody.'

'What about now?' Holly jibed humorously. Claire was still attractive at forty-one – when you looked past the extra weight, the tiredness that was psychosomatic. Why did Claire let herself go? That beautiful, near-black hair always used to be freshly done. She never used to walk around devoid of make-up.

'Who's got the energy to climb into stray beds? That's the suburban, the small-town scene. City wives don't have time for infidelity. Besides, you know – Bernie and I have a sensational sex life.' Claire was proud of that, after the rotten first marriage. 'But I'm amazed that Ron's bothering with us.' A self-conscious note colored her voice. 'He moves in another world now. No matter how Bernie breaks his neck, we both know he'll never hit over eighteen thousand a year. And my mother can't understand why I'm pissing up a storm about going back to work.'

'Fifteen years ago that sounded like a fortune.'

'We live in a different world from fifteen years ago,' Claire said defensively. 'Ron probably pays more than that in income tax. Oh, hell – I'd better go to Cindy. She's got the water running in the tub. That could mean another flood!'

While Holly was putting the sofa back into its daytime form, Jonny made his first overtures to breakfast. Holly raced into the kitchen for the bottle. Those first few minutes when Jonny

18

woke up were lovely. He was such a happy baby.

Give Jonny his bottle, change him, transfer him to the playpen. With luck she could sit down at the desk beside him and work for an hour. Thank God, he was willing to wait that hour for breakfast. But by the time he had finished his bottle, was changed and transferred to the playpen, the phone rang again.

'Hello—' Why had she answered? She needed this hour!

'Hi, darling. Feel like company for lunch?' Wendy's voice came blithely over the phone.

'Great!' Hearing the effervescence in Wendy's voice shot her back through the years. Wendy – who used to be a double for Rita Hayworth, in her prime. The auburn hair gone to gray at thirty-eight – and she wouldn't bother to color it, the sexy body girdled in a losing fight against overweight. How wrong, that nothing remained of gorgeous Wendy Meadows but the effervescent voice. 'Come over early,' Holly urged, brushed with nostalgia, pushing away guilt at cutting out from work. The young years – the years of coming into adulthood – were the ones that were indelibly stamped in your consciousness.

'I'll have to stop by the employment agency on my way in. It's back to the salt mines again.' Her voice was wry. 'I'm nuts to think we can manage if I don't work. We don't live in that kind of world.' She sighed. 'Eleanor Roosevelt said years ago that we live in a "two-pocketbook world" – it takes two incomes for a family to survive.'

'Oh, Wendy—' Holly knew how Wendy loathed that sweatshop typing she did – but it was the only kind of job where they put up with her recurrent swatches of absenteeism. The motherhood problem.

'The kid's birthday is coming up – I've promised her a party. She hasn't had a splashy one in three years.'

'Wendy, a party for a thirteen-year-old doesn't have to be a catered affair!' Why must Wendy have this compulsion that everything must be expensive where Carol was concerned?

'I'm running into a stinking situation with the party—' Wendy paused. 'There's this little girl in the apartment below us. She and Carol are real close.' Wendy took a deep breath. 'But Melinda's colored.'

Holly tightened in shock. Just yesterday they'd talked with such admiration for the dedicated Freedom Riders – some of them white college students – who were fighting so zealously for civil rights for Negroes. Both she and Wendy were horrified by the violence they encountered. 'So what, Wendy?'

'It's creating racial tensions right in my neighborhood.' Wendy was grim. 'Two mothers buzzed me. "You're not having Melinda, are you?" The kids are beginning to date. These creeps are worried about interracial dating. Up till Melinda's family moved in, the neighborhood was lily-white.'

'They're disgusting!' Holly blazed.

'We have to live with them,' Wendy said unhappily. 'The parents, I mean—'

20

'Why don't you make it an all-girl luncheon?' Holly suggested.

'Can't.' Wendy dismissed this with finality. 'Carol would be miserable – she says it's no fun having a party without boys.' Meaning, Wendy had discussed this with Carol. 'You know – she's at that age.'

'What are you going to do?' Wendy couldn't *not* invite that child.

'I'm not going to worry about it today,' Wendy said with a firm note of dismissal. 'Today I line up a job, come over to see you. Tomorrow I'm coming over to the dinner party. I'll worry Sunday. But let me get off the phone – if we sit here yakking, I'll never get over.'

Holly put the phone back in place. Ron Andrews' coming into their lives this way had thrown her – disconcertingly – into the past. Usually those early years – when she had first met Al and Wendy and the others – seemed a lifetime away. Now she could reach out and touch them. She had never known Ron herself – he'd disappeared from their group just as she arrived – but he had always been there, touching them.

How old had she been when she first met Wendy? Seventeen, lying herself into nineteen. What a nutty kid she had been. The frenzied rush to finish high school in three years, with inchoate fantasies of college – when she should have known it was financially impossible. Three weeks after her graduation she and her parents were on a Greyhound bus bound for New York.

Poor Dad, with high hopes of hitting a jackpot

– in a year when everybody was making money, except those in the armed forces. In some ways he was like Al – always ahead of his time. By August of that year, she was working – bringing home a paycheck to that drab Queens apartment. Wendy had been working in the same office for almost a year...

Three

Late August, 1943

Holly stood before the mirror in the company Ladies' Room – freshening her make-up before leaving the office. Wendy hurried in with an air of relief that the business day was over, fussed with her hair for a moment, then turned to Holly.

'Busy tonight? Have a cheap Chinese dinner with me?'

'Sure.' Holly glowed in anticipation, brushed aside the truant reminder that her mother would be furious when she phoned to say she was having dinner with a girl who worked in the office. But she was lonely in New York – knowing no one. And Wendy was so friendly.

'I've traveled to the Bronx straight from work for three weeks in a row – I'm ready to blow a gasket,' Wendy said frankly. 'Mom knows I'm trying like crazy to take off ten pounds, but what does she do? Shoves everything at me that I shouldn't eat. Besides, I go stir crazy in the apartment—' Her eyes darkened in discontent. 'Before the fellows got themselves drafted or enlisted, everything was so different.'

'I know,' Holly said. Not knowing at all. There had been no boys in her life – though there had been flattering overtures. Her parents had insisted she was 'too young for that craziness'.

'I remember when it was an absolute disgrace not to have a Saturday night date,' Wendy said and giggled. 'Now it's a miracle to have one. Who's left around town?'

Holly made a nervous, self-conscious phone call home. Her mother was shocked at her staying in the city after work. Annoyed. But she hadn't argued. In a corner of her mind Holly understood. Every week she brought home her paycheck. Mom gave her money for the subway and a cheap lunch. The family needed that check for survival.

Holly ached to be part of the world she read about in a small show-business weekly. She'd been enthralled when her parents decided to move to New York. Here was the Broadway theater – but she was an outsider, knowing no one. Ever since the third grade, she remembered, she'd been writing stories or plays. English teachers in high school had been encouraging – but here in the center of theater and publishing she felt adrift in a boat without oars.

'OK, let's get this show on the road,' Wendy interrupted her introspection.

Holly and Wendy left the office, joined the crowd waiting for a down elevator. The conversation noisy. Everyone seeming to relish the release from obligatory jobs, swapping cracks with the elevator operator as they crowded inside with a sense of freedom.

At capacity now the elevator zoomed down to the lobby. The pressed-together humanity dislodged itself, moved out into the twilight of Broadway. The home-going rush was in full force – people pushing towards the subways, buses, here and there trying to nab an elusive taxi. The cafeterias were crowding up rapidly, the Automat a carbon copy of the subway crush. If it wasn't for the brown-out, Holly thought, nobody would remember there was a war on.

Wendy prodded her towards the west side of Forty-Fifth Street, off Broadway. 'I hope you like Chinese. I always eat Chinese when I'm hungry and almost broke – which is always,' Wendy admitted with an air of levity. 'Where else can you eat for twenty-five cents?'

'I've never had Chinese.' She'd heard the other typists and stenographers talk about the neighborhood Chinese restaurants. So many things she hadn't tried, Holly thought, pleased with the prospect of adventure – even minute. 'But I'm willing—'

'Here's the place.' Wendy walked down the two steps, swung open a door. The restaurant was small, dimly lit, with most of the booths filled with young people like themselves – most of them girls in pairs or trios. 'Let's go on in the back – we'll find a spot.'

They settled themselves in a table at the rear. Holly inspected the room with voracious curiosity. The tablecloths were thin from frequent washings, the upholstery frayed – but the atmosphere was friendly, welcoming. A smiling Chinese waiter brought them menus, and for the next few minutes they devoted themselves to choosing.

Holly and Wendy shared steaming tureens of chow mein and chop suey, then focused on almond cookies and small, earless cups of tea. All at once Wendy squealed with delight. A lanky, army-uniformed figure was sweeping between rows of tables – obviously searching for someone.

'Mitch! Back here!'

He hurried to their table, swooped down to kiss Wendy on the mouth.

'Had a hunch I'd find you here.' Mitch grinned in high good humor. 'Your office was closed. You weren't at the cafeteria or the drugstore.'

'A lucky hunch. Most nights now I'd be on my way to the Bronx. When did you blow into town?' Wendy pulled him down beside her, face aglow.

'About three hours ago. On a forty-eight-hour pass. I'm still stationed in New Jersey.' He held up crossed fingers. A corporal, Holly noted from the stripes on his uniform. Not handsome but nice. Irregular features, hair that looked as though it were debating about taking leave of its owner, the lanky body associated with movie cowboys. 'What do you hear from Al? Still in the States?'

'He's still sunning himself in Florida. He said something in his last letter about a possible

25

transfer up here. Wouldn't that be something?' Wendy smiled fondly at Mitch – a hand clasping one of his. 'Almost like old times.'

'I'd love to see the old son-of-a-bitch,' Mitch said.

'Gosh, I'm rude,' Wendy apologized. 'Holly, this character is Mitch Garrison. The baby is Holly Woodridge.'

Mitch studied Holly with a thoroughness that made her self-conscious yet without angering her. 'Pretty baby,' he commented. He turned back to Wendy. 'How about getting out of here and going some place we can relax? Steve gave me the key to his apartment – I'm bunking there while I'm in town. We could pick up a bottle of wine and go up there. Steve would love to see you. Hell, it's a damn long time since we had a real brawl.'

'Sounds great.' Wendy exuded pleasure. 'What do you say, Holly?'

'Sure.' Holly managed an air of nonchalance, though the mention of the bottle had touched off a vague alarm in her. But Wendy thought it was OK.

Holly and Wendy paid their checks. Mitch took each girl by an arm, and the three of them – wallowing in high spirits – moved out into the humid August night. They made a swift visit to the liquor store two doors down, then Mitch flagged down a cab. Inside the cab, Mitch settled himself between Wendy and Holly. He kept up a barrage of mildly profane gossip that – at first – startled Holly. Mitch kept Wendy's hand tightly in his, and Holly was aware that one leg rested snugly against Wendy's. Holly enjoyed the frank, sensual pleasure the other two were finding in each other. To her it was new and refreshing.

The cab swung north on Eighth Avenue, cut through Columbus Circle with its soapbox oratory already well launched for the evening. Past the Circle, up Broadway into an area unfamiliar to Holly. West in the mid-Seventies, then halting before a high-stooped brownstone.

Steve's apartment was a typical West Side furnished studio. A studio couch and two easy chairs flanked one wall, with a Village Art Show painting hanging over the couch. A coffee table, chest of drawers, a small dinette table – all in typical maple. The kitchenette hid behind Venetian blinds. The girls collapsed into comfortable positions on the studio couch. Whistling, Mitch went into action with wine bottle and glasses.

Wendy leaned over to fiddle with the radio. Somebody – Holly thought it was Helen O'Connell – was singing 'I'll Never Smile Again', and Wendy hummed along. Now she learned that Mitch – before being drafted – had worked as a small-time music arranger but was sure he'd be another Cole Porter – 'with a little luck'. Wendy had tried – for the brief two years since high school – to launch a singing career.

Holly relaxed against a pillow, feeling a wistful envy for the way Wendy accepted Mitch's easy affection, the way she wandered over now for a casual kiss as he held out two wine glasses, purple with port. Holly leaned forward to accept a glass. Wendy sipped at her wine, then momen-

27

tarily abandoned it to dance with Mitch.

Holly started at a sharp banging on the door that brought a whoop of anticipation from Mitch.

'Steve,' Mitch announced and raced to open the door.

Steve rushed in amid an exuberant exchange of greetings, introductions. Laughter, music, high good humor blended into a convivial medley. To the lilting tones of 'That Old Black Magic', 'You'll Never Know', then the hopeful 'Comin' in on a Wing and a Prayer', Holly danced with Steve, then with Mitch, back to Steve again. Back home she'd danced only with other girls – in the high-school gym.

'Hey, I don't know about you characters, but I'm starving,' Mitch announced. 'You know what GI shit tastes like! How about a load of good old New York delicatessen? On me.' He grinned and pulled out his wallet. 'I did good in a crap game last night.'

'So let's go shop.' Wendy's eyes were luminous with anticipation. She turned to Holly and Steve. 'Don't drink up all the port,' she warned. 'The delicatessen I remember is four blocks away.'

'Wait, this is my party,' Steve objected, going over to haggle with Mitch. 'Come on, keep your frigging army pay. Let a defense worker shell out.'

While Steve and Mitch argued good-humoredly, Wendy explained that Steve gave up chasing after acting jobs when shipyard jobs started popping up. But he'd had a small part in a road-company production of *Oklahoma*, she added with deep respect.

Holly sat on the couch with an uneasy smile on her face. She was tense at the prospect of being alone in the apartment with Steve. What would they talk about? Was he annoyed at being left alone with her?

Churning with nervous anxiety, she launched into a recital of her first reactions to New York. Steve was amused. It wasn't so awful, she decided minutes later.

'New York's pretty sensational.' Steve poured himself a fresh drink. 'I'd sure as hell hate to leave – for more reasons than one,' he admitted with a chuckle. 'That job out at the shipyards is the best way I know to stay.' But he sounded guilty at not being in military service, Holly thought.

Now she learned that Al Rogers had been an entertainment field agent.

'Al did some writing, too—' Steve continued. Holly listened avidly. 'He's had a few short stories published – in literary magazines that pay peanuts. He even had a play produced by some experimental group. I hear it was good – but the producers were short on cash – it lasted four nights, until their money ran out.'

Steve told her how Al had gathered a clique around him – most of them a few years younger than himself – who looked upon him as their road to success.

'Al was the agent who was going to sell us into big time,' Steve said, his smile wry.

All with dreams, Holly thought, that were

interrupted on December 7, 1941.

'Hell,' Steve mused, 'all of a sudden there were real jobs out there – with real salaries. For those of us who could manage to avoid the draft.'

Twenty minutes later they heard Wendy's laughter blending with Mitch's as Mitch struggled with the key in the lock. The door swung open. Wendy's hair was disheveled, though there had been not a whisper of wind out tonight. Her lipstick was a pale blur. A smudge of bright color trailed across Mitch's jaw.

Holly slid to her feet, hurried to help Wendy with the sandwich makings. The four of them sat down with platters of towering sandwiches before them. The aroma of fresh coffee perking blended with the pungent spice scents of corned beef and pastrami, pickles and fresh rye.

Holly marveled at the capacity of Mitch and Steve – both for solid and liquid refreshment. They were not kids, she decided in respect – both Mitch and Steve must be at least twenty-three or twenty-four.

'Mitch, it's past eleven!' Wendy was shocked. 'I have almost an hour on the IRT. Holly goes out to Queens. Then the same old ride back in the morning.' Wendy shuddered expressively. 'You two characters walk us to the subway.'

They went out into the still well-traveled street, walked towards Broadway. Four high-spirited young people determined to find the world a good place in which to live – at least for the moment. Holly tried not to worry about her mother's reaction to her being out so late.

Here and there occupants of brownstones sought respite from the August humidity on a stoop. The night brigade of dog-walkers strolled along the curbs. Other couples like themselves making the most of the evening. An older pair – gone to fat and bickering because he had over-tipped a waiter. But there was an atmosphere of life being lived that Holly found exhilarating.

Mitch and Steve deposited light kisses on both girls' mouths, and then Holly was trailing Wendy into the depths of the IRT.

It had taken Wendy and Holly nine weeks longer to make their glorious escape from parental apartments into an apartment of their own. A miracle, too, to find an apartment that autumn of 1943. A friend of Steve's got drafted – he grabbed the apartment for them. With the proviso that – once the bloody war was over and he came home – they would relinquish it to him. That was how it began – the transformation of Holly's life.

Four

Holly was caught up in nostalgic recall. What would have happened if she hadn't worked in the same office as Wendy? Life goes along on its familiar pattern – and then one day the pattern shifts – and your life is transformed.

That furnished apartment – in a rundown brownstone in the West Seventies between West End and Riverside – had seemed magnificent. She and Wendy saw none of the shabbiness, the worn upholstery, the faded drapes, the antique kitchenette appliances. The refrigerator must have been the first GE ever made. To them the apartment was Old World Charm.

Eighteen years ago she and Wendy tossed their first party in the apartment. She closed her eyes – feeling herself there right this minute. The large, square somber wood-paneled walls, the closed-up fireplace flanked by built-in bookcases, the bay window jutting out into the yard, the minuscule bedroom with a window opening out into the branches of a sturdy old oak.

That first party was the night she'd met Al. Everybody was jubilant because Al had just been transferred from Florida to duty in New York. Wendy reported with an indulgent smile that he had just been busted again – back to PFC. How long ago it all seemed! Centuries...

October, 1943

The sky was pink-gray – hinting at imminent rain. An unseasonable bone-chilling rawness permeated the air. The homecoming horde – recently disgorged from the IRT or the Broadway bus – walked with shoulders hunched against the twilight discomfort. A reluctant pup tugged at a leash on a stoop – not wanting to venture out into the cold.

'Oh, thank God, we've made it home.' Wendy sighed with satisfaction while Holly and she trudged – clutching grocery bags – up the stoop of their West Side brownstone.

'Let's just get inside—' Holly juggled parcels in an effort to reach her keys. 'I'm sure one of these bags is just ready to burst.' She eyed the suspicious wetness with concern.

Holly maneuvered the outside door. They moved into the foyer, headed up the faded carpet of the stairway in the dim light offered by the twenty-five-watt bulbs the landlord fancied to their second-floor apartment.

'Let me open the door.' Wendy took the key from Holly, so that Holly could nurse the precarious parcel.

As usual, there was a minor struggle with the lock – but it was difficult to get any service out of the 'super' these days. Every delay in service was blamed on the war. Finally, the door was open. The two girls surged into the living room, dumped bags on the card table that did duty for dining.

'Sure we have everything?' Holly peered into bundles – anxiety overshot with delight. Every nerve in her body hammered with expectancy. They were giving a party!

'We've spent our whole food allowance for the next week,' Wendy reminded. 'We better have everything.'

Holly hurried over to the closet kitchenette for dishes, stared at the sugar bowl.

'We're out of sugar!' They were always out of sugar, with the rationing situation so stringent because of the war.

'Claire said she was bringing two pounds – she's on saccharine again. But I forgot about ice cubes—'

'I filled the trays last night,' Holly soothed. 'If we run out, we can borrow from Laura up-stairs—' Holly shifted food from bags to plates. She hesitated a moment, staring distastefully into space. 'Laura hinted again that if we were short of things – like sugar and coffee and stock-ings – she could help out.' For a price.

'We'll take her ice cubes. Screw her black-marketing.'

'Do you know, this is the first party I've ever been part of in my whole life?' Holly glowed. 'It's kind of a landmark.'

'I'm limited to kid parties myself – on the giving side,' Wendy admitted. 'Though I've been to plenty of brawls – high school on.'

'I've never even had a birthday party. Just a birthday cake every year with my mother and father. You know my mother by now. She was always too nervous to be bothered with parties when I was little. When I was older and might have put up a battle, we were too broke.'

She used to hate their deserted isle of a house, Holly recalled with recurrent distaste. Ever since she could remember, they'd moved every couple of years – always to something smaller and cheaper. Only once did she ever bring a friend home for lunch – she never dared after that.

Poor Daddy, he must hate coming home from his dismal cashier's job to their dismal little apartment – and Mom's constant nagging monologues. Only once did she ever hear him talk back to Mom: *'What do you want me to do – jump out the window?'*

Never once did they have a guest for dinner – not even Daddy's close friend, Mr Madison. Not even somebody in for coffee, or to sit – back home – on that neat row of rockers that was her mother's pride.

'You meet folks on the street to talk to – that's enough.'

Most Sunday mornings, Holly recalled nostalgically, Daddy used to go to visit Mr Madison at his pharmacy on the wrong side of town. Sometimes Daddy took her with him.

She loved to listen to their passionate discussions. Daddy was so concerned about the plight of the mill workers in town – and the awful one-room schools for the colored children. He should have been in politics – fighting to make things better. She yearned to write about these one day – to say all the things that needed to be said.

Wendy brought her back to the moment. 'Al gave me a wild brawl on my last birthday. You

35

know I worked for him until he enlisted. That was the nuttiest job – with Al half-agent, half-playwright. The agent part paid his bills.'

'He was your agent, wasn't he?' Wendy had dreams about being the next Marian Hutton or Helen O'Connell. But that would have to wait until the war was over.

'Oh, Al booked me into some two-bit night clubs for a while – and I started to work part-time in his office. Then he hired me full-time.' A wistful glint in her eyes. 'I couldn't afford not to take it. My folks were already making noises about jobs being out there now – forget about singing. I had to give money home.' Wendy was philosophical. 'Doesn't everybody?'

'Yeah—' Holly nodded in understanding.

'Al's something. People cluster around him like he was a grown-ups' Pied Piper. I was so proud when he took me into his inner circle. It was like belonging to a special club.'

'It's a miracle my folks let me take the apartment with you.' Holly moved about the closet kitchenette with an air of pleasure, put up water for cocktail franks. 'It wouldn't have happened if my mother hadn't been so upset when three girls in our neighborhood were attacked on the street.' *I'm still giving ten dollars a week home – a big chunk of my salary. They can't say I'm not helping.*

'This is the first of a long line of parties,' Wendy promised. 'What else have we got in this crazy, mixed-up world?' For a moment exuberance gave way to pain. Since the Japanese bombed Pearl Harbor, life in their world was

36

fraught with anxiety, fear. 'Honey, put up the coffee, will you, while I fall into clothes?'

Holly was in the bathroom – brushing her dark pageboy into gleaming beauty – when the guests began to arrive. In seconds the living room ricocheted with noisy greetings, high spirits. Holly's reflection in the mirror showed her own excitement.

She knew Mitch and Claire. Steve couldn't make it – he was working the swing shift now. Claire was fresh out of Hunter and in her first year of teaching. While she squeezed in occasional evening acting classes – with yearnings to be the next Katherine Cornell – Claire was realistic about the need for a steady job. The others would be strangers, part of the Al Rogers circle that seemed larded with talent.

Nobody will guess I'm seventeen. Tonight, twenty – like Wendy. Claire's twenty-three. I don't have to be nervous about meeting everybody. Wendy's here. Wendy won't let me make an ass of myself. But they're all so sophisticated. So what? I can play the game.

Stop stalling with the hairbrush. Open the bathroom door, go into the living room. No, no more eye shadow – it's OK. Now go out there – you're the co-hostess.

'Holly—' Wendy spied her, beckoned her to the trio with whom she was carrying on convivial conversation. 'Come over and meet people.'

'Hi.' She knew Mitch, of course.

'Linda and Eric,' Wendy introduced. 'Holly, the roommate.'

37

'Hi, roommate.' Eric – in civvies – inspected her with candid approval.

'Hello, Holly.' A whisper of condescension in Linda.

Holly recognized an undercurrent of competition between Wendy and Linda. Because of Mitch – or Eric? One rainy evening last week Wendy opened up about her personal life. She'd slept with Mitch, who'd been coming in on leave at a steady clip during the last year.

For an instant Holly had been shocked. This was a whole new world for her. Her sexual knowledge was derived from a sex manual shared covertly with a high-school girlfriend.

Linda dropped an arm about Eric with an air of possessiveness. Mitch sauntered over to the improvised bar to set up shop. Holly and Wendy had provided ice cubes and mixes. Eric and Mitch had arrived with bottles. Eric exuded a secretive air of amusement – as though part of him sat removed from the others. To Holly this seemed intriguing.

Linda was attractive. The auburn hair showed darker roots but was becoming. The body was tall, narrow, high-breasted – and Linda was determined the world should recognize her potential. When Linda bent over to adjust a stocking seam, Holly discovered she didn't believe in bras. Mitch discovered, too. He whistled, stared uninhibitedly.

'Know what's wrong with this frigging army?' Mitch announced. 'No broads in the barracks!' A glass in hand, he strolled over to Linda. Ignoring Eric at her side. 'Every company should be equipped with one of these.' He slid an arm about Linda's waist.

'Right now, equip me with one of those.' Linda pointed to the glass in Mitch's hand. 'I thought you were bartender for the night.'

Wendy propelled Holly away from the group, towards the kitchenette. It was time to set up the buffet table.

'What does Linda do?' Holly asked.

'She's a typist in a government office down near Wall Street,' Wendy told her. 'Eric's a glorified office boy in some important literary agency. He writes on the side. I think he's awfully good.'

Holly knew that Mitch was an arranger who was determined to write a Broadway musical. Al used to book him as a pianist in ten-dollar-a-night clubs. The same kind of joints where he'd occasionally booked Claire as a singer until she settled down – under pressure from home – into college and then teaching in a Bronx junior high.

Nobody – except Wendy – knew she meant to write plays and radio scripts. She'd made a down-payment last week on a Royal portable. By avoiding lunch she could make a payment each week. Soon she could type up all her notes on the radio script in work.

Holly's eyes were drawn to Eric. His lean, ascetic face was like a painting in a museum, she mused. He'd look at home in a monk's cowl – forsaking all worldliness. But from Wendy's report, Holly knew Eric was famished for the physical advantages of success – of high living.

'Sorry, I can't dazzle you babes with khaki.'

Eric's smile was bitter. 'I'm blind as a bat.' Without his glasses he'd look a lot like Leslie Howard, Holly decided.

'Be grateful, you dumb bastard!' Mitch slugged Eric between the shoulder blades. 'You don't hear me crying because I'm still here instead of overseas.' Then – with a triumphant, sly grin – Mitch dragged Linda down on the sofa beside him.

Holly caught the high-pitched, phony gaiety in Wendy's voice. She was centering her full attention on Eric, plainly happy to be the object of her affection. But Wendy was furious with Mitch for the byplay with Linda.

With a need to be active, Wendy crossed to the kitchenette. She brought out more cheese and crackers. Eric reached for Holly's hand, prodded her into the club chair – faded and bursting at the seams – beside their 'non-burning' fireplace, and settled himself on one arm. He seemed intrigued at her familiarity with American and European playwrights.

'I went right down the shelves in the public library back home,' she explained with an effervescent smile. This was comfortable territory. The local library had been her second home. 'I love O'Neill and Ibsen and Shaw – and the Phillip Barry comedies – and of course, Strindberg—' *Eric has already written two plays, Wendy told me. And she says they're good.*

Mitch remembered his bartending obligations. He brought belated drinks to Holly and Eric. Holly loved the song he was humming – 'Embraceable You'.

40

Linda leaned back – legs crossed high, short skirt riding about her thighs – swigged down her drink, demanded a replacement. Holly sipped at her drink – euphoric at meeting new people. Exciting people.

She'd had wine with Wendy and Mitch. Never cocktails. Wendy had told Mitch to make her a brandy Alexander. It felt good – sitting within her. The doorbell rang again. Wendy hurried to open the door.

Whoops of excitement filled the air. A dark-haired, compactly built man in army uniform – appearing taller than he was by virtue of his bearing – surveyed the others with a magnetic smile. The stripes on his jacket identified him as Private First Class, USA. Nobody had to tell Holly. This was Al Rogers.

Mitch charged towards Al, slapped him on the back.

'You old bastard! Why aren't you in the ETO by now?'

'What about you?' His voice was low and mellow. Fascinating blue eyes, Holly thought. They wore an aura of power.

Al kissed Wendy, handed her a package before turning back to Mitch. 'So why are you still hanging around?'

Eric and Linda were at his side now. He kissed Linda, shook hands with Eric. Eric, too, had looked to Al Rogers to push him ahead career-wise, Holly recalled – though Al wasn't a play agent. Wendy said they all looked to Al as their passport to fame – until Pearl Harbor short-circuited their lives.

'You know, it's almost seven months since I've been home? Damn this shitty war!' Al Rogers' eyes lingered on Holly now. Probing, evaluating. She felt a surge of excitement.

'Al, this is my roommate,' Wendy said. 'Holly Woodridge.'

'You wrote you had a roommate,' Al acknowledged, his eyes still on Holly. 'Seventeen?' He lifted an eyebrow. 'Eighteen?'

She felt color flood her face. 'Twenty,' she stammered. Wendy had told her Al was twenty-eight. The oldest in their clique.

Al's gaze traveled to the wall. 'What the hell is that contraption?' He pointed to the bulging towel that masked a protuberance on one wall.

'With our luck, we have the thermostat for the whole building in our apartment,' Wendy explained. 'You know the lousy landlords – they've got the great excuse about oil shortage these days – so we never get enough heat.'

'This is our heat-raiser,' Holly explained, laughter lighting her eyes. 'We tie a towel full of ice cubes around the thermostat. The reading goes down – the heat comes up.'

'Remind me to watch out for you, baby.' Al nodded in approval.

'They're bound to find out sooner or later,' Holly conceded, 'but until they do, we're living.'

'If we make a roast, the house freezes for days.' Wendy giggled. 'But who has money for roasts?'

The bell buzzed again. Wendy scurried to answer.

'Hi!' Claire stood there. Effervescent, exuding a zest for living. Her near black hair styled to enhance her resemblance to Claudette Colbert though she yearned for Colbert's sleek figure. 'I'm out of my mind. I walked all the way up to the top floor without thinking.'

'Good exercise!' Al crossed to Claire, kissed her. 'You're always dieting, anyway. You claim.'

Claire fell into his arms. 'Al, it's been forever.'

'You look great.' Al inspected her with exaggerated care. 'How's school?'

'Don't ask.' She shuddered. 'I almost got raped this afternoon.'

Claire tossed her coat to Wendy, reached with a sigh of pleasure for the drink Mitch extended. 'Mitch, I love you.'

'Say, what are you teaching, anyhow?' Al prodded Claire into a chair. There was a nice relationship between them, Holly decided. 'Biology?'

'You wouldn't believe this school if you weren't there. Leave it to me to get stuck in an area like this. These damn kids must have started with sex in the crib. This one was all of fourteen – so hot he's bursting out of his pants. I was in a closet dragging down supplies – and all of a sudden, there he is, with octopus hands. I swear, two minutes more, he would have had my dress off. I ran into the same situation last month. The boy's gym teacher crashed in, nearly broke the little monster's arm. The Board called the gym teacher up on charges for that.'

'Where's Skip?' Wendy demanded.

'Off to Larchmont, for an evening with

43

Mama.' From the tone of Claire's voice, Holly realized this was a rocky marriage.

A few minutes later, Norman – handsome, lavishly endowed with acting talent, Wendy vowed, but inhibited by his lack of height – charged in, with an obvious head-start on the drinking. At the moment Norman was still on what he hopefully referred to as 'permanent duty' at Governor's Island. He had been there since he enlisted seventeen months earlier – when his first Broadway play closed after two performances.

'Know what's wrong with this mob?' Bristling with scrubbed young American good looks, Norman swung his gaze about the room. 'No music.'

Wendy shoved him towards their small radio. She nodded in approval when the latest Glenn Miller recording filtered into the room.

'Let's talk,' Eric said persuasively to Holly when the others rose to dance.

Holly enjoyed the verbal sparring with Eric. Something in his barbed wit reached through to touch her. Wendy said Eric had grown up in an orphanage.

A couple of years ago, he bumped into his father at the Times Square subway station. He hadn't seen him in nine years. They both cried – but twenty minutes later his father disappeared into the subway crowd again. Eric hasn't seen him since.

Wendy and Eric had been in high school to-gether. At one time they must have been close – it was there in the way they looked at each other.

Had Wendy slept with Eric? Holly felt a self-conscious warmth ride over her. Three months ago that kind of question would never have passed through her mind. Wendy said the war changed people: *'You might as well live today – you don't know what tomorrow will bring.'*

'Hey, Eric, stop hoarding the broads.' Norman hovered over them in good-humored reproach. 'Come on, let's dance.' He pulled Holly to her feet. 'Gorgeous baby,' he crooned, drawing her closely to him. His face against her hair.

Fighting discomfort, Holly forced herself to follow him. Nobody had ever held her this way before. She could feel everything – even *that*. Did the others see the way Norman and she were dancing? She made a clumsy effort to pull slightly apart. He rejected the attempt. From the corner of her eye, she spied Al strolling towards them.

'OK, Norm, don't monopolize,' Al ordered with a grin – disentangling Norman and her.

Al stood with an arm about Holly's shoulders while he exchanged barracks jokes with Norman. Then the others rallied around, to make it a free-for-all.

Nurse this drink. Nobody will notice, as long as I have a half-filled glass in my hand.

Eric lighted a cigarette, gave it to her. She accepted it – fighting self-consciousness. A moment later she felt a surge of relief. It was a snap, so long as you didn't inhale. Some of her tension evaporated.

A mellow feeling permeated the smoke-filled room. They settled comfortably – in chairs, on

the studio couch, on cushions about the floor –
to listen to the poignant sweetness of current hit
songs. 'People Will Say We're in Love', 'As
Time Goes By', 'That Old Black Magic'.

Mitch stood up to switch off the high-wattage
lamp that bathed Linda and him in brightness.
Across the room – sharing a club chair with Eric
– Wendy flipped off the other lamp. Only a
trickle of light from behind the half-closed
kitchenette door filtered into the high-ceilinged
room – painted with shadows now.

In one corner, Norman – the others called him
'Norm', Holly noted – danced with Claire.
Claire's eyes were closed, her body fused with
Norm's. Mitch pulled Linda to her feet, disappeared with her into the blackness of the
minuscule bedroom. Holly exchanged a startled
glance with Wendy. Mitch and Linda had both
been drinking heavily. But not too heavily.

Holly tried not to think about Linda and Mitch
– in the tiny bedroom she shared with Wendy.
They wouldn't have the nerve to do it, would
they – with the others sitting right out here?

Wendy and Eric were in a heated embrace. In
the semi-darkness Holly saw Eric's hand fondle
Wendy's breasts. From the bedroom – behind
the closed door – Linda's throaty, keyed-up
laughter drifted out, then was hushed.

Al leaned back against the sofa, reached for
Holly's hand. Wendy told her Al knew all kinds
of gorgeous girls. They chased him like mad.
Why is he bothering with me?

'Do you want the rest of that drink?' Al asked.

'No.' He guessed she was just nursing it. He

was so sweet.

His mouth reached for hers. She closed her eyes – her heart pounding. This was a whole new world she'd joined. That small town in South Carolina had disappeared. This was exciting New York.

He didn't try to hold her tightly. He was letting her get used to this newness. Then his mouth grew urgent – eliciting unfamiliar emotions in her. This was part of the wartime syndrome they read about in newspapers and magazines, she thought in a corner of her mind. She was disappointed when Al's mouth released hers.

'Ever been kissed like that?' His voice was low, unheard by the others – all wrapped up in their own searchings.

'No.'

'Like it?'

'Yes.' Startled by her reactions.

He rose from the sofa – leaving Holly in the shadows.

'I'll get us some coffee.' He sounded pleased.

It was past five when the party began to break up. There was an air of reluctance in the room – as though each one loathed to shatter the spell of the past few hours. It had been good, Holly thought with recurrent satisfaction. A new experience for her.

Feeling maudlin, Norm insisted on kissing everybody goodnight – even the fellows. Who could remain angry at him? So warm, so puppy-friendly. Wendy was noticeably cool when she kissed Mitch goodnight. Mitch announced his next communication might be from the guardhouse – if he didn't make his bus, he would be AWOL. Eric was the last – and most reluctant – to leave. He was whispering entreaties in the hallway – about sleeping over. Wendy shipped him on his way.

Holly shut the apartment door. Wendy surveyed the littered living room with distaste.

'I'd love to leave all this mess until tomorrow. Only it'll be twice as bad then.'

'Let's go to work,' Holly decreed. Feeling an odd exhilaration. Tonight she had come of age.

Holly and Wendy moved in comfortable silence, dumped paper plates and napkins into a brown-paper bag, transferred remains of their spread to the refrigerator, stacked cups, saucers, glasses, serving bowls in the sink for overnight soaking.

'Wendy—' Holly dumped the last littered ashtray into the grocery bag.

'Yeah?'

'Mitch says the way the war's going it's almost certain they'll all be overseas in two or three months. Do you believe that?' She recoiled from the vision of Al and Mitch and Norm in battle.

'It's a miracle they've been home this long. Mitch teaches a class on machine guns – that's kept him here in the States. Norm's folks are supposed to have pulled strings. Al's plain lucky.'

Holly shivered. 'Doesn't it give you a funny feeling?' She would remember forever that Pearl Harbor Sunday – December 7, 1941. Up until that moment war was something you studied in history. Four months after Pearl Harbor she sat

48

on the porch with the afternoon paper reading and rereading the front-page story. The town had suffered its first casualty. Last year Joe Hill was a member of the high-school senior class. He used to deliver groceries to their back door. Now red-headed Joe Hill – whom just about everybody in town liked – was nothing. A dog tag sent home to his family.

'I've had a funny feeling for almost two years.' Wendy dragged Holly back to the present. 'Next month they could all be dead. It doesn't make sense.'

'I never thought we would grow up into a war, did you?' Holly pulled a pillow to her as she sat on the sofa.

'Cold?'

'A little,' Holly admitted. The heat had long been turned down – it was a miracle to get any after ten o'clock. The drinks had worn off. A somber chill invaded the room.

Wendy went into the bedroom, returned with two sweaters, tossed one to Holly.

'Eric's a character, isn't he?'

'I like him,' Holly said. She'd never known anybody like Eric. Nor any of the others in Wendy's small circle.

'I used to be nutty about Eric – my last year in school and the year after.'

'What about now?'

Wendy's smile was philosophical.

'I suppose I'll always be interested in Eric – as far as I allow myself. He was the first guy I slept with.' She giggled. 'Now I've shocked you.'

'No,' Holly denied. Wendy had made it clear

not long after they met that she had 'messed around'.

'Eric's impossible. You try to talk seriously to him – like about maybe getting married – and he runs as though somebody's after him with a hand grenade.'

'Claire says it's the psychosis of the '40s – all the fellows being marriage-shy.' To her marriage seemed light years away.

'The fellows *we* know are like that.' Wendy was grim. 'Remember the waiting lines down at City Hall? I'm fed up with the "let's live it up tonight because tomorrow we may die" brigade. So damn convenient for them.'

'Linda's another character.' How cool Linda had been when she and Mitch came out of the bedroom. When everybody knew what had been happening.

'Linda's oversexed. Anything gets Linda excited – but nothing's ever enough. She can be fun at a party – if she's getting most of the male attention.' Wendy yawned. 'Wow, it's late. But tomorrow's Saturday – we can sleep all day.'

Wendy untangled herself from the sofa and headed for the bedroom. Holly switched off the lights and followed. Minutes later they lay in their twin beds – with the autumn moonlight sending its final shadows of the night across the tiny room.

'Asleep?' Wendy's voice was soft.

'No. Suddenly I'm not sleepy.' Physically exhausted – but wide awake.

Wendy squirmed about – trying to discover a position more conducive to sleep.

'We ought to be snoring by now. Too much excitement.'

'Does Linda always pull off things like that?'

'Disappearing into the bedroom with Mitch?' Wendy shrugged it off. 'Linda was half-lit.' Wendy was silent for a moment. '*I* kid around. You know.'

'You're different.' Holly was defensive.

'How am I different?' Wendy challenged.

'I don't know—' How could she explain? 'When *you* do things, they don't seem messy.'

'Mitch claims that any girl past twenty who's still a virgin these days is doomed to frustration. I'll never know, of course,' she flipped.

'Do you suppose a lot of girls are just frigid? Maybe it doesn't mean anything to them.' She wasn't frigid. Tonight proved that to her. 'I mean,' Holly stammered, 'you read all the time about frigid women.'

'I'll bet half of them are just scared. We've been brought up with the nutty theory that sex is something women have to put up with. The girl's not supposed to enjoy it – that's the man's prerogative. Claire's like that – she comes right out and says so.' Wendy beat a fist into her pillow. Her eyes were troubled. 'How many guys make a girl a tramp?'

'I don't think it's how many – it's the way she handles herself.'

'When you dig down to naked truth,' Wendy confessed, 'I get so passionate sometimes even the milkman could get in. If he's there at the right time.'

'You have to like him an awful lot.' Holly's

51

face was suddenly hot. 'Don't you?'

'I'm not talking about sex with love,' Wendy said. 'I'm talking about pure physical need. OK,' she conceded with a giggle, 'so maybe it isn't exactly pure. I mean, sometimes you ache inside so much it'll be enough to find somebody fairly pleasant – that you can delude yourself into thinking is great – to plow in and fill that stinking emptiness. Plenty of married couples don't worry about love – they're happy to settle for liking when the sex part is good. Maybe that's how liking builds into love.'

'I'll bet Al knows how to make love.' Holly's face filled with heat. *Why did I say that?*

'The master.' Wendy's admission had slipped out, Holly realized. 'Well, I sure opened my big mouth that time.' The first tinge of dawn crept across the bed to show Wendy's rueful grin.

'Why not?' It was disconcerting, though, to think of Wendy and Al that way.

'We both knew it was just for the moment. No ties either way. There've been repeats,' Wendy conceded. 'Good for both of us.' She raised herself up on an elbow, leaned forward to switch on the lamp between the beds. 'Go on, say it. Wendy's a tramp.'

'No,' Holly protested. So much was happening, so fast. But Wendy could never be a tramp. She was warm, sweet, *honest*. 'I think you're getting melodramatic because it's five thirty in the morning, and you drank more brandy Alexanders than you'll admit.'

Wendy's smile was laden with affection.

'You'll get a liberal education around me,

Holly. Now let's stop this yakking, or neither of us will get any sleep.' Wendy swung over on her other side, hugged her pillow with a show of determination to end the night.

That was how it had started with Al and her – at that first party eighteen years ago. Only now – with Ron Andrews popping into their lives to thrust a mirror before their eyes – did the ghosts come out to dance.

Five

Holly finished spooning food into Jonny's eager, small mouth, wiped up the mis-aimed cereal. She enjoyed feeding him. It was a warm, private time that never bogged down into irritation except when she was desperately tired or upset. She enjoyed his pleased sounds of satisfaction when he drained a bottle. A child's substitute for sex, she thought with tender humor.

Last night, Holly recalled with a rush of guilt, she had yelled at Jonny. She had screeched at him because her mind dwelt on Ron Andrews' arrival in the city and the effect of this on Al. Poor darling baby, he had looked stunned, dissolved into tears of reproach.

'OK, pumpkin.' She gathered Jonny into her arms, lifted him from the feeding table. 'Let's get down to serious business.'

She scooped up a paper bag of special playpen-time toys, teased Jonny into abandoning his adventurous notions.

'Here you go, Jonny boy!' She deposited him into the round, meshed, deceptively imprisoning playpen.

At the typewriter now – in a corner of the living room – she hesitated. Part of her mind recoiled from the job at hand. Maybe some breakfast, she stalled. Put up a fresh percolator of coffee – Wendy would be along soon.

With coffee up, bread in the toaster, she returned to the typewriter. Be realistic. Get this show on the road. Where else could she pick up nine hundred dollars for two or three weeks' work? This was a job – as much as turning out the glorified garbage in advertising or publicity, knocking out TV soaps. Plenty of those writers rebelled at their straitjackets. How often had she shared a crying towel with one of them?

But the straitjackets are self-fastened. Nobody hangs over our heads and orders us to turn out this crap. I could quit tomorrow. But those cozy checks – rolling in religiously now – would also quit.

It had not disturbed her – that period of living in a near-slum, weighing every minor expenditure. She had accepted it as a challenge because there was the undeniable satisfaction of being her own master. Al was working at the store, she admitted with a guilty brush of reality – but she concentrated on writing. *Not for a market – for me.* The most absorbing experience she had ever encountered. The spoils of that small parcel of

54

time lay – waiting for the nebulous era when she might have time for polishing – in a file drawer along with Al's plays and his book-in-work.

Her mind darted back almost two years ago – to the day she'd got the results of a pregnancy test. Positive. She'd said nothing about her suspicions to Al...

She was impatient for Al to come home from the store to tell him the news. *After all these years I'm pregnant. Will Al be happy? Or upset? Our whole world will change now.*

They couldn't bring up their child in the East Village – prolific with fringe talents, the poor, and drug addicts. She'd go out and find a job – work up until the last minute. But what about after the baby was born? Oh, wow, she and Al as parents! It was both beautiful and terrifying.

In earlier years there had never been time to consider a family. Whenever she'd brought up the subject, Al had always backed away. *'I'd be a rotten father – I'm too old.'*

She heard the elevator stop at their floor. She was opening the door as he approached.

'You look like you just won a big-time lottery,' he joshed. 'What's up?'

'Al, I'm pregnant—'

Al stared at her as he walked into the apartment. Disbelieving. Stunned. 'You're kidding—'

'Don't you want the baby?' Her heart was pounding.

'You're sure?' he tried again.

'Sure.'

'Then I guess we're going to be parents.' His smile was shaky.

'You're not pleased,' she whispered.

'I'm surprised,' he admitted. 'But what the hell? Why can't we be good parents?'

'I'll get a job,' she began. 'We'll save—'

'Hey, this calls for a celebration,' he interrupted. 'Let's go out for dinner. Nothing fancy,' he anticipated her objection. 'We'll run up to the Second Avenue Deli and have corned-beef sandwiches and warm strudel.'

'You order corned beef, I'll order pastrami – we'll split,' she said in high spirits now. *It's going to be all right. Somehow, we'll manage.*

While they were waiting for a table, Al spied a newcomer. 'Evan!' he called out. 'Evan Ross! Where the hell have you been all these years?'

In moments Al and Evan Ross were exchanging stories. Evan was the editor all those years ago of the literary magazine that had published several of Al's short stories, Holly remembered. When they were seated and had ordered, Evan explained that he was a literary agent these days.

'Got something for me to sell?' Evan demanded. Holly gathered he was not at the top of the pile as an agent.

Al's face tightened for a moment. 'When do I have time to write these days?'

'I'm on to something hot,' Evan said expansively. 'This paperback house that's looking for writers. No Steinbeck or Phillip Roth, but stuff you could probably knock out in two or three weeks. And you can pick up a thousand-buck advance.'

'What have you been drinking?' Al scoffed. 'Who can write a book in two or three weeks? I can't type that fast.'

'These are very short – between fifty and sixty thousand words. Not porn,' he emphasized, 'but plenty of sex. It's a male readership.'

'You mean writers are turning these books out that fast?' Holly's mind was racing. He talked about a thousand dollars for maybe a month's work, she reasoned – guessing he was exaggerating somewhat. Far better than she could pick up as an office temp. If other writers could do it, maybe she could give it a whirl. 'And it's not an overnight deal that'll disappear in a few weeks?'

'I've got three writers working at it – and Cozy Books are after me to bring in more.' He inspected Holly with fresh interest. 'You're a writer?'

'Yes,' she said, ignoring Al's astonishment that she was interested.

'Holly's a quality writer – that crap's not for her,' Al dismissed this.

'Will they buy on an outline and a couple of chapters?' Holly pursued. *Even after the baby is born, I could be earning money.*

'They're hungry for writers.' Evan squinted in thought. 'I think I could persuade them to take a chance. Especially if you've got some background.'

'I've sold radio and television,' Holly told him. 'Nationally.'

'Hey, give me an outline and maybe twenty-five pages, and I'll go to bat for you,' Evan offered.

That's how she became involved in writing for Cozy, Holly remembered with wry humor. Almost two years now – but the bank didn't care that there were people who called her market soft porn. And she and Al were living in a life-style they'd be reluctant to lose now.

The doorbell shattered her concentration. As she raced to the door, she caught the pungent aroma of burning toast. Oh God, again? The damn toaster kept breaking down – and she could take prizes for burning pots. She detoured to the kitchenette, pulled out the toaster plug, then hurried to open the door.

'You OK?' Marty Kass – sixtyish, tall, spare, on one of his sporadic beard-raising kicks – hovered in the doorway. 'I smelled smoke.'

'I burnt the toast again.' Holly sighed. 'You know me, Marty. I'm probably the only woman in the state of New York who can burn hard-boiled eggs.'

'You and Betty.' Marty grinned, waved to Jonny.

'Come in for a cup of coffee,' Holly invited. Al and she knew no one else in the building – beyond elevator conversation – other than Marty and Betty Kass. Marty and Betty were mental fellow-travelers. It was pleasant to know they were next door.

'I'm taking off for a day's golf.' Marty pointed to the bag of clubs leaning against his door. 'A beautiful day like this I get claustrophobia. I got plenty of leave coming at the office, so why not?' He was silent for a moment. 'Betty and I made a big decision last night. You talk to her this morning?'

'Are you kidding?' Holly laughed. Betty had to be at her office by eight thirty. 'But what's the big decision?'

'Oh, it's been bouncing around in our minds, but we finally made it concrete. We're both retiring within the next six months.' There was little relish for Marty in the announcement, Holly sensed in surprise. 'Why not? Betty's been with the Welfare Department for thirty years, me with the state for thirty-eight. Know what our pensions come to after all that time? Between us we figure on over six hundred seventy a month – and we've saved through the years.' He chuckled, a momentary glow in his wistful brown eyes. A faint, palliative pride. 'We'd like to do some real traveling for a while. Like a year in Europe, maybe. Really see it.'

'Sounds marvelous.' How remote such thinking was from their existence these days! They lived in such a tight, narrow, isolated world. There had been a time Al and she had talked about Europe – before Jonny. She fidgeted – enjoying the respite from the typewriter but guilty because Jonny was behaving himself and she should be working.

'It's a little something to show for thirty-eight years.' Marty's eyes held a quality that reminded Holly of Al's – since he had come face to face with Ron's success. 'I never thought I'd be working at that same crappy office for thirty-eight years. I was twenty when I went there – it was going to be temporary, until I found myself

59

something real.'

Holly remembered Marty's collection of small talents. For writing poetry, composing music, sculpturing. A little talent in a brash, pushing world could be a curse. 'They never used me to my full potential in the job. Not in all those years. Anything I had was wasted.'

For a moment he stood there stripped of all pretense – in the poignant hurt, the bewilderment of the army of people whose talents never developed beyond the budding stage. In the beginning – when Al and she first moved into the building – she'd considered the Kasses the rare couple at peace with the world. The Kasses knew how to enjoy urban living as it was seldom enjoyed. Museums, concerts, theater, political events – Betty and Marty, with their civil-service job security, lived in a world many people viewed with envy. Betty with that striking contempt for money that frightened Marty at times.

'How's the golf score?' Holly asked awkwardly – to hide the rush of compassion that today was especially facile.

'Could be better,' Marty shrugged, the personal moment retreating, leaving behind a trace of self-consciousness. 'If I don't get out, it'll be worse.'

Marty left for his day of golf. Holly returned – without toast but bolstered by the mug of freshly perked coffee in her hand – to the typewriter. Jonny wanted out, became vocal in his demands. She scrounged around for a fresh supply of toys to delay the ultimate moment.

She couldn't erase Marty's face from her

mind. Al could be Marty a dozen years from now, her mind taunted. When you're young, you believe with such intensity that anybody with genuine talent will make it. Then you get older – and you're still sitting at the starting gate. You don't make it – and you wonder, 'What's missing?'

She was getting older, Holly reminded herself. Thirty-five. Being the youngest in their group, being eleven years younger than Al, had sheltered her. But Ron Andrews had come into New York for his Broadway production – and a lot of things that had not shouted in their faces before shouted now.

Jonny was making vociferous objections to the limitations of the playpen about the time that Holly was reaching her self-imposed quota of work for the morning. She shut up shop, cast an appraising eye about to make sure the room was fairly baby-proof, and lifted him out to the freedom of the living-room floor.

The downstairs bell buzzed, with the familiar two shorts and two longs that was Wendy's long-established signal. She hurried to answer. She spoke with Wendy over the phone several times each week, but it was close to two months since Wendy had managed to get over. Somehow, traveling to the Bronx with Jonny seemed an insurmountable project.

She opened the apartment door – listening for the sounds of the elevator.

'Hi, darling,' Wendy called exuberantly from the opening elevator door and rushed down the corridor in her perpetual high heels – because

Wendy took pleasure in that her showgirl legs remained fabulously unchanged.

They kissed with deep affection, walked back into the apartment arm-in-arm. Holly remembered with amusement how a girl who had touched the fringe of their small clique once asked Mitch if Wendy and she were lesbians.

'I think you lost half a pound,' Holly jibed gently.

'I have to have a nervous breakdown to lose five pounds.' Wendy sighed, making a beeline for Jonny. 'I swear I don't eat that much. It *has* to be glands.'

'The doctor still giving you hell for not taking it off?'

'I'm scared to go in,' Wendy admitted, in deep conference with a happily squealing Jonny. 'I'm about five weeks late for my last appointment.'

'Wendy, that's awful.' Holly shook her head in futile reproach.

'Maybe I pick up a few things along the way that I shouldn't,' Wendy conceded in a moment of somber candor. 'For the weight and for the blood pressure. I guess I don't care that much, Holly.' She stared into space. 'I have to have something. Everybody does.'

'Sure, Wendy—' Softly, compassionately, unhappily.

'But tomorrow night we have a swinging party – that'll brighten up my life for a while.' Wendy's smile was dazzling. On the surface she had shooed away the somber note.

'How's Jerry?' Holly asked, going towards the kitchenette.

'Oh God, don't get me on that track. He's carrying on like crazy – again – about how much he hates his job, and how he'll never have any security keeping books for a lousy living. So you can figure it out – it's been hell living with him these last couple weeks.'

'Any chance of Jerry's coming to the party?' Did every man hate his job? Did anybody in this world enjoy their work? 'Maybe the change will do him good.'

'He's still working Saturday nights at that shitty supermarket job. I don't know, Holly. The two of us work like dogs, and still we never get our heads above water.'

'Al's carrying on, too. I can't say I blame him for not liking that stinking job—' A shocking comedown at his age.

'So who says we're madly in love with what we have to do?' Wendy challenged. 'They're married men – with families and responsibilities. Men are all cut from the same mold – the lot of them. Oh, Jerry's latest kick – he's considering selling insurance! I'm trying to get it through his thick skull that we can't live on a job that depends on commissions.'

'Al just deliberately hexed a promotion. It smacked of permanency.'

'When's Al going to grow up?'

Holly moved into the dining area with a tray of sandwich makings. 'He's so demanding of himself in a job. He expects other people to be the same way – and you know and I know most people won't be.'

'Al and his precious individuality,' Wendy

63

grumbled but with affection. 'Can't he just once in a while run with the mob?'

'Coffee's on the strong side,' Holly warned. 'I got carried away.'

'I can use it, honey.' Wendy lowered herself into a chair at the dining table – releasing Jonny to play with a cluster of blocks close by. 'Al may not have written a smash Broadway play,' she said with breezy humor, 'but he made a most adorable baby.'

Thank God, Al had found the transition from one form of writing to the other so comfortable. In truth, the switch had been in the back of his mind for years. But there was the frustrating problem of never having time to work on the novel.

'Jonny, no!' Holly called out. He was making a tentative move towards a lamp. The base fascinated him at regular intervals. 'I told Al – the ideal home for kids would have everything up on the ceiling on pulleys. You pull down whatever you need when the time arises.' Her smile softened because Jonny had swerved away from the lamp with a beatific grin on his small face.

'Remember before Jonny was born?' Wendy's face was alight with humor. 'The way I phoned the hospital – four weeks early – because you weren't here when I called? I was certain you were in the delivery room if you weren't home by midnight! I was a wreck. I was supposed to be there to hold Al's hand.'

'You instead of my mother,' Holly laughed. 'She didn't want to know anything until it was over.'

'Where were you?' Wendy squinted. 'A party, wasn't it?'

'Playing charades four blocks away. You caught us at 2 a.m. – when we'd just walked in.'

'It's going to be wild seeing Ron after all these years,' Wendy detoured. 'He never impressed me in those days. If anybody was going to make it big, it was Al.' She paused, a hint of apology in her eyes. 'And for a while he did.'

'Al and Eric, I figured.' Holly fought down annoyance that Wendy talked as though it were all over for Al. For all of them.

'Eric had that ugly bitterness from the start,' Wendy reminded.

'I remember one summer night when we sat on the grass in Central Park.' Holly gazed somberly into space. 'You and I and Eric. The other guys were overseas by then. I said something about the apartment houses along Central Park South, and he said— "You might as well look at them because sure as hell we'll never live in one of them." It shocked me that Eric could feel that way.'

'Maybe all that talent we saw wasn't there.'

'Eric was *good*.'

'So Eric was good,' Wendy picked up. 'It's Ron who's living off the fat of the land.'

'Ron had something to offer, too,' Holly reminded.

'But it takes more than that. It takes drive and guts – and luck. No room for the squeamish. Oh—' Wendy's voice took on a fresh tone, as though she were determined to blot out such

65

sobering thoughts. 'Did I tell you I bought the kid a great hi-fi? Cost a bundle.'

'Wendy—' Holly smiled with a mixture of reproach and affection. 'For a thirteen-year-old kid?' Wendy and Jerry couldn't afford that.

'She's nuts about music. Let her at least hear it on something good. OK, so I'll kill myself paying it off for the next eighteen months. A hi-fi is something else to keep the kids coming around. I know where Carol is nights – that means a lot.' The phone rang. Wendy scurried to answer. 'That's probably my little chickadee.' Her face wore a maternal glow. 'I told her I'd be over here.'

Holly reached into a closet for her purse, debated about what to put on Jonny for his afternoon stroller ride. There was a sharp chill in the air. No sitting in the park today.

'Well, that finished that,' Wendy said with a note of uneasy finality – putting down the phone. 'My little darling has been issuing verbal invitations already to her birthday brawl. It's definitely coed—' She sighed, avoided Holly's eyes.

'What does that mean?'

'It means I'll have to be honest with Melinda's mother. How can I invite Melinda and leave her open to insults? It would be awful for that sweet little kid.'

'How can you do that?' Wendy, of all people!

'It's too late to do anything about it – Carol's *invited* the boys.' Wendy seemed relieved that the matter had been removed from her hands. 'It's a stinking, bloody mess, but what can I do?'

She gazed at Holly. 'Look, we do the best we can for our kids.'

Holly and Wendy – with Jonny between them – were heading for the elevator when the phone rang again.

'It might be Al,' Holly said, running back to the apartment. 'I won't talk long.' She hurried to unlock the door, clumsy in her rush. Inside, she grabbed for the phone.

'Hello—'

'How's everything?' Al, as she'd suspected. 'Jonny sleep late?'

'Not much after you left,' Holly reported. 'Wendy's here. We were just going out.'

'Hear anything from Ron?'

'Was he supposed to call?' Holly was startled by the question.

'I figured he might try to back out at the last moment.' Al was self-conscious despite his effort at nonchalance. 'You know the kind of people Ron runs with.'

'He ran with you for quite a while,' Holly shot back – a touch of hostility undercoating her voice.

'Ron doesn't usually bother with anybody unless they can do something for him.' Al was blunt. 'I just wondered why the hell he was wasting an evening on us. Go on out with Wendy – I'll be home early.' A note of defeat crept into his voice again.

Was the party a mistake? Doubt tugged at her while she locked the apartment door again. It had seemed a great idea, born of impulse. Their social life was practically extinct these days.

That alone could be a reason for this depression that had taken root in Al.

No. Don't run away, Holly exhorted herself. Al's depression didn't come from their lack of social life. It didn't come from Ron's sudden appearance in their lives, after such a long absence. Ron's appearance only drew the festering abscess to the surface.

After this weekend she and Al must sit down, talk everything out, stop dodging around corners. It tore at her nerves to live in an aura of constant discontent. Rebellion was for the teens, the twenties. So Al hadn't written a Pulitzer Prize-winning play – it wasn't the end of living.

Six

Holly guided the stroller from the carriage room in the basement into the elevator. Wendy walked alongside with Jonny balanced on one hip – ignoring his absorbed demolition of her painstakingly nurtured hairdo.

'Feel like a long walk?' Holly asked on impulse. Maybe she could walk off some of this simmering unease.

'A day like this, why not?' Wendy agreed. 'Not that it'll do a lousy thing for my figure.' She sighed without losing the aura of good humor. 'The legs are still OK, but the bust line's nothing to write home about any more. I remember when

Al said I had a pair that could give a Civil War veteran an erection. Now nobody but a Civil War veteran would be interested.' She grinned. 'Anyhow, Jerry still likes.'

'Let's walk downtown, then cut across to the Village,' Holly planned, anticipating a stroll across Eighth Street. Window-shopping, maybe browsing in a bookstore or two. Then south again to Washington Square. The Village wasn't just a place; it was an atmosphere. 'I wish we could afford to live over there.' The new apartment buildings catered to the high-salaried. To acquire an apartment in the older, rent-controlled buildings required grapevine knowledge of impending vacancies.

Wendy stared in disbelief. 'Worse rents than you pay? When I think what you lay out for rent every month – even us, stuck way up in the Bronx – it makes me sick. If it was just Jerry and me, I'd settle for a one-room efficiency, smack in the middle of Manhattan.'

'Oh, let me check the mailbox,' Holly remembered this morning routine as they approached the door. 'It'll only take a sec.' But the mail had not been delivered yet. 'I don't really expect anything except bills and catalogues.'

The crisp autumn air was exhilarating. Normally a day like this would lift her spirits. Not today. Too much tugged at her subconscious. She slowed down, gazed at the taxi pulling up at the curb.

'Hi, Betty.' Holly waved while her neighbor emerged from the cab. 'What's the matter? You get jealous because Marty took off for golf?'

'I got fooled by that damn weather report last night.' Betty's smile encompassed Wendy and Jonny as well as Holly. 'So there I was at the office, like sitting in Dante's Inferno. Thank God I live so close.'

'I heard the repairman in your apartment yesterday,' Holly recalled. 'Did he get the dishwasher working?'

'At last. It's something, you know? I made a remark to Rolfe – just before he left for Paris – about being upset because we were having so much trouble with the dishwasher, and he said to me—"My mother, who was born on Jefferson Street, is worried about her dishwasher!" On Jefferson Street it was the bathtub in the kitchen that bothered me.' Her smile contrived to blend wryness with good humor.

Someone who didn't know Betty well, Holly mused – who was aware only of the lavish outlay of money on theater tickets, concerts, the steady parade of deliveries from Sak's and Lord and Taylor – would never guess her preoccupation with the underprivileged. Checks flowed to every cause.

Odd that Betty and Claire – the three or four times they'd met in her apartment – had not clicked the way she'd expected. For years – like Betty – Claire had been wedded to causes. She could close her eyes and hear Claire talking about her childhood on Essex Street. The Depression still lingered in her mouth.

'You know, I never tasted an orange until I was nine years old,' Claire had recalled in a rare moment. 'We never wasted money on toilet paper – Mom would save the tissue from the fruit they sold in the store. That Goddamn grocery store – always in the red because Mom couldn't refuse credit.'

But just these last few weeks a doubt budded in Holly's mind. Was Claire changing? Were Claire's *values* changing? Little things that bugged Claire now – like problems with schools, integration – came into fresh focus.

'There's the mailman.' Betty's face wore an incandescent glow as she spied the mailman emerging from the next building. 'Maybe there's something from Rolfe. We haven't heard in several weeks.' Then Betty shrugged. 'Oh, I'll pick it up on my way back down to the office.' Ashamed, Holly guessed, to admit how anxious she was for a letter.

Betty bolted into the lobby. Wendy prodded the stroller towards the corner with an air of candid enjoyment – keeping up a flow of gibberish with Jonny.

'You get hold of everybody?' Wendy's voice was undercoated with expectancy. 'I know you talk with Mitch regularly. What about Eric? Linda?'

'I've left word at half a dozen places for Eric. Do you know, it's at least six years since we've spoken? And we didn't honestly speak that time. I was coming out of an express subway car and he was dashing into a local. The door closed before we could get together for a few minutes, at least.' Eric had made no effort to elude that closing door, Holly recalled.

'What about Linda? Mitch still sees her,

71

doesn't he? Even after everything?'

'Once in a while. She's back in New York again. Mitch says she's marrying some character in the diplomatic service.' Wendy made a disrespectful noise. 'Anyhow, that's the way I heard it.' No time in her harried days now – and meager interest – to speculate about Linda's romp from nymphomania to lesbianism and now – presumably – back to what society labeled normalcy.

'Holly, you think I'm kind of creepy cutting Melinda out of the kid's birthday party, don't you?' Wendy threw at her in a sudden somber switch.

'I didn't say that,' Holly hedged. She'd never been able to dissemble before Wendy. 'But that little girl is going to be awfully hurt. Why can't you juggle to make it a lunch party for girls?' Holly tried again. Again, she asked herself – how can Wendy of all people do this?

'It won't work,' Wendy insisted. 'Carol would be heartbroken – she's already invited three boys.' The traffic light changed. They crossed. 'Look, for Carol it's no fun having a birthday party without boys. You know that age.' Apology blended with guilt in her voice.

'Put it squarely to Carol.' Holly was stubborn. 'Point out how Melinda is going to feel. She has to learn someday she can't have everything.' An unplanned sharpness laced her words. Why must Wendy make such a fetish of keeping Carol in a make-believe, goody-goody world? She'd have to live with reality. 'You could change it – Carol could tell the kids you put your foot down.'

72

Something Wendy never did with Carol.

'Look, *we* know what a rotten world it is. Let the kid at least dream a while.' Wendy was silent for a moment. 'OK, maybe I'll beat around the bush with Carol. If we don't ask Melinda, we have to discuss it.'

'No chance of your sleeping over?' Holly asked. All the passing years, their living in separate worlds – except for these snatched moments maybe a dozen times a year – didn't lessen the closeness she shared with Wendy.

'No such luck.' Wendy sighed. 'Tonight Jerry's kid brother – you remember Tim – he's coming over with his girlfriend for dinner.'

'He's getting married soon, isn't he?' She recalled meeting Tim once, when Carol was a toddler. A lean, sensitive-looking teenager then – the kind who seemed born to be hurt.

Wendy gazed into space. 'I don't know – something's happened. This is a new girl. I have a funny kind of feeling about it. Anyhow, Jerry and Tim talked forever on the phone last night, then Jerry told me he'd asked them over for dinner tonight. He hasn't got around to confiding in me yet about the marital situation.'

'Wendy, you knew Ron. What was he like?'

'You'd never notice Ron twice – unless he was turned on at a party. Sharp, though. Ron used everything and everybody that came in touch with him. We had a mad old time at a party once – I think he just wanted to see if he could make it with me. There was a kind of competition – about girls – between Al and him.' She chuckled. 'Would you ever think I lived it up that way?

73

Good old reliable Wendy, the staid Bronx house-wife loyal to one bedmate these many years!' Her eyes took on a yesteryear's glint. 'Jerry would die if he knew about those years when I was the belle of the ball. You know—' Laughter welled in Wendy, spilled over. 'I think back, and I can't believe it sometimes. Was I actually that swinging babe?'

'I thought you were absolutely marvelous,' Holly said softly.

'Did you?' Amazement, mixed with pleasure, shone from Wendy.

'To me, you were the ultimate sophisticate. I'd been brought up with such a blackout on sex, remember. The inference was you could get pregnant by holding hands. I couldn't share a Coke straw with somebody else – male or female – without recriminations. I might pick up syphilis.'

'We were pretty kooky – the way we had such confidence in good old US Rubber. I didn't have the nerve in those days to go to a doctor and buy a diaphragm.'

'I was sure you had the nerve for anything. You and Claire and Mitch – no inhibitions about anything.'

'So now I'm the Bronx housewife with budget problems.' Wendy's eyes were rebellious. 'It scares me, the way you can lose your identity. I'm never *Wendy* any more. I'm "Carol's mother", or "Jerry's wife". What about Wendy? Don't I have a right to be me? Thank God for the years of sleeping around!' Wistful defiance laced her voice. 'It wasn't always this rat trap.'

'Oh, Wendy—' Holly shook her head in affectionate reproach. 'You talk like a regenerate prostitute. You didn't sleep around that much.'

'Let's say I was shopping for a while. Anyhow, Jerry knew he wasn't getting a virgin.'

'That makes two of you,' Holly reminded.

'Holly, it was different with guys,' Wendy reminded. 'Especially in those years. Despite all the yakking about modern sexual freedom. Besides, he'd spent three years overseas.'

'We weren't having a ball here at home. Chewing our nails, scared to death of every news bulletin, writing V-mails—'

'You didn't mess around, Holly—'

'What would you call Al?' Holly retaliated. 'So we got married later – after much travail.' She smiled faintly. 'You know, it's wild the way you hear so much talk about promiscuity these days. Today's kids are just more honest. We did and shut up. They talk.'

'There were other fellows interested besides Al – nobody got close.'

'It was a closed corporation. I was tied up with Al and the Great Career. Most of the time.'

'Most of the time?' Wendy jibed.

'When he was shipped out, I stared at the ceiling plenty of nights and wished there was a pill to replace sex.'

Holly's mind dwelt on those early days with Al. Once Al made the pitch, nobody else had a chance. Al was a man – the others were boys.

How fast things moved after that first party. Al transferred to Governor's Island. Constantly underfoot. Wendy was working overtime like

75

crazy – eager to buy herself a fur coat. Muskrat was big those years. How long was it after that first party? Five weeks? Seven? How long before she was in bed with Al?

Time was a different dimension in those days. The future was scary. How could they know when Al would be shipped overseas? How could they know there'd be a tomorrow for them?

Six weeks – she pinned down the time she'd known Al before they made love all the way. By then, she'd been briefed on Al's reputation with women. Wendy was blunt. *'God – it's unbeliev-able the way girls are ready to stretch out on the couch for Al. Not just kids – women.'* Still knowing this she'd offered no resistance when Al made a big pitch for her. It was as though she knew this was predestined...

Seven

Mid-November, 1943

On a bitter cold November afternoon with the scent of snow in the air Wendy told her she'd be working late.

'Probably till ten or eleven,' Wendy reported blithely. 'I want to make a fat down-payment on the coat by Christmas.'

Holly went home alone – telling herself she

ought to take a shorthand course, go after a higher salary. But she wasn't genuinely concerned about money – just so there was enough for her own limited expenses, the ten dollars a week to go home. She was absorbed in trying to crack the freelance radio markets. Free writing time was more important than overtime dollars. But only Wendy – who talked about resuming a singing career 'after this bloody war is over' – knew her determination to be a writer.

She prepared herself a fast dinner, sat down to eat at the tiny table by the window. The radio switched to WQXR. Classical music filtered into the cozy warmth of the room, brought about by its contrived heat-raiser. For a while Holly relished the solitude. Not even a phone to disturb the quiet. Who could get a phone in the middle of the war? They were lucky to have one in the hall.

The doorbell buzzed. The apartment door. Someone had left the front door ajar again – the super would be livid. Holly ran to answer. Guessing it would be Al.

'Hi.' It was always a small miracle that Al came here on his time off duty – instead of to what Wendy called 'one of his glamorous, show-biz broads'. The tall, svelte type who wore silver fox before noon and would die before being seen in anything but spiked heels.

'Hi, baby—' Al's gaze caressed her, then swept about the room. 'Where's Wendy?'

'Working late. She won't be home until ten or eleven.' All at once there was a sudden electricity in the air. Holly's heart began to pound.

She knew this evening was going to be different. She could step outside of herself and watch. Al had kissed her often in these past weeks when they'd been alone briefly. She knew the taste of his mouth, the excitement aroused in her by the touch of him. Always a sense of waiting.

'We'll run out to the cafeteria for dinner later,' he said. 'But what about coffee for now? I hate the bilge we get at the mess hall.'

'Sure—' Holly hurried to the kitchenette while Al fiddled with the radio until he approved of the music. The poignant strains of 'Be Careful, It's My Heart' drifted into the room.

They sat over coffee – knees touching beneath the table. Al reported on barracks activities – slightly salacious, but she gloried in being considered grown up enough to be amused. If he had rushed her, she knew in a corner of her mind, she would have been scared off. She grew up in such a narrow little world. Coming to New York, meeting Wendy and her friends had catapulted her into a whole new – exciting – existence. That and the war, she thought defensively – nobody knew what lay ahead. All they were sure of was today.

Al pulled her to her feet, prodded her towards the sofa – coffee forgotten now. His mouth reached for hers. His arms closed in about her. She felt the heat of him. No stopping tonight. Instinct promised her this. Then he was drawing away, and she silenced a protest.

He leaned forward to switch off the lamp by the sofa, left her to switch off the other lamp.

The room bathed in darkness now. He returned to the sofa, pulled her close again. She was trembling. He coaxed the pale gray sweater above the rise and fall of her breasts. Even the kids in high school did this much. They used to talk about it – in the gym, the locker room, in low triumphant whispers.

His hands moved behind her. He unhooked her bra. The material went slack. Oh, his fingers were cold against her back! His breath touched her ear while his hands roamed.

'Know what you're doing?'

'Yes,' she whispered. Not knowing at all.

'Scared?' he asked after a few moments.

'No.'

'It's going to be great, Holly.'

For a little while part of her remained disengaged, observing – and then she was swept up in new, tumultuous emotions.

After that night Al and she were together every minute he was able to make it to the apartment. The specter of separation – a fear of what the future might bring – hung over them. To Holly it was a constant miracle that Al was clearly as totally in love with her as she with him.

In late January, 1944, he was put on alert. They knew he'd be shipped out any day. To Europe or the Pacific? That last evening when Al came in, he didn't have to say a word. Holly looked into his eyes and she knew. Looking stricken, Wendy kissed Al goodbye, and made the IRT trek to the Bronx to sleep over at her parents' apartment.

She and Al knew this would be the last time they could be together – for nobody could guess how long. She wouldn't allow herself to realize it might be for the last time.

'When do you have to report in?' This had happened to so many other couples since Pearl Harbor – and now it was their turn.

'Five a.m.' Al stood before her – clenching and unclenching one fist in helpless frustration. 'I'll have to leave about a quarter past four—'

Seven hours – perhaps for the rest of their lives. So senseless! How had the world allowed this insanity to happen?

Al left at twenty minutes past four. They clung together for poignant moments – and then he was gone. The hands on the clock were forever engraved on her memory. She stood – small and chilled – behind the closed door, then turned to gaze about the room –as though to will his presence here. Oh, he'd forgot his cigarettes, his lighter.

Instinctively Holly crossed to pick them up. Her impulse to run after him. But it was too late for that. He was out of the house. And he would not be back tomorrow night. He would be on a troop transport. In a blackout.

Holly dropped to the edge of the sofa. Her eyes fastened to the half-filled pack of cigarettes. She'd always meant to buy a can of lighter fluid. Al was forever running out. Her throat tightened. How did they survive – all those others whose men fought a war across an ocean? *How am I to survive?*

The first gray-pink streaks of dawn pushed through the blackness of the night. Wrapped in her robe – a present from Al – Holly huddled on the sofa. She couldn't bring herself to go back into the bedroom. Not yet.

Three hours later Wendy's voice – warmly compassionate – rocketed her into the painful new day.

'Hi. You plan on going in to work today?'

Reluctantly Holly opened her eyes. Still in coat and kerchief, Wendy hovered above her.

'Let's both call in sick.' Holly shivered, though the room was comfortable.

'Why not?' Wendy accepted. 'I never have any trouble. I leave off my make-up, look miserable, and everybody believes me. You get dressed, I'll make breakfast.'

Holly forced herself to go into the bedroom now. Where was Al right this minute? Was he on a ship already at sea? Was he quarantined with his company for secret departure? She wouldn't know anything until a postcard with his APO number arrived. Europe or the Pacific?

She shivered when she emerged from the shower. Sure, she thought with momentary rebellion, there was a shortage of oil because of the war. But landlords took advantage. Her hand was unsteady with lipstick and eyebrow pencil. Yet the face in the medicine-cabinet mirror looked the same. How could that be – when her whole world had fallen apart?

Ten minutes later she sat across the table from Wendy and pretended to enjoy breakfast.

'When you were a little kid, did you ever think we'd see a war? You learned, 1066, Battle of Hastings – but it had nothing to do with *us*.'

81

'I don't suppose any generation expects it.' Wendy was somber. 'You think – my generation's too smart. Until a nut like Hitler gets loose – and we land in the history books.'

'How did he ever crawl into power? How did people let him?' Holly's eyes were dark with reproach.

'Maybe we were lucky in this country,' Wendy said after a minute. 'Instead of Hitler, we had Roosevelt and the WPA and farm relief. Living in a small town during the Depression, you didn't feel it the way people did in the cities. The bread lines, the soup kitchens. So many people on Relief – you didn't feel shame – at least, that's what you told yourself.'

'My folks weren't WPA poor, but just one step behind. Dad was forever being swamped with some idea that was ahead of his time. And the way he worried about people! Still does. I remember how he used to rail about the starving Southern farmers who insisted on planting cotton year after year, and the people who worked in the cotton mills. We lived in the middle of cotton country – in a mill town. The mill workers worked twelve hours a day – for a dollar a day! Before the war, I mean. They lived in factory-owned houses, were scared to death of being thrown out if there was no work and they couldn't pay the rent.'

Wendy gazed into her coffee. 'Without money it was lousy everywhere.'

'I remember when I was in the first grade – I found out about the school's free-milk program. I was shocked when I realized those kids *wanted* that milk. My mother bribed me to drink Ovaltine. I brought two kids home for lunch with me when I found out milk was all they had for lunch. My mother fed them for two days. Then she must have talked to the teacher because they weren't allowed to go home with me after that.'

'In New York people with no money gathered on street corners and listened to the Socialists atop soap boxes. It was a weekend entertainment program. Not for me – I wasn't the Cause type. There was that big career waiting – only I never got to first base.' A rare bitterness tainted her smile. 'Maybe if the decent jobs hadn't come along, I might have stayed with singing. But there's that check every week – I can't let go.'

'Wendy, when is it going to be over?' Holly felt sick with anguish. 'When?'

'I don't know, baby. I don't know.'

Four days after Al sailed, Holly received the official postcard with his APO address. And then came the frightening delay of weeks before the first of a long line of tiny folded scraps of paper that was V-mail arrived. The lifeline between reality and unreality.

'We're in London,' Al wrote, 'though nobody knows how long we'll stay. The city's really taking it. Sightseeing through London, you begin to get an idea of what war is really like. Back home, Holly, you just don't *know*.' Then a two-line chunk deleted by the army censor. 'Bumped into a terrific character onboard ship – named Jake Saunders. With luck you'll meet him some-day.'

There was another deletion because Al became too detailed about the frantic training being thrust at them for a coming invasion. A final paragraph about places he had visited with the new buddy, Jake. Such a tiny space when there was so much to say, Holly thought in frustration – though Al had made a determined effort to cram as much as possible into the one small sheet. But V-mail was speedy.

Al's next letter arrived four days later. A half-dozen tightly packed pages of regular mail. He told her about the trip across, the crap games that helped kill the hours each day. About how weird it was to travel across the ocean in a blackout.

He had started kidding around with a revue for the men – writing the sketches, directing. His lieutenant had received sanction from head-quarters for Al to proceed with the revue. This was a real deal, Al boasted – he was being relieved from practically every duty in order to get the show on the boards.

He went on to marvel about the terrific talent he kept running into among the men. His enthusiasm and high spirits sang out from his rapid scrawl – and Holly was grateful.

As with so many others, Holly and Wendy lived in a maleless world. Al in England, Mitch in the Pacific, Norm in Italy. Male fringe members of their circle scattered among the armed forces. The apartment – which had seemed such a delightful oasis – was now a prison, inhabited by ghosts. The hours away from work dragged on endlessly. They pushed away time in the huge cafeteria on Broadway that had become a sort of club – lingering over Danish and coffee. Once a week – on occasion more often despite their limited budgets – they went to a neighborhood movie.

For those on the home front, movies were a drug, an escape from the real world. Holly and Wendy wrote a steady stream of letters – to Al, to Mitch, to Norm. Again, Eric had drifted out of sight. The radio was a constant source of war news. They never missed an Edward R. Murrow broadcast from London. It was a period of waiting. A world of achingly lonely days and nights.

Wendy loathed her new job as part of the steno pool in a major advertising agency – but the money was better. Now Holly moved into a new job. Before his latest disappearance Eric had introduced Wendy and her to an eager group of young people with entertainment-world dreams. They congregated in a spot ebulliently labeled the Genius Club.

At a reading of a play she met Sandra, who had set herself up as an agent four years earlier. Right away they clicked. Sandra offered Holly a job as her assistant – at ten dollars a week less than she was earning, but the prospect of working for Sandra was exciting. She accepted, clinging to the promise of an early raise. She'd manage till then, she promised herself.

Al wrote steadily. Between the lines Holly sensed the tensions eating away at him. She wished with painful urgency that she could reach out to touch him, even for an instant.

'The show's running smoothly,' Al reported. 'Of course, nobody gives us any inkling of how long we'll be allowed to keep running. Some of the material isn't bad. I feel real puffed up about it. Incidentally, from now on address your letters to Sgt. Al Rogers. The big brass put through the stripes for me because the revue's such a hit. Not bad, huh? If you can manage, send more salamis and cigarettes and chocolate bars. They're great!'

As with girls across America, Holly and Wendy connived to gather together salamis and cigarettes and chocolate bars. Covering the length of Broadway to buy a bar here, a bar there, cigarettes wherever they could find them. Conning everybody they knew for help until they'd acquired a respectable total.

Al wrote that his captain offered to pull strings to have him transferred to Special Services. He refused. 'I can't stomach the idea of messing around any longer with entertainment,' he wrote. 'Not after what I'm seeing in London.' The English astonished him with their unruffled acceptance of the bombings, of the destruction that inevitably was part of this. Then in the midst of a bombing, a GI appearing in Al's revue was killed.

'Twenty-two and loaded with ambition,' Al wrote. 'He might have made it, too. One minute I was talking to him. The next he was in my arms with his guts hanging out. It makes you sick to your stomach. Everything's quiet, and life goes on for a while like the world was normal – and suddenly all hell breaks loose. Across the way you saw a building five minutes ago. Now it's a shambles. You hear people screaming – kids crying. When you reach in to help, God knows what you pull out of the wreckage. Last night, I brought a five-year-old out of the rubble. He had nothing where there should be arms and legs. I sat down there with that half-dead kid cradled in my arms and bawled.'

Eight

Al tried to be patient with the woman shopper – in the midst of her tenth debate about which shirt would make a suitable birthday present for her husband. He felt guilty at his lack of patience – he railed religiously about the rotten attitude of sales help in general. Their credo, Al had long ago decided, was to do as little as they could and still draw a paycheck. GI thinking, he scoffed.

'Maybe I'd better just go sit down over a cup of coffee and think about it,' the woman hedged finally and took off.

'Why didn't you tell the old bitch where to go?' a fellow salesman demanded in disgust. 'I'll bet if she bought something, she'd bring it back for a refund tomorrow, anyhow.' The sales-man inspected his watch. 'Coffee-break time.' Suddenly he nudged Al. , get a load of that!' He whistled suggestively. 'That give you ideas?'

Al inspected the tall, heavily made-up blonde sauntering through the aisle. She wore a white knit suit that hugged her jutting breasts so snugly the nipples stood out in bas-relief, closed in about the overly ample buttocks in a way that was almost obscene.

'A dog.' Al withdrew his glance.

'Come off it, Al,' the salesman protested. 'That ain't foam rubber sticking out into your eyes, man.'

'I get the picture,' Al drawled. 'But if she stretched out for you, you'd run like hell.' Frank had a wife and six kids. He made a lot of noise about his sexual urges, but he'd probably drop dead if a babe offered it to him. All noise, daydreams – and at six o'clock he hurried home to wash the dishes, make bottles, help his wife with diaper changes.

Frank strode off for his break. Al straightened the disheveled counter. Straightening up was a compulsion with him – just standing still drove him nuts. Here it drove him nuts. But the blonde in the torso-hugging knit suit lingered in his mind – for some inexplicable reason. Until his memory jogged into position.

Rita. The blonde slut reminded him of Rita. Wow, that was going back! He wasn't apt to forget their first encounter. In London...

London was a mass of nerves. The American army was working feverishly with the British in an all-out defense of London. Al felt hemmed in, ripped apart inside with the need to strike.

Now there were times when he reproached himself for acting like a jerk. When the captain offered to pull strings to have him transferred into Special Services, why in hell hadn't he snapped at it? Jake told him he'd had a screw loose somewhere.

Fighting an attack of deep depression one night, he strolled about aimlessly, ended up in a bar on Piccadilly. He sat on a stool, ordered a drink. Moody, restless, hating the war, hating everything. And then he saw her. Sitting at the other end of the bar – only empty stools between them because it was early for business. She sat there in her Red Cross uniform – frankly appraising him. Which surprised him. Red Cross gals went for officers' brass and high spending. He was a lowly sergeant.

Heat rising in him, he stared back. Nearly as tall as he was. Large-boned, attractive. Twenty-eight, thirty. She picked up her glass and moved nearer.

'Hi.'

'Hi, yourself.' Automatically he offered her a cigarette. Conscious that she wore perfume. Perfume on a sexy bitch like this one belonged to another world.

She took the cigarette. 'The name's Rita, in case you're interested. Rita Maxon.'

'Al Rogers – and I'm interested.' He reached for his lighter. For a moment an image of Holly rebuked him. But that was another world.

'Over here long?' Her voice was low, caressing.

She had spent hours developing that voice, he decided. Nice developing. That went for the rest of her, too. High, full breasts, inviting hips. Legs tapered just right. His mind made guesses about the rest of her.

'Since late January,' Al told her finally – their cigarettes lighted. 'Four long lousy months.'

'Gruesome, isn't it?' She crossed her legs and his eyes lingered on the view of silken thigh exposed.

'You don't have to stay here,' he reminded. Excitement rising to high tide. No brass around? Or was this her night to slum?

'I'm not the type to sit at home and knit. I like things happening. All kinds of things.' Her hand brushed his as she reached for her glass. He knew it was deliberate.

'Another?' He was already signaling the bartender.

'You're from New York,' she guessed – head tilted back, breasts thrust forward. Every move calculated.

'Right to the head of the class. You?' His knee moved, encountered hers, remained with it.

'Kansas, but I moved around a lot before the war. I like excitement.'

'This kind?'

'Any kind.' She reached for the fresh drink – her eyes sending messages. 'To excitement.'

He grinned, a stirring low within him sending out messages. 'To excitement.'

They talked another few minutes, then he suggested dinner – though it was early.

'Great. I know a place where the food isn't too bad and the drinks are decent.'

The restaurant was a short walk away. The waiters knew her, hovered about eager to please. She traveled with heavy tippers, he told himself.

'You're a gal who gets around.' Under the table his knees jogged against hers as they sat sipping what passed for coffee.

'Would you like to sleep with me?'

He drew his breath in sharply, crushed out his cigarette. His thighs trembled with anticipation. 'I'll go crazy if I don't.'

He paid the check. They went to find a hack. He let Rita give instructions to the driver. She kept a hotel room five minutes away. There was no elevator. They walked up the five flights – Al swearing all the way. Rita was laughing with frank pleasure while she unlocked the door.

Inside she allowed him only a momentary brush of her mouth.

'Sit down and relax.' Rita shoved him into a chair.

She opened a cabinet, pulled out a bottle of Canadian Club, glasses. Al whistled in appreciation. She crossed to a makeshift closet, reached inside. With a smile of sultry promise, she disappeared into the bathroom. Even a private bath. Leave it to Rita Maxon.

Al heard the water running into the tub. A faint, heady scent seeped through the door. Bath salts blending with steam. He took off his jacket, tie, shirt, stretched out on the bed. This was every GI's fantasy.

Sooner than he'd expected, he heard the water chugging down the drain. He tensed in anticipation. The door opened. Rita appeared in the doorway.

After months of women in drab wartime English clothes, women in uniform, Rita was potent. War and dirt and death faded into the background. If you were a man, he thought, at this moment you were conscious of one thing. A sheer black nightie caressed her full figure. She made no effort to close the equally sheer negligee.

Wow, what an overheated bitch this one was! She knew what she was doing to him. Standing there with those tits shoved out towards him. Dark circles – big as silver dollars – surrounded the stiffening duskiness of the nipples. She would be as passionate as hell.

'You're a sight, baby.'

'You're overdressed.' She slid her hand beneath his undershirt.

'We'll take care of that,' he promised. Hot as eighteen.

After that night, every moment he and Rita could filch they spent together. Intuitively Rita knew when he wanted to make love, when he wanted to talk. Between his outbursts of hatred of the war, Rita waited. They both were sure this could end any day. Rumors were rampant about a coming invasion.

And then it came. D-Day. June 6, 1944 – and five thousand Allied ships were steaming across the English Channel to land over a hundred thousand troops on to the coast of France – and he was smack in the middle of it. The greatest mass invasion in history.

After D-Day his company was on the move, he remembered. But in September he ran into Rita for a frantic forty-eight hours. Close to Christmas, 1944, he stood waiting for Rita again with fevered impatience. In Paris. Wondering through what devious routes she had contrived to meet him. Through what beds?

To hell with that, he ordered himself – standing restlessly before the pension. He had a forty-eight-hour pass and empty nights to compensate. Hell, he hadn't had a chance to shave or bathe for days. They had been constantly on the move these last weeks. Once he swung the pass, he lit right out for Paris. Rita wasn't even sure he'd be here.

Then he saw her – swinging down the street. He strode forward to meet her. Every nerve in his body tingling with awareness of her.

'Looking for someone?'

'Al, you made it,' Rita crooned, clutching at him until a passer-by – laughing – ordered them to stop blocking the way.

The weeks apart had not dulled the memory. Now everything came rushing down on him like a spilling-over dam.

'Miss me?' A pain in his gut because there was this need for byplay.

'What do you think?' Her breasts jutted against his chest.

He glanced up at the entrance sign above them. Their designated meeting place. 'We staying here?'

'Everything's set.' Rita reached into her bag for a key.

He followed her inside, up the dark, narrow stairway. Then they were standing in the darkness of the room – the door mercifully shut behind them. Body to body in the darkness for an instant, then Rita reached for a light cord.

'I'm a wreck.' He grinned. 'Haven't had a bath or a shave for a lifetime.'

Rita brushed her cheek against the heavy stubble on his chin. 'We'll fix that.'

She pulled away from him. She was hot as a pistol, but she had to play games. She walked across the small room to the ancient but beautifully polished dresser, pulled shaving gear from a drawer, held up a bottle of shaving lotion.

'What's that thing?' he demanded, pointing to the galvanized-iron tub sitting in the middle of the floor. No private bath this time.

'What does it look like, sweetie?' Rita's smile was dazzling. 'You're having a shave and a tub. Start shaving!'

Rita picked up a kettle, sauntered out of the room, down the corridor. OK, play it her way. He crossed to the dresser, reached for the shaving cream. Rita made six round trips, until the iron tub was half-full. While he finished shaving, she dumped bath salts into the water. The heavy scent of honeysuckle filled the room. Al walked to her, held out a shaven cheek with a mute appeal.

'Later,' Rita rejected, eyes sparkling. 'Strip.'

Passionate as hell, but she was going to have it her way. Deliberately, he took his time undressing. Rita slid out of her jacket, kicked off her shoes. How long was she going to stay in the rest of that uniform? He could mentally see her without the clothes. Christ, she was built!

'All right, into the tub.'

'Yes, ma'am.' His eyes mocked her while he
94

stepped into the tub, sat down at her feet.

'I showered before I met you—' Her eyes were full of promises. In an era when a bath or a shower was the supreme luxury, Rita found no problems. In whose quarters had she showered?

'You're going to get all wet,' he warned when she reached to dip a washcloth in water. His hand reached beneath her skirt to brush her thigh.

'Wait,' Rita insisted.

'Enough playing games—' She was no longer in command.

Later – much later – they were lying naked across the bed – smoking the American cigarettes Rita had collected along the road. Neither of them heard anybody at the door. They both were startled when the door swung wide.

'Whoops!' The two fellows hovering there took in the situation rapidly.

'Sorry! Wrong room!' one of the men apologized as he reached to pull the door shut again. But Al recognized him. Knew *he* had been recognized.

'Hell!' He sat upright, scowling. Ted Conway, a character actor he knew from New York. Probably here with a USO troupe.

He was uneasy. No way this could get back to Holly, he soothed himself. Holly was reality. Tomorrow and the rest of his life. Rita was today, in the ugliness of war.

Al frowned – his memory trying to jog facts into place. What was it he heard lately about Ted Conway? Ted went down with a California-bound jet. He'd finally landed himself a part in a major new movie – after twenty years of small roles on Broadway – and zingo, he cracked up with ninety-one other people. Fate. How can you beat it?

Nine

Holly and Wendy moved leisurely across Eighth Street. Both for the moment content with being together, with Jonny crowing happily in the stroller. A sense of well-being flooded Holly. This was one of those little pockets of time when the world stood still, when you could exist for just that moment – enjoying the act of being. Time out of the jungle.

'Anyhow,' Wendy bubbled, 'this is one place we can walk along holding hands and nobody cares. I suppose they'd figure me for the butch type, and you're the fragile feminine flower.' She giggled. 'Carol still loves to crawl in bed with Jerry and me to cuddle. I suppose that would smack of incest.'

'I wouldn't worry about it,' Holly jibed affectionately. Her eyes searched along the street. Was the coffee shop still in existence? With the way the low buildings were being ripped down to make way for high-rise apartments, you never knew. 'There's the place.'

'Can we take the stroller inside?' Wendy

squinted at the small interior. 'Nice atmosphere,' she grinned, 'but not at the cost of losing a stroller.'

'We'll take Jonny in. Sit in a booth by the window to keep an eye on the stroller.' How many coffee shops had she occupied in these months of walking Jonny? Sometimes she just couldn't take another hour of the park. 'Jonny will probably grow up with a memory pattern of me with a mug in my hand. My coffee consumption is fantastic.'

'So is your work capacity,' Wendy reminded.

'It's a grind.' Holly slipped back into reality. 'You keep turning out this garbage – and you wonder, what in hell am I doing with my life? All this crap being sold, millions and millions of copies, Wendy. Even my junk – you know the print run of each is eighty thousand? If I do one a month, multiply that by twelve!'

'Don't run yourself down,' Wendy ordered. 'You pull down a healthy check each month. You're earning a living in a profession that's damn tough.'

'Mitch was dumbfounded when he found out how many titles I'm turning out.' Holly frowned, visualizing the peculiar look on Mitch's face when he realized this had become a full-time occupation. 'He gave me the old cliché about "prostituting my art".'

'Mitch is jealous,' Wendy dismissed this. 'He wishes to hell he could do what you're doing.'

'It's shit.' Distaste rode hard over her. 'But it's a steady market. They get shelf space in most bookstores.' Holly grimaced. 'My wonderful high-school English teacher would be horrified to discover I'm writing men's sex novels.'

'You don't use four-letter words,' Wendy reminded. 'To me that's clean.'

'My publisher would collapse,' Holly admitted humorously, 'if I ever used f-u-c-k. You just hint – suggest. But there's got to be a sex scene every twenty pages.'

'As long as there are men and women, there'll be sex, drinking, and dirty books.' Wendy looked at her watch, eyes narrowed in concentration. 'Carol's still at school. I'll give her a buzz later.'

Inside the coffee shop they settled themselves in a booth flanking the window. Jonny was content to concentrate on the passing crowds. 'Wendy,' Holly was pensive, 'how would you feel if Carol picked up one of those paperbacks? My brand?'

'Oh, come on, honey, don't develop a sticky conscience. Carol won't pick one up because I make sure I know what she's reading. And are you forgetting how it was when we were kids? We cruised through all the sizzling bestsellers, not reading plot or character – just looking for the sex scenes. You expect this generation to be any different?'

'The other day I decided I ought to inspect the field. You know – find out what's going on among the competition. Trying to take the professional approach,' Holly mocked herself. 'You should have seen me, self-conscious as hell. Walking back to look at what paperback stores like to call their "intimate novel section".' Laughter welled up in Holly. 'There I was – in

98

blue jeans and sneakers – clutching Jonny and trying to get a look at the titles of purple passion. I couldn't get *near* a book. The whole section was bottle-necked. There were these Madison Avenue, briefcase-carrying characters clutching at books for dear life – not moving for anybody. They probably figured me for some sex-starved little housewife. One of them was fastened to my latest release – I don't even remember what it's about.'

'Why don't they buy the books?' Wendy scoffed. 'Don't they know the high cost of living today?'

'Maybe they were afraid to take the books out of the store. Maybe it was their sex for the day, and they felt great about not having to pay for it.' Holly's eyes were aglow with amusement. 'So Jonny and I slunk out. There are four stores near the house, but I can't bring myself to go in and spy because they know me. The other day I went in to pick up another paperback thesaurus – Jonny made confetti out of mine – and I'm standing there talking to two women from our building, and all at once I'm mesmerized because there're about four of my titles in the rack beside us – and these babes are yapping about the current drive against hard-core pornography!'

'You don't write pornography,' Wendy emphasized. 'And you don't use your own name except when you go to the bank.'

A waitress came over to the table, took their orders, and whisked herself away. Wendy was enmeshed in thought.

'Maybe I'll phone up Jerry while we're waiting,' Wendy decided.

She fished in her purse for a dime, then sauntered towards a vacant phone booth.

'May I speak to Jerry?' Wendy was startled that somebody else answered his line.

'Just a minute. I may be able to catch him at the elevator,' a friendly male voice offered. Probably somebody who recognized her voice. Yes. She could hear the echo as he yelled to Jerry: 'Hey, Jerry, your wife's on the phone!' Where on earth was Jerry going in the middle of the afternoon?

'Hi, honey.' Jerry's voice, breathless from running back to the phone.

'Where are you headed in the middle of the afternoon?' she jeered. 'Off to meet some blonde?'

'To tell the truth, baby,' he began, 'I was kind of nervous about telling you—'

'Telling me what?' A premonition of trouble taking root in her.

'I promised Tim I would take the afternoon off—' Dead silence for a moment. 'To stand up with him at City Hall.'

'Tim's getting married?' Wendy gasped, incredulous. Tim just broke up with his last girl three months ago – when they were already talking about shopping for the rings. Nobody ever said why they broke up, but Jerry admitted her folks were to blame. 'I thought he had just begun to date this new girl. They're supposed to come over for dinner tonight.'

'I figured maybe once you got to know her,

you might feel better about it.' Jerry was stammering – which he did when he was deeply disturbed.

'What about this girl?' What was there for her to feel better about?

'She's about twenty, just out of nursing school. Tim's batty about her. Good looking, nice figure, brains—'

'Jerry, why are you trying to sell Tim's bride to me?'

'She's colored, Wendy.'

'Oh, Lord!'

'A hell of a sweet kid – I met her last week. Tim asked me not to say anything yet – not even to you. Mom's going to blow the roof off.' Jerry's voice held a note of humility that was poignant to Wendy. She wanted to reach out and cradle him, as she might Carol in a moment of hurt.

'Jerry, it's Tim's decision to make.' She strove for calm. 'If they're happy, whose business is it?' *But what a wild scene when Mom finds out!*

'We'll have them over for dinner tonight,' Jerry went on. 'They'll go to a hotel for the weekend. Tim's supposed to be driving out to the country for a weekend with a friend.'

'Mom'll have to know sometime.' Yet it would take time – even for her – to accept the full impact of this. Right now it was like something happening to somebody else.

'If Mom phones up, don't let on,' Jerry warned.

'Don't worry, I won't,' Wendy promised sharply. 'You can have that pleasure.' Poor Jerry, he always drew the dirty jobs in the family.

'I'd better run. I have to meet them at City Hall in twenty minutes,' Jerry said with a note of apology. 'Wendy, there's nothing we can do about it—'

'It's none of our business.' Amazing, how calm you could sound, when you didn't feel that way at all. 'Take them to a bar for a drink, Jerry – after the ceremony.' The mind seemed to work on a sort of independent, automatic push-button system. Her kid brother-in-law Tim – the sensitive, idealistic, neophyte social worker – was about to be married to a colored girl. And she, Wendy Meadows, was giving a birthday party for Carol, and *not* inviting a delightful, sweet thirteen-year-old because she happened to be black. 'I'll try to get home early and prepare something festive.' Shrimp cocktails for an opener – the frozen kind, she planned. Strawberry shortcake for dessert.

She walked back to the booth where Holly and Jonny waited for her. In this world you were always thirty seconds from tragedy. Pick up a phone, open a door – and there it was. Poor Jerry, he was a nervous wreck.

She felt the closest to Jerry when he was so humble. Fearing to hurt Carol and her – when no act of his was responsible. And so determined to do the Right Thing by Tim.

'You look upset.' Holly was anxious.

'Jerry pitched me a curve,' Wendy said with an attempt at humor. She sat down, sighed. 'I told you about Jerry's brother coming over for dinner tonight? With this new girl? Well, things have

102

been moving rather fast. He's marrying her this afternoon. Jerry was just about to leave the office – to meet them at City Hall. Mom doesn't know about it yet. Jerry and Tim are scared to tell her.'

'Why? Tim's twenty-six. It's his business if he decides to get married.'

'You know Jerry's mother by now.' Wendy sighed. 'She's got such definite ambitions for her children. I'm sure she's never been satisfied about Jerry and me, though she puts up a good front most of the time. Right color but wrong Church.' Wendy was Jewish – her mother-in-law Episcopalian. 'This will really knock her off that lower-middle-class perch of hers.' Wendy took a deep breath. 'Tim's marrying a black girl.'

'His mother will flip out.' Even with the civil-rights movement growing in strength, demanding changes, the subject of interracial marriage could be explosive. But this wasn't exactly an interracial marriage.

'Mom spent all these years weaning the family away from anything that smacked of black – and here Tim throws them right back to their dear old Jamaican grandmother.'

'She'll have to know sooner or later.'

Holly remembered all those years ago – when Wendy first began dating Jerry. She had noticed the golden warmth of his skin. They had talked together in candor.

She had not worried for Wendy and Jerry. They were adults. She had worried for their children. The world could be such a monstrous place for children of blended strains – who

103

found they were ostracized by both communities – belonging neither one place nor the other. But Jerry and Wendy were married. Carol was a lovely child – full of warmth and happiness and a personality that drew youngsters to her.

'Hell of a mess,' Wendy conceded, 'unless we keep it in hand.'

How was it going to look, in Wendy's all-white neighborhood – except for Melinda and her family – when Wendy opened her door to welcome a black sister-in-law? How did you break the news to a thirteen-year-old – in the protective womb of middle-class Bronx – that in reality she was one-eighth black?

Ten

Washington Square was autumn-tinted earlier than usual this year, Holly thought as Wendy and she lounged on a bench and watched Jonny crawl with absorbing curiosity over a patch of browned grass directly behind. She loved autumn. A season pregnant with sweet promise – a welcome relief from summer.

She loved this park – that was like none other in the city – with its potpourri of people, its sequestered corners for small children, its ice-cream wagons, its central fountain, its benches and expanses of grass. An urban campus for

NYU – shared with the long-time Village residents, the newcomers with creative and rebellious inclinations, nursemaids shepherding children from the newly sprouting luxury apartments. Two summers ago – protesting the heat – she had shed her sandals to wade with others in the fountain. Since then air-conditioning had entered her life.

'Holly,' Wendy pricked their introspective mood, 'would you mind if I left early? Maybe if I'm lucky, I'll get back home and find Carol there ahead of the others.'

'You want to pick up a subway downtown?'

'I'll walk back to the house with you. I know Carol can't be there much before five.' Wendy squinted in thought. 'They're going somewhere after school – Carol won't race right home. I'd like to be there by four thirty, though. Besides, I have to go back with you,' she said with an effort at humor. 'I haven't a thing to read on the subway. You wouldn't expect me to squander fifty cents on a paperback, would you?'

'We'll start back now,' Holly offered, rising to collect Jonny.

'I told Jerry to take Tim and his bride to a bar when they left City Hall.' A fatalistic somberness overtook Wendy. 'That'll give me a little extra time.'

'I know it's easy to say, don't get into a stew – but everything will work out better than you anticipate.'

How *could* it work out well? Holly taunted herself. Tim – who appeared white – and his bride would be another interracial couple – who could move about New York unnoticed only in the Village. She remembered inquiring about an apartment at a broker's office when she and Al first came back into Manhattan. She had gone in with the purpose of having a lease drawn up – and the broker had said to her, 'What about your husband – is he like you?'

She'd stared without comprehending until he added impatiently, 'Is your husband *white*?' There had been a charming Korean man – alone – in the next apartment when they moved in. But the rental office wanted no interracial couples.

But at this moment it was not Tim and his bride, their future, that was uppermost in Holly's mind. Nor in Wendy's, Holly guessed. How would Carol react?

'You know how I feel about people,' Wendy said after a moment as though reading her mind. 'They're all the same – whether they're white, black, or purple. But there's Carol, and no matter how many ways I try to look at it, this has to affect her. I remember the time Jerry's grandmother came up from Florida with his oldest sister – just that one time when I met her.' Holly knew Wendy meant the time when Jerry had let her confront the fact that his grandmother was black – and he had let her face it with no forewarning. No doubt scared and sick inside because this was still the kind of world where skin pigments have status values. 'Carol was just four then – and she wanted to know why GeeGee had brown skin.'

'Has she ever said anything about it since?' But kids were so complex. You never knew what went on in their intricate little minds.

'The old lady died two years after that. Carol never saw her again.' Wendy contrived a smile. 'Carol will have to marry a man who's broad-minded. I couldn't let him walk in blind.'

They strolled in silence for a few moments – both inwardly involved with Carol.

'I have a batch of paperbacks for you,' Holly recalled, anxious to rout out somberness. 'Al went on a kick a couple of weeks ago about finding himself a commercial market. Of course, it died a-borning.'

'I'll take as many as I can carry. Carol's almost up to me in reading now – though I still censor. It's a scream – when we go into one of our restaurants for a cheap dinner the nights Jerry's working late. We sit there – each of us with a book propped up before us – while we eat.'

'You don't know if you're eating porterhouse or hamburger,' Holly chided affectionately.

'I know,' Wendy chuckled. 'On my budget who can afford porterhouse?'

They began to walk more briskly – aware of the passage of time. Reluctantly they headed back to the apartment. She had much to get done, Holly reminded herself – and Wendy was nervous about getting home.

She should salvage a couple of hours to work on the current book. Maybe she could manage that. Al was working late tonight.

She was going to make Al cut down on the overtime, Holly promised herself. With him everything was one extreme or the other. As long as she was working the way she was, he was insane to torture himself with overtime. He earned a savage satisfaction, though, sweating out those extra hours at time and a half. In the evening, he admitted, he was too bushed to sit down at the typewriter and write.

It was terrifying to look into the past and recognize the wasted time – the years when they should have managed time for Al to write. For her to write. Now it was becoming an obsession, a constant frustration for Al. She tried to ignore her own distaste for what she was writing these days.

Yet in those years Al was not ready. The old quotation – that she had once thought came from Shakespeare but in reality derived from the Bible – sprang into her mind again: 'To everything a season—' Now was Al's season to write.

Sixteen years after WWII – when he was sometimes overwrought because American soldiers were going into South Vietnam as advisors – he was bursting with a need to write about the blessings of peace and the curse of war.

She had just unlocked the apartment door when the phone began to ring. She raced to pick up.

'How's everything?' Mitch asked. 'Pretty much set for the brawl tomorrow night?' Mitch was depressed, Holly sensed.

'Just about. A few last-minute details. You gave Linda the address and all?'

'I had lunch with her today. I try to keep my nights clear for work. I've made up my mind to finish this book before the first of the year.'

Holly was familiar with Mitch's book and his play that had been making the rounds for the last three years. 'Shall I bring a bottle?'

'No need,' Holly reassured. 'We're stocked. Al collected several bottles at the store as Christmas gifts. We never seem to drink any more.' She glanced at Wendy, who had deposited Jonny in the playpen and was busy repairing her make-up. 'Wendy's here – but she's racing to leave,' Holly added because Wendy was pointing to her watch. 'You'll see her tomorrow night.'

'You believe Ron's going to show?' Mitch was skeptical.

'Why not?' Holly was taken aback by the question.

'That's right,' Mitch said drily. 'You never knew Ron.'

They talked another few minutes. Mitch hung up. For no reason that she could pinpoint, Mitch's preoccupation with Ron's arrival in town disturbed her.

'Mitch sounds depressed,' she told Wendy.

'Didn't you expect that?' An unfamiliar acerbity colored Wendy's voice. 'The towering success comes home to roost. Mitch won't like that.' She headed for the kitchenette. 'I'm going to have one more cup of coffee before I make the trek back to the Bronx.'

Holly followed Wendy. Did Mitch have any real talent? She'd long been ashamed of doubts. 'Mitch sounded terribly depressed—'

'Mitch has been depressed for years. Before the war he was sure he was going to be the next Cole Porter. After the war – when he switched to novels – he was going to be the next John Steinbeck. We all run into stone walls somewhere along the way.' Wendy shrugged. 'We learn to live with our banged-up heads.'

'When I first met Mitch, I thought he was all breezy optimism. Until that time with Linda. Remember?' Holly winced in recall. 'He came in on a pass, and wound up at our apartment because Linda wasn't home. That was the night he told us he was going to ask Linda to marry him.'

Wendy nodded. 'So he goes charging over to her place after midnight and finds her between the sheets with the air force. Then he got stinking drunk, came back to us, and would have been AWOL if we hadn't sobered him up.'

'Do you think it would have lasted – Linda and the air-force captain – if his plane hadn't crashed?'

'Who knows? Maybe we were romanticizing when we figured that was the reason for Renée. I always wondered – how could a man-eater like Linda change to the lesbian scene?'

Holly tried to rationalize. 'Linda had tried everything else, I suppose—'

'I'm old-fashioned in some things,' Wendy chuckled in a spurt of good humor. 'Some things I prefer the old, reliable style.'

In retrospect those years seemed another world. And now Al – who seemed to her perennially young – was haunted by birthdays.

Wendy concentrated for a few absorbed moments before Holly's catholic collection of paperbacks, chose one for subway reading, stuffed three more in a tote, then breezily kissed Jonny goodbye.

'Back to the sticks.' She walked to the door with Holly. Her breeziness not quite camouflaging an undercurrent of frustration. 'Off on another rat race. It never stops, does it?'

'Tim and his girl are married. That should concern only them.' But Holly understood the complications ahead.

'Every neighbor on my block is going to consider it their personal business. Carol oughtn't to be hurt – but she will be.'

'Don't get an ulcer over something you can't help. Save your energies for things you can rectify.'

'I'll come over as early as I can tomorrow,' Wendy promised, pausing at the door. 'Don't try to do everything all by yourself.'

Eleven

Holly walked back into the living room, checked the clock. Too early to start Jonny's dinner. Maybe she could get ahead on the book. Jonny sprawled across the playpen like a relaxed puppy – yawned. His eyelids drooped. He was going to sleep, she thought – momentarily upset. But today it wouldn't matter if he took a nap again, stayed up till all hours. Al wouldn't be getting home before ten thirty.

Within minutes Jonny was asleep. She lifted him in her arms – feeling a rush of warmth, a sense of exhilaration that this small, beautiful bundle of humanity was hers – and carried him into the bedroom.

The buzzer in the foyer sounded. She walked swiftly to the intercom. 'Yes?'

'It's me,' Claire said. 'Buzz me in.'

'I'm parked downstairs,' Claire announced when Holly opened the door. 'Cindy's asleep on the back seat and my mother's reading a newspaper. I can just stay a few minutes. We were downtown shopping.'

'You losing weight?' Holly asked, inspecting Claire's ample frame.

'God, I hope so. I feel so damn self-conscious at going out on job interviews when I look like a cow.'

'You slimmed down before you got pregnant with Cindy,' Holly reminded. 'Do it again.'

'I'm trying.' Claire held up crossed fingers. 'I'm going to the doctor again. He said if I lost twenty-five pounds, he'd be in the mood to make a pass at me himself. I'm not sure if he was kidding or not. We've had one of those on-the-fence relationships for years. As long as nothing happens – and it won't,' Claire reminded, 'it's marvelous for my ego.'

'You mean it about going back to teaching? How are you going to manage with Cindy?'

'I'll have to get a woman in – that's all. Millions of other mothers do it.' Claire collapsed on the sofa. 'I'd rather not teach in private schools. I'm hoping for a city appointment. Not

112

only is the money better – I like the fringe benefits. By next September Cindy will be three – I'll be able to put her in a nine-to-three nursery school. That'll be helpful.'

'She seems young for a long stretch like that.'

'Holly, I'll flip my lid if I have to sit at home until she's five or six. Besides, how the hell can we get anywhere on Bernie's salary? You know what the apartment looks like! I haven't bought a piece of furniture since we got married – and that's fifteen years ago. We should be entertaining. Bernie ought to be bringing professional associates home socially – you know what contacts mean. But I can't stand having people see the apartment the way it looks.'

'How's Todd? Glad you took him out of private school?'

'I think it's the worst mistake we ever made. But Bernie hates the idea of private schools – he's got some mental fixation about their being breeding places for a future snob generation. Plus, of course, it made an awful hole in our budget – even with the scholarship. And now we've got this bussing bit hanging over our heads.' Her grimace was eloquent.

'I wouldn't expect that to bother you.' Holly was startled.

'When things touch you personally, they take on a new coloring. I can rationalize all I want – but when I see my kids on the point of getting an inferior education, you can be damn sure I'm going to balk!'

'What's inferior about Todd's education?' Holly challenged. Claire, the great social reformer? Claire, who was forever emotionally aroused over social injustices? Or was it that – through the years – she had failed to notice the shifting in values in Claire and Bernie? This afternoon she was conscious of problems that normally remained in the background of her mind – except for outbursts of indignation about school segregation in Little Rock and the bus strikes in Montgomery. 'I thought you moved near that school because it was one of the best in Brooklyn.'

'That and because it was also close to Bernie's office,' Claire acknowledged. 'But it's the fringe area that bothers me. They've got these kids coming in – real hoodlums. I have to be afraid to let Todd go to school with money on him because some little shit might slug him to get it. It's time to be disturbed!'

'Don't they police the school areas?' So soon public schools would be a problem close to Al and her. 'They can't terrorize little kids like Todd inside the school.'

'They're doing it.' Claire's face was grim. 'And if they start bussing in, it'll be worse. Why can't they leave the few decent schools alone? No, they've got to wreck what little remains open for the middlc-class parents. Today, you have to be either culturally deprived or rich enough to afford private schools.'

'Al and I won't ever get into the private-school rat race.' Holly was firm. 'At least a thousand a year for one kid, two thousand if we have an-other. How do you raise a family and maintain your sanity?' *How many years can I stay on this grind of a book a month? Just to keep above water!*

'That's what Bernie's been saying all along,' Claire picked up. 'Our kids are going to public schools. But even Bernie's beginning to realize we're a vanishing breed. Holly, be realistic. When you have bright kids, you want the best for them. Our public-school system is geared to the deprived child. Screw the middle-income families. You know how many schools in the city are losing their specialists? Every school in an area of comfortable family incomes!'

'We didn't go to private schools.' Holly was faintly defiant. 'We survived.'

'This is a different world.' Claire was brusque. 'The great affluent society.'

'That lives on the brink of bankruptcy,' Holly expanded. 'We're greedy, Claire. We demand so much.'

'Oh, come off it.' Claire checked her watch. 'What was so noble about starving to death, living in decrepit flats? Twelve years ago my mother-in-law and father-in-law made a bonfire on a farm up in Connecticut – to burn their books. They were supposed to be card-carrying Commies. So put them into an affluent society – and what do you discover? My mother-in-law wears an autumn-haze mink stole, and every summer she runs to the Concord for three weeks. Times change. *We* change.'

'They were never real Commies,' Holly scoffed.

'Give anybody a piece of affluence – they forget about being Communists. Look at Bernie's two older sisters. Stiff-necked Republicans these days. Only the kid sister writes songs for Freedom Riders.' Claire paused. 'Did I tell you what a scare we had last week?'

'No.'

'An FBI agent showed up at Bernie's office. He nearly collapsed, until he discovered the FBI character was looking for information on a family he's been working with. For one wild minute, he thought— "Joe McCarthy rising from the grave." '

'Claire, that's past.' Holly's throat tightened. She didn't want to remember the Joe McCarthy period. She had to be hit over the head to realize it could even reach out to touch Al and her. The dark days of democracy.

'I'd better get down to the car before Mom has a fit,' Claire said reluctantly. 'She's burnt up enough because I'm trying to get back to work. "You're a terrible mother! How can you do this to your children?" All that hogwash. What am I supposed to do? Vegetate before a gas range and a kitchen sink because I went through the biological act of having kids? They won't be cheated because I'm working. They'll have more.'

'I don't know.' Holly was honest. 'I look at some of the nurses and kids in the park – and I'm uneasy. Some are great – but how do you know what you're getting?'

'You pay top wages, you get top people.' Claire rose to her feet. 'I didn't sweat my ass off to get two degrees just to throw them overboard. I wish to hell I could go back for my doctorate, teach at college level.' She walked to the bedroom door, opened it, gazed inside. 'Ah, he's a gorgeous one,' she crooned. 'I was sure you two would never have kids.'

'Jonny was an accident,' Holly admitted. 'Al always insisted he had no room in his life for kids – he would be a terrible parent. You heard him, Claire. But somebody at the store gave him a bottle of champagne for Christmas. Then at New Year's Eve we had ourselves a high old time – just the two of us. Zingo, Jonny.'

'I figured,' Claire grinned. 'Even though you said you just got careless. I had a hunch it was less prosaic.'

'Now you know.' Holly's smile was tender. 'Anyhow, I'm grateful for that bottle of champagne.'

Claire squinted at her watch again, sighed. 'Damn, where does the time go?'

'Too fast, it goes.' Forty-six years of it gone for Al.

'I've got to run,' Claire apologized. 'Todd'll be coming home from his woodworking group. You'd think that at eleven Todd would be no trouble at all with Cindy – but sometimes I feel like a referee instead of a mother. Oh, shall we bring a bottle tomorrow night?'

'We have plenty around,' Holly assured her. 'If we drink once a year these days, it's a lot.'

'What about Linda?' Claire lingered at the door. 'You expecting her tomorrow night?'

'She said she wouldn't miss it. I haven't seen her in years. Mitch says she hasn't changed a bit.'

'I'd hate to think that,' Claire drawled. 'Or was Mitch referring to the "before Renée" Linda?'

Holly started at the low, fretful cry from within the bedroom.

'Go to him,' Claire said briskly. 'I have to run.'

Jonny was asleep, in his cherished frog position – face burrowed in the pillow, rump raised high, firm small legs tucked beneath him. He'd cried out in his sleep – that stinking tooth trying to push through.

The door chimes tinkled. Holly hurried from the bedroom to the foyer. Probably Betty. She knew this was Al's night to work late. Holly cast a cautious glance in the direction of the clock. Still too early to phone her mother.

'I brought along my own percolator.' Betty greeted her with a whimsical grin. 'I knew you wouldn't throw me out with fresh coffee in tow. Or are you working?' She inspected the cluttered work corner.

'It's futile,' Holly admitted. 'It's like my whole past rose up to hit me in the face today. All because of that lousy dinner party tomorrow night.'

'I'm not sure I'll be welcome after tomorrow night,' Betty jibed. 'Not after you've entertained a Broadway playwright at dinner.'

'Marty was telling me about your plans to retire.' Holly went into the kitchenette for mugs. 'Sounds fabulous.'

'I figured it was about time. Give us a chance to travel. All we've actually had in close to thirty years was two weeks in Europe, eleven years ago.'

118

'What do you hear from Rolfe?' Holly asked. 'I haven't heard a thing for three weeks,' Betty admitted. 'I'm dying to know what's going on. But I told Marty – we've got to take a "hands off" attitude. It's Rolfe's life – he has to find his own path.' She was silent for a moment. 'He probably didn't write because they're so busy with sightseeing trips. He and his roommate go chasing off weekends to other countries. It's marvelous how close everything is in Europe.'

'Think you'll miss the job?' It was difficult to imagine Betty not involved with the cases that made up her daily life. If there were ever a dedicated social worker, Holly thought with respect, that was Betty.

'I might for a while,' Betty conceded. 'When you've lived with something for thirty years, it can be a wrench to leave it behind.' A compassionate smile lifted the corners of her mouth. 'Like eleven-year-old Pedro. That kid keeps me awake nights. He was sent to me because he's having such trouble in school. Not the language problem. He's been here over a year – he's picked up English. But he has to share a bed with his mother. The trouble is,' Betty chuckled ruefully, 'Mama brings business home. Pedro never knows what man he'll find in bed with Mama.'

'Oh God!' Holly shivered.

'Too bad Marty isn't in my job – he could have written a dozen books by now.' Betty glanced at her watch. 'I'm keeping tabs on time because I have to meet Marty for dinner and then we're going to an Off-Broadway play.'

'I shudder to think when Al and I went out together last. Before Jonny was born,' Holly surmised. 'It's wild, how you get turned into a narrow little world of bottles and diapers, and feeding schedules.' The only time she went out now was when Mitch prodded her into going to the theater with him and Al babysat.

'I don't know how you manage to work.' Betty shook her head. 'You turn it on and off like a spigot.'

'It's formula stuff.' Holly shrugged.

More and more, discontent was seeping through the surface – despite the welcome checks. She had to stay on this for an unforesee-able future, she reminded herself realistically. Three years ago she would have considered what she was earning a fortune.

Where did the money go every month? All the extra expenses of the baby, the high rents, sitters when she had to go in to the office with a finished assignment, the dentistry that cropped up when you least expected it. And she needed help to keep up with the writing.

She didn't count the check to her mother each week – that was a responsibility. One she'd never shirked. Even when Al and she were scrounging for dimes – when a trip to a hock shop was necessary – the money was there for her mother.

'One gorgeous thing about retiring,' Betty sighed pleasurably. 'No getting up in the morn-ing until I'm ready – I can lie in bed and read till four in the morning if I'm in the mood. I'm looking forward to it, Holly.'

'Like I'm looking forward to nursery school,' Holly said, and laughed. 'He's only fourteen months but the time goes so fast.'

'Don't push Jonny out too quickly,' Betty cautioned. 'Sometimes I think that's why Rolfe is so independent now. We *planned* on Rolfe. We wanted him. But I was in a rush to get back to work again. We had to lie about Rolfe's age – make him five months older than he was – to get him into a nursery school from nine to three, five days a week. When I think of it now, I wonder if it was a mistake.'

'Jonny's awake.' Holly leapt to her feet. 'I'll go collect him.'

Jonny was trying to climb over the crib bars. Holly reached to scoop him up. She relished the weight of him in her arms, the soft face against hers with its sleep-warmth. The most fulfilling emotions in all of life were not bound up with income and status and the towering rat race, she thought. They were evoked in moments like this.

Holly walked back into the living room. Betty sat with shoulders hunched in tension. Her usually serene eyes stripped bare.

'Rolfe won't ever come back to us, Holly. He may come back to the city – but he won't come back to us.'

You held him in your arms like this, Holly thought in compassion – and eighteen, twenty years later, you have to let go. The basic pattern changed little. Only the characters, the costumes, changed.

Twelve

Wendy closed the paperback with a sigh of relief. The train was pulling into her station. There was no such thing as missing the rush hour any more – unless it was by traveling at five in the morning. There was the working crowd, the school crowd, the shopping crowd – and then the reverse trips all over again. No matter what time you tried to push yourself into the subway there was the shoving, the sweat and – too often – the standing. Damn!

She allowed herself to be prodded to the door and on to the platform with the disgorging hordes. You lost your identity on a subway – you were part of the mass. Where didn't you lose your identity in this highly refined civilization? You were a number on a computer card, so-and-so's mother, so-and-so's wife, a social-security statistic. What had happened to *people*?

The outdoor air felt refreshing after the hour of standing, jammed into anonymous bodies. Right now she relished the chill, dreaded the evening ahead. No matter how they tried to rationalize about Tim's marriage, this evening would be nerve-wracking.

Dusk was beginning to close in about the rows of two-family houses, with here and there an apartment house. Lights glowed from kitchens where housewives were beginning the rites of preparing dinner. Small boys skated along the sidewalks. Women hurried home with supermarket bundles, piled high with the day's specials, pushed shopping carts of bulging laundry. Students caught in late sessions walked in noisy clusters.

Just ahead of her a middle-aged couple squabbled, ignoring passers-by, embroiled in their personal, private hardship. The woman's voice soared perilously, shrieking out her recriminations. Men were a race apart. After the first few years of marriage you learned that fast enough.

Jerry and she fought a lot – mostly about money – but she could never in truth say that she regretted the marriage. Sexually, they were fabulous together. She could never have lived with a man who was not passionate. She knew that, long before Jerry. She had been ready for marriage at eighteen.

Had Eric ever been anything more than a habit with her? Her first big love. Her first complete love. He had been so ashamed of himself afterwards – that first time. Blaming himself for letting it go so far. Their last year in high school, and both of them deeply involved with the Glee Club musical. God, how young they had been!

She walked up the hill towards the row of two-family houses where they had been living for almost six years now. At first it had been a joy to spill over from three tiny rooms into the luxury of a six-room flat. But the six rooms were a work trap. The house was never honestly warm

123

enough in winter, deadly hot in summer. Maybe next summer – if she kept working – they could afford to put air-conditioners into the bedrooms.

She slowed down as she neared the stuccoed house that was a replica of every other house on the block. Was Carol home? She didn't want Carol to walk into the house and see Tim and his bride sitting there together. Her hands were unsteady as she fumbled for keys. Her ears strained for sounds from the upstairs flat. The minute Carol walked into the house, she flipped on the record player or the TV. The house was silent. She pushed open the door, girding herself for the evening.

'Ma?' Carol's voice drifted from the bathroom.

'It was so quiet,' Wendy bubbled in relief. 'I thought you were still out.'

'I wanted to try out a new hairstyle.' Carol sighed. 'I just hate the way I've been wearing it.' She inspected her reflection with impatient young disapproval.

'It looks right for you.' Wendy searched her mind for words. 'Tim's coming over for dinner,' she began.

'Some of the kids are coming over after dinner, but Tim won't care.' Carol loved the way she allowed the house to be a sort of teenage club. 'Tim's sweet.'

'Head off the mob tonight,' Wendy told her.

'Why?' Carol swung about to face her mother. Her blue eyes mirrored astonishment.

'Honey—' How did she tell Carol? 'Honey, Tim got married this afternoon – we're having a sort of wedding dinner tonight.'

Carol's mouth hung open. 'Why so sudden?' She giggled, pleased that she could talk so frankly to her mother. 'She isn't pregnant?'

'Absolutely not.' Wendy managed a look of amusement. 'But it's hardly the time to have a gang over.' That wasn't the main reason, Wendy reminded herself. Why couldn't she come out with it?

'OK,' Carol accepted calmly. 'I'll pass the word along.'

'Carol,' Wendy tried to maintain a casual tone, 'there's something else you have to know.' She cleared her throat as Carol faced her with a sweet, inquiring gaze.

'What, Ma?' Carol frowned, puzzled at her mother's reluctance.

'It's about Tim's wife,' Wendy said slowly. 'She's colored.' For an instant Carol's face mirrored shock, then her face was impassive. Only her eyes showed that the knowledge startled her.

'Does Grandma know about it?' Carol asked.

'Not yet,' Wendy admitted.

'Oh, boy, will she blow her stack!'

Carol concentrated again on her reflection in the mirror. She lifted the brush to tease a flip about her face. Whatever went on in Carol's mind, Wendy thought, she was not going to find out.

'I think I'll run down to the supermarket again,' Wendy decided. 'I should have picked up a couple of chickens to throw into the rotisserie.'

She must do something about Carol's birthday party, Wendy admonished herself. A shudder racked her as she remembered her first protective instinct – to go along with Carol's innocent insistence that a party without boys just would not be any fun at all. *How could I have considered not inviting Melinda?*

It must be an all-girl luncheon, with Melinda on the guest list. Carol would have to understand. Later, they would talk about it. Carol must learn the necessity of compromise.

By the time she arrived at the supermarket, the lines at the checkout counters snaked far back into the store. She shopped what was essential only, hurried to wait her turn at the register. If the party tomorrow night was anyone's but Holly's, she would have begged off.

Maybe she could persuade Jerry to take off, go downtown to a movie with Carol. *The Music Hall*, maybe. For Carol, Jerry might give up overtime.

Thirteen

Al shoved his way through the influx of after-office-hours shoppers who were beginning to clog the store aisles. With luck he'd be able to clock out ahead of Bill. Tonight he'd prefer to sneak off alone to the delicatessen, eat there instead of the store cafeteria – where dinner was provided on the house. God, he loathed the slop they dished out in the cafeteria – or did it taste that rotten because working in the store depressed him so?

He made it to the time clock five minutes ahead of normal Friday night dinner punch-out time. Damn, there was Bill. Normally, the old man's company was a pleasant break in the day. He was a real character.

'Hey, Al,' Bill McHenry yelled with his booming voice that belied his sixty-two years. 'Wait'll I clock out of this fleabag.'

Al reached for a cigarette, lit it, drew a few drags before he hid it in the palm of his hand. It gave him a small satisfaction to thumb his nose at store regulations. Now he was going to have to sit down with Bill and be tortured with more tales about the house.

'Seven weeks more,' Bill breathed reverently as he fell into step beside Al. 'Seven weeks and I'll be out of this rat race forever.'

The two men shoved through the aisles, emerged into the early evening briskness.

'How did you ever stay for thirty years?' Al asked, a coldness clutching at him. *How much longer of this penal servitude can I handle?*

'I'll be damned if I know where those thirty years went. First there were the kids, one after another for ten years – and nobody was making much money in those days. The union came in, conditions got better, I worked enough overtime to put some money by. The missus and I decided to try swinging the house up in the country.'

'How the hell did you manage it on a salesman's salary?' He knew in his heart that he and Holly couldn't deal with buying a country house. Not without going into painful hock.

'Prices weren't so crazy fifteen years ago – and the house is three hours out of New York. How many city people would go for that much driving on weekends? But I tell you, Al, without that house and those acres up there I would have blown my cork long ago. That's living. The old lady and I split the driving – but I cussed a lot through the years.'

'But now you want to sell it,' Al reminded. God, he needed that house. The book was ready to pour out of him – but not in an hour grabbed here, an hour grabbed there. No phone calls, no interruptions – sleep when he had to, eat when he needed a break. A year of solid work, and he'd have it. 'You're bluffing,' Al tried to be jovial. 'You'd never sell that place, you old dog!'

'I'm retiring – and the pension's not good.' McHenry shrugged as he and Al walked into the deli – lightly populated this early. 'And I won't be drawing social security for another three years. The old lady and I figured it out – time to sell the house.'

They chose their regular table near the rear. Al sat back, inspected the older man in friendly scrutiny. How did a man stay in one dull job for thirty years? How had he let himself fall into a rut like this? It was supposed to be temporary – a few months.

'We're buying a trailer this weekend,' McHenry announced. 'We've been dickering over the price about ten days now.' He chuckled. 'But they've seen the light. We go over to pick it up tomorrow morning.' His eyes narrowed. 'When are you going to get off the fence and make up your mind about the house? It's a sensational deal – I'm not conning you, Al.' His voice took on a serious note. 'I tell you frankly – it takes time to sell a house that far out of the city. And if we want to eat something besides hamburgers and spaghetti, we'll need the extra money each month that comes from the payments.'

'Why do you have to worry about payments? If the buyer gets a bank mortgage, you've got the whole thing at once.' Al was startled.

'Don't want it that way. Didn't I explain that? We'll hold the mortgage. We're better off getting checks each month to tide us over. If we get a big chunk of dough, Molly's going to blow it on the kids. One of 'em will need a new refrigerator, another down-payment on a house out on the Island, one or two with a whopping big dental job. That money won't last if we get it in hand,' McHenry said with dry practicality.

'It's a big step,' Al hedged.

Holly and he had a wild battle each time he tried to talk about buying Bill's house – if they could persuade a bank to give them a mortgage. The idea of another bank loan threw her into panic. So in the past they had got burnt good. That didn't mean it would happen again. And Bill wanted to hold the mortgage himself.

'You won't find a piece of property like mine every day in the week,' McHenry warned. 'Nice little house – I'm not saying it's a fancy show-place, but it's comfortable. Big kitchen, a working fireplace in the living room, two bedrooms.

Taxes low, don't cost much to heat.' His eyes took on a glint of satisfaction because Al was listening with hunger in his eyes. 'Seven acres of God's country. You sit out there in the back and you look over the hills. A brook that keeps running when every other one in the county goes dry. A man who wasn't as lazy as I am might make a swimming pond out of that brook. A big wooded parcel out back, chock-full of chipmunks, coons, cottontails – more than once we seen deer drinking down there by the brook. And when it snows, you never saw anything like it – unless it's the autumn when everything changes color, and you wish you knew how to paint.'

'We're living high right now,' Al admitted. 'Crazy rent. We've been talking about getting a car in the spring.' A car loan would bring their monthly expenses up another eighty a month. Neither Holly nor he wanted anything to do with a second-hand car. A new one – no headaches every time you turned around. Holly was talking about hiring a woman to help with the kid, he remembered uneasily. 'Even if I could make the down-payment, it would be rough. And what's the use?' Al forced himself to be candid. 'I can't raise four or five thousand to plunk down on a house now.' The couple of thousand they'd squirreled away had to stay for emergencies.

'No down-payment,' McHenry said after a flicker of hesitation. 'All you'd need would be closing costs.'

Al stared in astonishment. 'Nothing down?' Excitement spiraled in him.

'I got a feeling for that house – like it was a kid
130

of mine. I'd like to see you up there. You'd be surprised,' McHenry said with unexpected gentleness. 'You won't even hate the job so much if you have the weekends to tide you over.' He'd never mentioned to Bill that what he wanted to do was to chuck the lousy job, move out there on a full-time basis. 'So it's a hell of a lot of driving. It's worth it. And you can spend your vacation time up there.'

Al cleared his throat. 'Let me talk to Holly. Maybe we can take the train out Sunday afternoon.'

'And drive back into the city with Molly and me.'

Al scrounged around in his pocket for his wallet. 'I think I have your country phone number some place. I'll buzz you Saturday.' Hell, Holly could work anywhere – as long as she had her IBM. He craned his neck for a view of the phone booths, spied an empty one. 'Order me a corned beef and French fries,' Al said. 'Let me see if I can get a call through to Holly.'

He dialed the apartment, swore quietly at the busy signal. He might have known it. This time of day Holly would be phoning her mother.

Holly sat on the arm of the sofa – her shoulders tense while she listened to her mother's current store of unhappiness. Jonny was content – for the moment – to explore the box of miscellaneous toys that masked the fact that he was her playpen captive. How had she forgot to call last night? Holly searched her mind, only half-listened to the recounting of a restaurant slight. They

131

had been so involved, Al and she, with the discussion about Ron. Then Al had started up again on that country place. How could he be so unrealistic?

'People seem to look for me to be nasty to,' her mother droned. 'I should be used to it.' She was still flipping mad because of the missed phone call, Holly thought tiredly. 'Even as a child, I was the one who got the short end of the stick. Rhoda was the oldest sister and Jack was the baby and Anne was delicate. I was always the leftover one.'

How many thousands of times had she heard this? She should be sympathetic. There was a reason when people faced the world as her mother faced it. If her mother was a character she was writing, she'd dig down to the roots. *Understand.*

'The ceiling's damp again in my room,' her mother's voice dragged Holly back to the present. 'But I'm not going to say another word about it. And the light in the hall just outside my room blew two days ago. You think anybody bothered to fix it?'

'Mother, tell them.' What did her mother expect *her* to do?

'There're other people on the floor – let them complain. Why should I always be the one?' Again, the familiar self-righteous disposal of a problem.

'About the ceiling, Mother.' Holly fought a losing battle to remain casual. 'A piece of wet ceiling can fall and hit you on the head.'

'Don't shout. You never know who's listening

on the switchboard.'

But her mother launched forth on a lengthy dissertation about the manners of the hotel help, her personal sufferings at the hands of unfeeling humanity, on and on. It was a familiar litany – repeated endlessly through the years.

'What happened last night?' The real core of her mother's anger surged to the surface. 'I waited and waited for you to call.'

'I'm sorry – I forgot.' Her mother was never in the hotel before five thirty. In the summer – with the days longer – it was later when she returned from her circuit of cafeterias, park, and library. By eight o'clock she was in bed with a magazine – annoyed if it was necessary to get out to answer a wall telephone. 'It was a madhouse here,' Holly apologized. 'Jonny took a fall. I burnt a pot. I'm sorry.'

I know she's lonely. That's the reason for the daily phone calls, the twice-weekly visits. Why can't she find friends for herself?

The outraged refusals every time she suggested her mother join the neighborhood Golden Age! She'd find companionship there. Activities. Older people did nothing but complain, Mom scoffed. They always wanted something of you. Nobody would get the chance to use *her*.

'How's my precious little darling?' her mother demanded finally.

'Into everything,' Holly reported with a tender smile, and launched on the expected recitations.

'Well, I suppose you're busy. I'll see you in the morning.' The aggrieved note was still there.

133

'I'll make it nine o'clock, to be sure. So I won't be in the way.'

'Al's out by eight thirty,' Holly said tiredly. 'Eight thirty is fine.'

Fourteen

Holly dropped Jonny into the feeding table, placed dinner before him. A sandwich and coffee for herself. It was absurd to prepare a meal. The whole evening work schedule was shot – the way Jonny grabbed the nap earlier.

Damn, if the walls in these so-called luxury apartments were not so thin, she could type late at night. *No point in stalling any more. If I'm going to have to keep up with deadlines, I'll have to get help with Jonny.*

Jonny enthusiastically tackled the challenge of feeding himself. Holly ordered herself to ignore the mess – it was great for him to have this experience. She sat down – her mind pushing ahead to the party. After all these years of Ron's being a shadow in their lives, she looked forward to meeting him.

She finished the sandwich, poured herself a coffee refill. Al hadn't phoned on his dinner break – that was unusual. But he was so worked up over the house he probably forgot. Why couldn't Al be realistic? He *knew* they had responsibilities now, with the baby. They had to think ahead.

Restlessness tugged at her while she tried to relax with the second cup of coffee. She had no reason to feel guilty at refusing to go along with this new obsession of Al's. Between her mother and Al, she was forever feeling guilty.

Jonny was done with dinner. He sat back in the table with a complacent grin. She made a swift surface foray over the messy areas, reached for the bottle that had been sitting in a pot of hot water, and scooped Jonny up from the feeding table. He would curl up at one end of the sofa with his bottle. She would collapse at the other end with the remainder of her coffee.

She and Jonny were settling themselves on the sofa when the phone buzzed. Without lowering her feet to the floor again, Holly reached out to pick up.

'Hello—' A bright, determinedly cheerful greeting because she expected it to be Al.

'Holly, I'm ready to kill myself.' Claire's voice was grim.

'What happened?' Holly knew Claire well enough not to be unduly concerned. Not yet.

'I turned my back for two minutes – and Cindy has the living room littered with cornflakes! While I'm cleaning that up, I realize things are too quiet. Cindy was in the bathroom, standing on the washbasin. She'd pulled open the medicine chest and was all set to sample an antibiotic!'

'How did she get up there?'

'Who knows?' Claire sighed. 'How do you live through this?'

'Move to higher shelves,' Holly warned. 'I've told you. The ideal, childproof house would have everything at ceiling height, with pulleys to bring down whatever you need. And locks on the pulleys!'

'I called to see what you're doing about dishes. I have a service for twelve that we keep for special occasions. Want me to bring it down?'

'I'm borrowing from Betty. We're down to a service for four,' Holly said wryly and chuckled. 'It started out as a service for eight.' She remembered Al's exhortation about buying. She'd worry about that later. 'Thanks, anyway.'

'Oh, I'm sending Bernie down to the store tomorrow to pick out shirts. Al can still get them at his discount, can't he?'

'Sure thing. I'll tell Al to watch out for him.'

'I never thought he would stick to the job through the years this way. I thought he'd throw in the sponge and land in some comfortable hack-writing set-up.'

'There's nothing comfortable in writing,' Holly pointed out. 'Not when you're having to write for a market.'

'So he won't write the Great American Novel,' Claire said with a touch of impatience. 'At least he wouldn't have to stand on his feet all day behind a counter.'

'He'd rather stand and sell shirts than sit and write shit.' Holly repeated Al's personal dictum. 'That's my scene.'

They talked a few moments longer, until Claire was summoned to referee between Cindy and Todd. Holly pondered about phoning Wendy.

Better not. Wait for Wendy to phone her. She lunged for Jonny, just in time to rescue him from tumbling on his head.

With Jonny absorbed in a fresh activity, Holly moved about on the endless picking-up routine. Her mind returned compulsively to the money situation. She ought to try for another market – in case something went amuck with this one. The time was *now*, before they were caught short.

So she hated hack writing. Most writers felt the same way. But how much easier – and more remunerative – than the nine-to-five drudgery of an office or shop job? She forced herself to be realistic. There had been a time when she showed little concern for money – but now money was important.

The phone rang again. Crossing the room to answer, she gazed in Jonny's direction. No potential dangers in sight. She could sit down and talk for a few minutes. God, without the phone she might as well be living on a Pacific Ocean atoll! The phone was her whole social life these days.

'Hello—'

'Who were you talking to so long?' Al was mildly irritated. But then, everything irritated him lately. 'Your mother?'

'Mother first, then Claire.'

'I went out to eat with Bill. McHenry,' he amplified. 'The fellow who has the—'

'I know—' Holly was surprised at the sharpness in her interruption. It was involuntary. 'The one who's retiring.' *Don't be hostile – not in Al's present mood. But please, don't let him start up again about that country house!*

'Bill's buying a trailer, getting set for his take-off.' Al cleared his throat, a giveaway of his tenseness. 'He wants us to come up Sunday. We can take the train up – he'll drive us back into town.'

'Al, how can we? Heaven knows when the party will break up tomorrow night. We'll be falling on our faces Sunday morning.' *Can't Al understand? We can't handle a house at this point in our lives!*

'How's Jonny?' Al diverted himself into safer channels. 'Behaving himself?'

'He's fine. Except the tooth bothers him every now and then.'

'Poor little guy,' Al commiserated. 'Wouldn't you think the doctors would have figured out something about that by now?'

Al talked until his dime ran out, then got off. Holly sat motionless for a few moments – staring into space. Why did Ron Andrews have to come back to New York just now – with his possible Broadway hit?

Jonny became querulous when she was half-done with his bath. By the time she had him in his sleeper, she knew this would be a disturbed night. Don't put him in the crib – stretch out with him on the bed for a while.

If things were slow at the store, Al might buzz her again. She wouldn't fall asleep – just try to relax, get rid of some of the tenseness between her shoulder blades. *Is Al right?* Have I lost my drive?

138

I had tremendous drive in those early years –
I'd try anything. Maybe because Al was across
an ocean fighting a war. It was my way of telling
myself he'd be one of the lucky ones – the one
that would come home. I wanted so badly to
have something to show him – when he came
home...

Fifteen

Spring, 1945

The earth was shedding its winter cold. Fresh
green sprouts thrust into view. Hope surged
again in the hearts of Americans. It appeared that
hostilities might be drawing to a close. The
Russians had taken Warsaw. The Ledo Road in
China was in operation. McArthur had landed at
Manila. Roosevelt, Churchill, and Stalin sat
down at the Yalta Conference. The world waited
on tenterhooks.

April was an eventful month for history. On
the 12th, Franklin Roosevelt died in Warm
Springs, Georgia. People cried unashamedly in
front of radios throughout the country. A woman
in the apartment across the way rang Holly's
bell, stumbled in – red-eyed – to tell her of the
sudden death. To Holly, the only President her
generation had ever really known had been

struck down, with the war not yet done. A nation mourned.

Sixteen days later, Mussolini and his mistress were shot to death trying to escape into Switzerland. Mitch wrote that he saw them – hanging upside down – in that city square in Italy. A woman pinned the murdered Italian's dress between her legs for the sake of the living. Two days after Mussolini's death, the world rocked with the news of the suicides of Hitler and Eva Braun. Peace was en route.

Holly was sitting in the office of a television-package producer – avidly discussing a possible assignment. An office boy thrust open the door without bothering to knock.

'Hey, the war's over in Europe! VE-Day! The bulletin just came over the radio!' the office boy yelled in jubilation. He sped on his way, like a modern-day Paul Revere.

A chill went through Holly as she sat there – trying to assimilate the news. The man across the desk from her was ashen.

'Thank God,' he whispered. 'Thank God! I was shipped home seven months ago. Some-times we were damn sure it would never be over. I was lucky – I collected enough shrapnel in the legs to get me out of it.'

Holly and the television producer sat wrapped in a strange, reverent silence while outside the office erupted into a madhouse. One thought ricocheted through Holly's mind. One joyous thought. *Al will be coming home.* For a while, at least.

She left the office. This was no time to talk

140

about prospective writing assignments. Call Wendy! In the lobby she waited impatiently in line before the pair of phone booths. Nobody could get a call through, it appeared.

After an interminable wait she was in a booth, dropped a coin into the slot. She dialed Wendy's office. No answer. There had to be somebody there. And then realization shot through her. Switchboards throughout the city – the nation – must be deserted.

Work was brushed aside for the day. The bars were swamped with customers. Holly pushed through the people-clogged streets to the subway – heading home. She tried to reach Wendy again from a booth on the subway platform, once again on emerging from the subway.

Coming out of the cigar-store phone booth, she collided head-on with Ted Conway, an actor she had met through Al. And a close friend of Mitch.

Ted swooped her to him, kissed her soundly. 'Hey, isn't this terrific? Come on, let's have a drink!'

Ted pulled her along with him into a bar a few doors down. The place was doing a capacity business, but a waiter signaled them to a tiny rear booth just being vacated. Ted was talking non-stop about his USO tour experiences.

'When did you get back?' Holly asked when Ted stopped for a deep breath.

'Three days ago. Boy, home never looked so good!'

The waiter hovered over them in high good humor while they consulted briefly about their order. The jukebox began to fill the room with a

Harry James recording. Ted hummed along to the tune of 'You Made Me Love You'.

'Say, guess who I saw in Paris a while back.' Ted grinned, leaning forward with a conspiratorial gleam in his eyes.

'Somebody I know?'

'Al Rogers, in the flesh.'

Holly sat upright in astonishment. 'You saw Al?'

'Big as life.' Ted chuckled reminiscently. 'Surprised to see us. We didn't stay to chat,' he said, his eyes eloquent.

Holly walked right in. 'Why not?'

Ted leaned back, nearly choking with laughter. 'You should have seen Al's face. I can't figure out how it happened – we opened the wrong door in the hotel. There was Al – in the hay with some Red Cross broad. We could tell because her clothes were all over the floor – and they had the lights on. Wow, what a dish!'

Holly listened with a stiff, fixed smile while Ted poured forth a colorful recitation of the Rita–Al exploits.

'Back at headquarters they howled when we told them,' Ted recounted. 'Half the Red Cross knew about this Rita babe chasing all over Europe to catch up with Al.'

Somehow, she managed to carry on casual talk until it was possible to break away from Ted. She hurried home, by some miracle crossing the streets safely. Hearing Ted's voice repeating the flood of latrine gossip over and over in her mind until it was a full chorus beating her into insensibility. All around her radios blared joyously with the news of VE-Day – but Holly was a bystander now, feeling none of it.

Two hours later, Wendy arrived at the apartment. Holly told her about the encounter with Ted. Wendy listened – shocked, sobered, but not without comprehension.

'Holly, it's a war,' Wendy said softly. 'I guess lots of guys write home one way and behave another way.'

'This isn't a girl he picked up for a night! It's been going on for months! All that sanctimonious garbage he wrote about how lousy some GIs were when it came to women. He didn't have to worry – he had the Red Cross!'

'How can we figure out what goes on inside a guy's head when he doesn't know if he'll be alive the next night? It was tough for us. How do you suppose it was for Al?'

Suddenly Holly felt exhausted. 'Let's pretend I never bumped into Ted Conway. Don't say anything to Al.'

'Oh, sure, I'm going to sit right down and write Al,' Wendy derided gently. 'Why couldn't Ted have kept his big fat mouth shut?'

Holly searched for a way to forgive Al. Not for taking himself a girl – for lying to her.

The war in Europe was over. The world took a deep breath, girded itself for the final push. Then the civilized world was shaken. Stories poured forth about the atrocities in the German concentration camps. Buchenwald – Dachau – Auschwitz. Crimes against humanity that bore sick resemblance to the horrors of the Spanish Inquisition. American soldiers – who had held

143

their stand behind machine guns and heavy artillery while buddies were cut down beside them – turned white when survivors of Hitler's torture chambers crept out to meet their liberators.

The roads in Europe were a frenetic maze of people moving in every direction, meager possessions heaped on carts or reduced to a pathetic knapsack – the spoils of a lifetime. Frightened swarms of humanity searching for lost relations, for a haven to catch their breath, for a place to live again.

The American armed forces began to send men home under the point system. Despite the continuing fighting in the Pacific, an aura of hope shown through.

At four in the morning – early in July – Mitch phoned Holly and Wendy. For almost six months now they were the proud possessors of a phone. He had just landed in Virginia.

'Mitch!' Wendy screeched and yelled for Holly.

A few minutes later Holly was on the phone, heard Mitch laughing at the other end. 'Mitch, are you all right?'

'Great, kid,' he crooned. 'I'll stop off in Jersey to see the folks. Be on your doorstep Friday night—'

Wendy glowed. 'Let's throw a party for Mitch!' It was as though it were four in the afternoon, instead of four in the morning. 'Who shall we call?'

'Claire, Linda and Renée,' Holly began, and stopped short.

'Don't worry about Linda. Not with Mitch

practically ordering the orange blossoms for that girl in Italy!'

'I can't believe Mitch is marrying a girl we've never even seen.'

'It burns me up,' Wendy said in sudden fury. 'Thousands of American girls who're dying for husbands – who in any normal period would be marrying nice American boys – have to sit on the sidelines while European babes grab off GIs. Most of those girls are just after a passport to the good old USA!'

'I suppose some marriages were bound to happen,' Holly admitted. 'Look how long some fellows were overseas.' *What about Al and that Red Cross girl named Rita? Are they thinking about marrying?*

'There's this girl in my office—' Wendy's voice exuded defeat. 'All she talked about for three years – everybody said – was her air-force lieutenant who was fighting in the South Pacific, and how she couldn't wait to marry him. So four months ago she met some guy with a desk job here at home, and last week she married him.'

'Stop being morbid, Wendy,' Holly scolded. 'We've got a party to plan. We'll call Claire – and Linda.' She ignored Wendy's grunt. 'Mitch is home – and Al and Norm should be next.' Holly struggled for a light mood. 'We'll dig up Eric – he's around town somewhere. Ted Conway,' she went on.

'Sure you want Ted?' Wendy looked startled, compassionate.

'Mitch has known him forever. He'd like to see Ted.'

Al was coming home – to her or to the Red Cross girl he had loved in strange rooms in strange countries?

Holly was still in the bathroom – pulling a dress over her head – when she heard the doorbell, then Wendy's shrieks of greeting. Mitch had arrived.

'You louse, you look terrific!' Wendy was bubbling affectionately – half-strangled by Mitch's hugs – as Holly scurried into the living room.

Mitch was tanned, bright-eyed, brimming over with pleasure at being home again.

'Holly!' he grinned, and made a dive for her.

'Oh, Mitch!' Holly clung with genuine delight. 'Oh, golly, I can't believe it!'

'Pinch me, I'm real.' With an arm about each girl, he searched the room with his eyes. 'OK, where's the liquor around this joint?'

In a turmoil of excitement and high spirits, the others poured – almost simultaneously – into the apartment. Claire – with a strange man in tow, Ted Conway and acting buddy Joe, Eric. Linda and Renée were the last arrivals. Holly caught the startled suspicion in Mitch when he inspected Renée. But in a moment it was masked, and Mitch was kissing Linda soundly in welcome.

The room resounded with laughter, backslapping, ribald humor. Perfume, cigarette smoke blended with the aromas of still-warm pastrami and a turkey roasting in the oven. The war in the Pacific seemed remote. Mitch was home. Al seemed close.

'Got a minute?' Claire asked Holly. 'I broke

my bra strap – come fix it for me.'

'Let's go.' Holly prodded her towards the bathroom. The party was launched! All by itself it was launched.

'What do you think of Bernie?' Claire wanted to know, when Holly and she were secure in the privacy of the bathroom.

'I like him. He's warm and real.'

'Our second date,' Claire confided with a self-conscious grin, a lilt in her voice. 'Coming over tonight, he asked me to marry him. Once I get untangled.'

'Going to marry him?' Holly asked, startled. 'Second date's awfully fast.'

'Bernie won't rush me. He knows we need time to get used to each other. But I'm not letting this one get away. He makes me realize I'm a woman!'

'You have a glow about you,' Holly said softly. 'You look sensational.'

'Bernie spent three years overseas, then he was sent home to recover from a wound. He has a BA in psychology. He plans on going back for his MA – so he can work in the public-school system. He inherited an apartment – all his own,' Claire confided, her eyes bright with daring. 'If he asks me to go up to his place after the party, I won't say no.'

'You might be asking for trouble,' Holly warned.

'I know how to take care of myself by now,' Claire said frankly. 'One thing's sure, Bernie won't have to read any books! Like Skip.' Some of the glow diminished as Claire lapsed in fleeting silence. 'Of course, if you listen to my mother, I'm practically a prostitute because I'm dating at all. I moved back home, but to her I'm still Skip's wife. Skip wants out himself now – he came over to the house this week, while I was at school – practically bawled on Mom's shoulder about what a terrible time I've been giving him.'

'What's holding up the divorce?' Holly inquired, knowing the answer.

'Building myself up to letting go.' Claire grinned. 'I know it's nuts, but don't forget I was reared on the belief that you had to have a husband or starve to death in the gutter. My mind says it's time to call it quits, but there's that crazy little thing inside that has to be appeased. I'm throwing out the old – but I have to have a feeling that the replacement is close.' Claire made a determined effort to concentrate on her reflection, reached into the medicine chest to borrow Holly's eye shadow, touched one finger lightly to the eye shadow then to her lids in a flip gesture of confidence. She turned away from the mirror with a satisfied sigh. 'Come on, let's get back to the party.'

In the living room Claire walked straight to Bernie, settled herself beside him. His arm tightened about her waist. Claire and Bernie might have been alone in the room, Holly thought tenderly.

Across the room Wendy – flushed with pleasure – was leaning back against the sofa, Eric's arm snugly about her. Ted and Mitch were keeping up a steady barrage of GI jokes. Holly roamed restlessly about the room – emptying ashtrays, freshening drinks, painfully conscious of Ted's presence.

It was barely one o'clock when Linda – after silent communication with Renée – rose to announce that Renée and she were leaving.

'Early appointment tomorrow,' Linda murmured, without looking directly at anyone. Holly realized with a rush of sympathy that Renée and Linda had been uncomfortable.

'Hey, we're out of soda,' Mitch discovered. 'Ted, let's walk the girls to the subway and pick up some bottles.' He made a point of helping both Linda and Renée with their coats.

An air of mellow intimacy settled about the room when the other four left. Holly switched on the radio, moved the dial to WPAT. The poignant strains of 'You'd Be So Nice To Come Home To' drifted into the room. *Does Al want to come home to me?*

'For Christ sake, turn off some lamps!' Eric exhorted.

Grinning his approval, Bernie switched off the lamp beside the chair he shared with Claire. Joe turned off another. Only a wall sconce cast a faint glow into the center of the room. Joe pulled Holly to her feet.

'Pretty baby,' he crooned. 'Let's dance.'

Sixteen

Early October, 1945

In August, VJ-Day electrified the world. Holly knew that soon Al would be coming home. Still, when their phone jangled in the 4 a.m. silence on a Friday in early October, Holly scurried to answer with trepidation.

'Hello—' Her heart pounded against her ribs.

'Holly—' Al's voice a rich whisper of satisfaction.

'Al!' He'd been away over a year and a half, but now it was as though he had just walked out the door and had stopped to phone from a drugstore on Broadway. 'Oh, Al.' It was a benediction.

'Baby, it's great!' His voice was husky. 'I'm at Fort Dix.'

'When will you be home?' Her heart pounded furiously.

To hell with the Red Cross gal. To hell with everything. Al's back in the States. I'll see him soon.

'This afternoon,' he said. She shivered with anticipation. 'It'll be late – not before five. Check the schedules from then on. I'm coming from Fort Dix,' he pinpointed. 'Into Penn

Station, I'm pretty sure – check that, too.'

'Sure thing.' She would remember ever afterwards the sound of Al's voice calling from Fort Dix at 4 a.m.

Al talked another couple minutes, then she heard a clamor at the other end. 'Holly, I have to get off the line.' He chuckled good-humoredly. 'These guys are going to break down the phone booth. There's a line a mile long.'

Holly said goodbye, put down the phone, looked up. Just now realizing Wendy was her side.

'Al?'

'He's home. He's home!'

They didn't even consider going back to bed. They sat in the raw early morning chill of the apartment and talked in low tones over cups of coffee. It was the end of an era. The beginning of a new one.

Wendy left for work. Holly called in sick. At 10 a.m. – when she knew the beauty salon would be open – she went to have her hair washed and set. A rarity for Wendy and her because of the tightness of their budget.

She managed to carry on a coherent conversation with the operator, shared in talk with two other patrons – but all the while in a corner of her mind she savored the joy of knowing that in a few hours she would see Al. No more nightmare fears of his dying in battle. No more sleepless nights when there was a delay in his letters – though sometimes they arrived in bunches.

'I'm so upset—' the girl in the next chair confided loudly to the operator who was adjusting her hair dryer. 'How can my landlady put me and my roommate out of the apartment we've had for three years just because her son is coming home and she wants the place for him and his bride? Some French girl he met over there,' she added with rage. 'All those girls coming over here in droves – taking our guys. It's sick.'

Out of the beauty salon – dreading the empty hours before it would be time to go to Penn Station – Holly decided to squander some time in the cafeteria. She lingered over a Danish and coffee, then headed home. Her eyes drawn compulsively to her watch. Al said he couldn't be home before five o'clock – but he was guessing. She'd be there at four, she promised herself.

On her lunch hour, Wendy phoned.

'I'll go up to the Bronx after work,' Wendy told her. 'I'll call you some time during the evening. Kiss the big lug for me.'

'Wendy, I can't believe he'll be here in a few hours,' Holly whispered. 'I can't wait to see him!'

At last she decreed it was time to leave for Penn Station. Walk slowly over to the IRT. Take the local down to Penn Station. Encased in unreality, she left the apartment.

She forced herself not to race to the subway, yet on the platform she fretted over the train's delay in arriving. She stared in impatience down the dark tunnel – watching for the swaying dark red-eyed monster. At last the train shuffled into the station. No mob at this hour. She found a seat right at the door, sat down. Her heart already pounding at the knowledge that soon she'd be greeting Al.

People moved out at each station, were replaced with invaders. How many others – like her – with this sweet destination? Troops were coming home daily. You couldn't walk into a supermarket or a drugstore without hearing comments, seeing a returned GI not yet changed into civvies.

Finally the train lurched to a stop at Penn Station. She walked out of the subway into the Indian-summer sun of early October. Today everything appeared different. The streets. The people. The buildings that climbed into the cloud-free sky. She studied the clock in a shop window. Twenty past four. Too early, her mind admonished. Yet something drew her here.

She walked into Penn Station – conscious of the surge of vitality that sprang from every corner. Men in uniform – army, navy, marines – dominated the scene. Duffel bags deposited here and there in reckless abandon while their owners clung to wives, sweethearts, mothers, sisters. Fathers hovering proudly nearby. Tears in abundance. Happy tears. Everywhere a feeling of exultation. Their men had come home.

Holly stared tenderly at a young sergeant clutching an ecstatic redhead as though he could not have waited another instant. At the escalator a father was tossing his two-year-old son into the air with smug satisfaction – the son he'd never seen.

'4:33 from Trenton now arriving on Track Three,' a railroad employee intoned. '4:33 from Trenton, arriving on Track Three...'

The Fort Dix train came from Trenton. It was

153

thirty minutes before Al could be arriving. Still, she followed the others – moving swiftly, with towering excitement – to the waiting point at Track Three. Exhorting herself to realize that Al surely couldn't be on this train. He might not arrive for two hours. Even later.

And then she saw him. Halfway up the down escalator. He hadn't seen her yet. He was carrying on an animated conversation with another GI on the step above him. But it was Al! Sunburnt darker than she ever remembered. Duffel bag thrown over his shoulder.

He swung about, searching the faces clustered at the bottom. Spied her. Grinned and waved. Practically knocking over the GI ahead of him in his impatience to reach her. Holly laughed as he nearly collided with a cluster between them.

'Hi, baby.' Al dumped his duffel bag to kiss her – as though he had just returned from a weekend in the country – then turned from her to exchange addresses with the fellow who had been behind him on the escalator.

She waited – caught up in the joy of his presence.

'OK.' Al swung the duffel bag over his shoulder and with one arm about her, propelled her towards an exit. 'Let's grab a cab.'

He talked compulsively as the cab rolled through the streets. He gaped out the window as though hungry for familiar sights – all the while holding Holly's hand in his own. He started a discussion with the cabbie – whose words tumbled over one another in his rush to tell about his three brothers in the service. Holly inspected the battle stars, the unit citation, the campaign ribbons on Al's jacket.

At the apartment she pushed the door wide, watched as Al gazed about the room as though he couldn't see enough of it.

'God, if you knew how many times I lived through this minute, Holly! Sometimes I wondered if I'd ever make it.' He dragged his duffel bag into the room, deposited it in a corner. 'Now, know what I want?' He grinned down at her. 'I want to soak in that four-legged antique tub in there, with the water loaded down with bath salts – till I smell like a two-buck whore. I can't wait to get the stench of this damn lousy war right out of my pores!'

'I'll fix it.' Her face luminous, Holly moved towards the bathroom.

'Wait a minute, baby.' He reached to pull her close, kissed her. He released her, swatted her across the rump. 'OK, draw my tub.'

She tested the water. Hot enough – but not too hot. She dumped quantities of the honeysuckle bath salts he liked. He had come home – to her. His mouth, his hands, his body assured her of this. Ted was wrong about Rita, she told herself defiantly. GI barracks gossip – a fast fling overseas. Holly felt washed clean with gladness. *Al came home to me.*

She wandered about the living room – listening to Al splash with noisy exuberance in the tub. She switched on the radio. Al made it a duet with Sinatra. It was twilight already. She switched on a lamp, then closed the drapes as though to shut out the world.

Al was here. She could walk a few feet, see him, touch him. The melody of it resounded from every corner. Feeling another presence, she spun around. Al stood there in the doorway, smiling down at her, a towel about his middle, the heavily sweet scent of the honeysuckle bath salts clinging to him. She smiled, motionless, waiting. The air was pregnant with the knowledge of their reunion. But Al just stood there, drinking in her presence.

'Whenever you're ready, we can go out for dinner.' Al had written in such stubborn little-boy detail about the magnificent dinner they would have his first night home, with champagne and an orchestra in the background.

Al lowered himself on to the couch. He cleared his throat. 'Couldn't we eat here instead of running out?'

'Sure.' Holly's eyes shone with tender approval.

Al leaned over to fiddle with the radio till he found – with a smile of remembrance – the station that provided uninterrupted dinner music. Holly moved about the kitchen, grateful that she had gone out in a flash of prescience and loaded the refrigerator. Grateful that she had learned her way with food in the year and a half Al was overseas.

'Any wine around?' Al searched about with the old ease of familiarity, found the bottle of sherry as Holly came towards him with glasses. Eric had brought the bottle his last time over, Holly recalled.

Al brushed his face against hers as he filled the

glasses. He waited until she drained her glass, then pulled her to him.

'Miss me?' Al's voice was a caress.

'What a question!'

'You grew up,' he said after a few minutes.

Close to midnight the phone rang. Holly tiptoed into the living room to answer.

'I'm in the Bronx. I'll stay over until Sunday night,' Wendy announced blithely.

'You doll!' Holly whispered into the phone.

'Everything all right?'

'Beautiful. Al looks wonderful! And, Wendy, he's so glad to be home.'

'I'll get off the phone before he shoots me. Night, darling.' Wendy rang off – satisfied that, for now at least, all was well.

Hearing Al stir in the bedroom, Holly moved over to the stove to put up fresh coffee. Al said that after the mud overseas, he felt like drowning himself in freshly perked American coffee. With a rare sense of well-being Holly busied herself with food – knowing Al would be out in a moment for this late snack.

Afterwards they slept – entangled together – in one twin bed. In the morning Holly crept out of bed and into the living room – determined not to disturb Al. Dressed, she puttered about the apartment – waiting for him to awaken. Feeling refreshed despite little sleep.

Around noon the phone rang. She hurried to answer. It was Mitch. She told him Al was home. They talked in muted tones for a while. He had been working on a piece of music. Now he played it for Holly – the phone resting near the

157

keyboard so she could hear.

Off the phone, she tiptoed into the bedroom to see if Al was awake, tiptoed out again. Start breakfast preparations, she told herself. Ten minutes later, she heard his extravagant yawn. She hurried into the bedroom with a frosted glass of orange juice – squeezed in readiness for this moment.

'Hi!' She hovered above him, offered the glass.

'I haven't slept like that in years.' He yawned again, enjoying it. 'What time is it, anyhow?'

'Almost one.' She sat at the edge of the bed while he swigged down the juice.

'Let's not go out today, hunh?' Al slid an arm around her waist. 'Wendy's going to be away?'

'Until tomorrow night.' Holly felt his arm tighten in approval.

'Good girl.'

After breakfast Al lay full-length on the couch – with Holly sitting alongside – and talked for hours. As though driven to compensate for all the twenty months he had been away, she thought. Each meal became a major production. They conferred absorbedly over the problem of sausage or bacon for breakfast, Russian or French dressing for the tossed salad with lunch, whether to bake or mash the potatoes.

Again they slept in the one small bed – Al's arms tightly about her. They made love, and moments later Al was asleep, his arms about her.

It was a restless slumber. He tossed about, began to mumble. At first unintelligible – then his words took form.

'Rita, you gorgeous bitch! What are you trying to do to me?'

Over and over, Al repeated the name. Holly lay motionless, too stunned to move. Everything she had erased from her mind came tumbling down in mad, painful confusion. What was this, this dream turned nightmare? How could he make love to her in the darkness – and in the refuge of sleep cry out to some strange woman named Rita?

After a while he flung himself against the wall. Holly crept out of the bed, hurried into the living room. She stared out into the darkness, tried to conjure up a vision of this Rita. A dish, Ted had said. What had brought Al running home to *her*? Had Rita thrown him over?

'Holly?' Al's voice – brushed with concern – pierced the stillness.

'Yes?' She struggled to sound casual.

'What are you doing out there? Come back to bed.' Al sounded irritated. When she walked back into the bedroom, he was sitting up. The night-table lamp on.

'I was thirsty—'

Eyes averted, she reached to switch off the lamp. Al drew her down beneath the blanket with him again. His arms encircling her.

Seventeen

Mid-October, 1945

Logic commanded her to make a sharp, clean cleavage with Al. Now – before further hurt tore her down. Each night she swore would be the last. Each night was the same. She was sick with the weakness in her that refused to listen to reason.

Two weeks sped past. Al made no effort to search for an apartment. Wendy slept on the living-room sofa, tossed blunt hints in his direction. Then she breezed into the apartment one evening with the news that she had just cemented a deal for Al.

'The couple upstairs are moving to Texas. They'll hand over the apartment – for a "going-away" present of a hundred dollars. That's dirt cheap in this day and age,' Wendy pointed out.

Al moved upstairs the day of their 'the war is over' party. He was unfamiliarly withdrawn as Holly and Wendy helped him. As though he were being dispossessed, Holly thought with illogical guilt. But once he finished hanging his things away, he rushed back down to the apartment below.

Wendy was still racing about knocking on

doors – trying to borrow ice cubes – when people began to arrive. Breathlessly, Holly rushed to answer the doorbell summonses. First Norman, then Mitch and Linda – but no Renée. Holly recalled how Mitch had recoiled from the obviousness of Linda's relationship with Renée. Eric arrived, and Wendy blossomed into vivaciousness.

Within half an hour the room was pleasantly warm with laughter, cigarette smoke, and Haig and Haig. Holly was drunk on the feeling of friendship and conviviality that pervaded the apartment. Two years ago, she had been wide-eyed, awesomely impressed by these people – now she was part of them.

The doorbell rang again with ebullient insistence. Holly hurried to respond, grateful for activity. She swung open the door, to find Claire waiting – with Bernie.

'Hi!' Claire sang out – clutching tightly to Bernie. 'We come bearing news!'

'Come inside and spread the word,' Holly caroled, guessing the news.

'I'm flying to Reno next week. Skip's dear Mama is paying the bills. The minute it's legal, Bernie and I get married.' Claire kissed him soundly, as though to prove it.

'Claire, that's wonderful!' Holly kissed her on one cheek.

'Hey, you're supposed to kiss the bridegroom,' Bernie protested.

'What's this?' Al strode over with a hand extended to Bernie.

'The marriage business is booming, haven't

you heard?' Claire tossed off. But she looked at Al in a way that made him self-conscious, Holly noted.

'Yeah, wouldn't you love to corner the market on wedding rings?' Mitch joined them in high good humor. 'Look at the business right here. Claire and Bernie, Maria and me – as soon as I get her over—' Mitch caught himself – because he had nearly added 'Holly and Al', Holly guessed.

'Come on, let's get the drinks flowing around here,' Al ordered. 'Who wants a dry party?'

The doorbell rang again. Wendy raced to answer.

'You took long enough to answer,' Norm scolded but clearly in a high mood.

Moments later Ted Conway, with a bottle of Scotch and a uniformed buddy – whose hash marks indicated long overseas service – burst into the room. A frantic gleam lit Al's eyes. He broke away from Holly, dragged Ted off into a corner.

Probably swearing Ted to secrecy about Rita, Holly guessed. It was obvious from Ted's embarrassed grin. At least, Holly thought with relief, Ted was not letting on to Al that he had already spilled this choice morsel of gossip.

Fortified with drink and food, Mitch embarked on a series of bawdy latrine reminiscences. Soon everyone was caught up in shrieks of laughter. Holly was relieved to be able just to sit back and listen.

'Say, Al,' Bernie demanded. 'You were in France – what were the French broads like?'

Al shrugged. 'Broads. Standard equipment.'
Ted – his inhibitions destroyed by several
straight shots – broke up. Holly reached for
empty glasses, headed for the kitchenette to
avoid witnessing Al's discomfort. She kept herself busy for several minutes with sandwich
makings. When she walked past Al with the tray,
he took it away, deposited it on the coffee table
where the others could help themselves, pulled
her down beside him.

Feeling the tension in Al's body as it rested
against her own, Holly recognized his need not
to lose touch with her. Like a child, she allowed
her spirits to shoot up. After all, what was so
special about her that she should be immune to
the heartaches of war?

How many thousands of girls like her loved
soldiers who had lain with others – wherever
men in uniform had spent long months and years
in barren beds? The war was over! Pride was a
dead thing on a cold and lonely night.

As the evening mellowed, the myriad side
conversations dwindled away as each became
drawn into the central discussion. The unreal
years of the war, which still clothed them with
more reality than the present, dominated. This
was a strictly male give-and-take – the girls
listening with quiet absorption.

Inspecting the serious, intent faces about the
room, Holly wondered in how many rooms
across the world women were sitting like this
while their men relived the years of the war.
Their voices, their faces, wore a sameness in
reminiscence – the brotherhood of men who had

163

gone out to kill or be killed.

'Boy, the North African deal was something.' Bernie carried the ball now. 'One afternoon we'd be lying on our backsides soaking up sun and Mediterranean sea breezes, and the next the Germans would be strafing the hell out of us. We never could figure out their schedule.'

'I hear some of you guys in North Africa did a thriving business in black-market sheets—' Mitch chuckled. 'Fact or fancy?'

'You bet.' Joe, Ted's buddy, picked up. 'You'd think the army was a subsidiary of R. H. Macy, running a whitc-goods sale year-round. The Arabs were practically bawling to hand over twenty bucks in American money for each sheet they could grab. They'd fold the damn thing down the middle, cut a hole for their heads, and, zingo, new dress!'

'You'd be amazed,' Al contributed, his voice coated with sardonic humor, 'how many GI blankets went into wool dresses and suits for French babes. A package of dye and they were in business.'

'Boy, you must have been living!' Joe said admiringly.

'I wasn't collecting,' Al said. 'Not for blankets or food.' His face was tense, eyes somber in remembrance.

'About those Arabs,' Bernie picked up. 'Ten to one some Frenchman would come along, grab the merchandise from the poor Arab and accuse him of stealing it. The French character would beat the hell out of him, and the Arab would run back to his cave. You think we've got low living

164

standards in the hills of Kentucky? You haven't seen anything until you've run into those Arabs.'

'There were some enterprising ones,' Joe corrected drily. 'I remember when we got into Algeria. We saw this whole company lined up in front of a tent. Like a chow line – only it wasn't chow that waited inside. Some little Arab chick was taking on the whole blasted company! Forty guys waiting there, I swear. She must have cleaned up a fortune.'

'I guess all the black-market operators weren't here at home,' Holly said quietly.

'You can't even imagine what it was like over there.' Al was brusque. 'You never saw such thievery in your life.'

'What the guys took for themselves, though, we never counted,' Norm recalled smugly, grinning. 'We'd draw straws to see who'd go steal a case or two of beer on Saturday nights. This wasn't to sell – it was for us. We just stole it back from black-marketeers who stole it from the army. Even our chaplain counted it as an OK operation.'

'My big deal was swiping jeeps.' Al relaxed into a grin. 'I had a captain who was a hell of a nice guy, but wouldn't you know it, every month he'd have a jeep stolen on him. If it was in the front lines, no problem – he could write if off as shot up. But when we were back of the lines, he'd have to produce that hunk of junk or pay off. So he'd say, "Al, take inventory of our auto pool." And I would survey the situation and make sure our inventory was jake.'

'I remember our captain.' Mitch reached to

refresh his drink. 'You think it gets hot here sometimes in the middle of July, say – but that's like winter until you've served time in the tropics. We used to sprawl over that hot sand and dream about ice cubes. We didn't care what surrounded it, so long as we could taste an ice cube. So this captain made a deal. He swapped a PT boat for a portable refrigerator-bar. Boy, did we have a ball making ice cubes!'

'That reminds me of another boat.' Norm squinted reminiscently. 'A top brass latched on to a junior-sized yacht somewhere, and we had the honor of lugging that damned hulk up half the mountain passes of Italy – and those mountains in Italy!' Norm whistled expressively. 'Anyhow, he finally made it through the Po valley, planning to cross the river on his private battleship, and what do you know, the river had run dry!' Norm sprawled back against the couch, pulling Linda back with him. 'It was a real riot. Here I am, a character who used to get dizzy looking out of a third-floor window – and I have to fight a war all the way up the Italian mountains. You think, finally we're getting to the top. So you trudge along for a hundred yards or so – and more mountains! With a shrine stuck in every corner. It's lucky I'm not the religious type – I'd have a broken arm from crossing myself.'

'If I hear another GI joke about candy bars and matches,' Bernie contributed, 'I may throw up. Makes you think of the old classic about the little match girl – all jazzed up for the twentieth century. The little Italian girl doesn't *have* any matches. And don't believe all the crap you read in the papers,' Bernie warned, his eyes sweeping the girls. 'Not all the Italians were greeting the Americans as the great liberators. The Germans left a few friends behind. Every once in a while the MPs used to capture some German soldier who'd sneak back to spend a night with his Italian girl.'

'We had plenty of bastards on our side.' Al spoke with a vehemence that startled Holly. 'It's a laugh, when you think of the glorified picture of the good-hearted clean-cut GI that's supposed to personify the American in uniform. How many drunken GIs did you see in action that you wanted to punch in the nose? Knocking on doors in the middle of the night, yelling – grabbing any woman unlucky enough to open the door.' Contempt laced Al's voice. 'It didn't matter if she was sixteen or sixty! Did you ever think of the poor little bastards the Great American Army left in its tracks?'

'That must have been a bumper crop,' Ted guessed, but there was no humor in his voice. 'Poor little kids who'll hear all about Uncle Sam – but they'll never see him.'

'Children born of lonely nights and rashes of homesickness. Children born of stolen love, or callousness, or plain rape. But children with a stigma.' Al's sigh was deep with compassion. 'We won't write that off easily.'

'What was that shit about the Congressmen?' Joe demanded. 'All in an uproar because the GIs' morals were being impaired with pin-up girls. So they looked at a pair of big tits and got an erection. What else were they getting? The army should have sent the Congressmen over for a while – if they caught a bullet in their asses, they might have worried less about our wall decorations.'

'And that business about the monastery.' Al's voice was laced with contempt. 'Our guys were being picked off like sitting ducks – but they worry about a building. God, the stupidity all around! We had a great rule, right in the ranks. Don't give food to the civilians,' Al mimicked. 'Throw it in the garbage – but don't give it to the civilians. So you sit there at chow time, and you nearly choke to death because you feel the eyes of those half-starved kids hanging around, hoping you'll drop a piece of bread. You feel those eyes right down to the pit of your stomach. But the army makes its sanctimonious rule: dump the leftovers into the garbage.'

'Al, that's sacrilegious,' Holly protested.

'Haven't you heard? The army's short on common sense – long on rules. Believe me, baby, plenty of GIs forgot about that rule. Your insides churn like a mix-master when you watch good food being dumped into the garbage cans instead of into empty stomachs. After chow, I used to swipe piles of pancakes and scrambled eggs and bread before they cleaned off the tables. I was a one-man good-neighbor team. To those poor bastards over there cold pancakes and eggs tasted like filet mignon.' Al's eyes were dark with intensity as he relived his frustrations.

'Remember the deal about not picking up civilians?' Bernie grimaced. 'That was a stinker.'

'That was a bastard!' Al's voice reeked with disgust. 'You're driving along in your jeep, and you see an old couple – just about able to put one foot ahead of the other. They've got miles to go yet – but the army says no civilian pick-ups. Or a mother with a baby in her arms and two or three small ones hanging on to her skirts gives you this look – and you know and she knows the brass says no.'

'The Germans were smart,' Bernie recalled cynically. 'They gave anybody a lift.'

'Hey, anybody hear from Steve?' Mitch demanded. 'He gave up the shipyard job to enlist – and was shipped quick to the South Pacific. I told him he was nuts – why didn't he stay where he was?'

'We heard from Steve for a while.' Holly went cold with recall. 'Wendy and I used to write him – Claire, too. Then we didn't hear for about a month. We decided to give his mother a call.' Holly's voice choked. 'To reassure ourselves.'

'Our timing was great,' Claire picked up. 'I was here when Holly called. His mother must have thought it was a macabre joke. Holly asks, "What do you hear from Steve?" and his mother tells us about the black-edged telegram she got that morning. "My son gave his life for his country," she said.'

'Christ,' Al muttered. 'Nobody ever wrote me.'

'It wasn't a thing to write,' Wendy said quietly.

'Say, what in hell goes on around here?' Mitch broke through the somberness that enveloped them. 'I went out to buy some civvies. For a few pairs of slacks and a half-dozen shirts they expect you to hand over half of Fort Knox!'

'Yeah!' Norm jumped on this track. 'What goes with these birds? We chase half around the world to fight for their hides – and when we come back, they try to take ours.'

'Don't forget the rents,' Bernie contributed from the darkness of the sofa. 'To get married today you have to make sure the gal has a good job.'

'Aha!' Claire chortled. 'So that's the secret of my charm.'

'Anyhow, it's great to be home,' Al said softly, and there was quiet – like a moment of benediction.

Eighteen

Al emerged from the store into the balmy warmth of an Indian-summer night. He rejected the prospect of climbing down into the subway to wait for a train that would be slow in arriving at this hour. But the buses took forever. A taxi? He scanned the light traffic. He might wait twenty minutes for a taxi. All right, walk home.

He enjoyed the solitude that this area of Manhattan acquired past the shopping hours. What a rotten day at the store! What day wasn't rotten? Walking into that stupid job had been a trap. He had almost a third of the book written – with the

170

crucial rewrite ahead of him. He would never finish it, never do the rewrites, he thought with a tightening in his throat. Not without solid chunks of uninterrupted time.

Why couldn't Holly understand he had to have that house? They could swing it – they'd taken gambles before! He was forty-six years old. He had to make it now – or never. Ron had nearly pissed in his pants walking into *him* behind a counter that way.

He swung down Third Avenue. How the city had changed since the old Third Avenue El came down. Luxury apartments everywhere, with their patches of dirt coaxing evergreens into life. It was funny today – the way that broad walked into the store to remind him of Rita. Now it was like she had never existed. It had been part of the war – a separate life.

Coming back home he had been determined to go straight back to writing. No more side paths. At the very last Rita had leveled with him. She was married. It wasn't a working marriage, but she was in no mad rush to divorce Paul. Al and she would live together for a while – to make sure this would last, she'd decided. *But the war was over – and Holly was waiting for him. That was the real world.*

Rita finally handed him an ultimatum. Meet her out in Reno – or it was over with them. She'd finally decided to divorce the old boy, marry him. Remembering Rita – in London and Paris and the other places – he could feel a cold, white heat low within him. Yet all the time there was Holly. Holly was reality.

It was over – unless he'd hop a plane to Reno. He never considered that. An era just died. Al's pace quickened as he neared the tall white-brick evergreen-bordered building that was a facsimile of dozens of other new apartment houses about Manhattan. He had really reared when Holly first pulled this bit about moving out of the old apartment. Sure, he had bitched regularly about the lousy neighborhood, the smallness of an efficiency apartment that cramped him like a straitjacket after eight rooms and three acres near Yorktown Heights.

Al ducked into the building with a broad smile for the doorman. Poor bastard, probably figured them for living high on the hog. He made a point of being heavy on the tips.

He waited for the elevator with impatience. He had not called Holly tonight, the way he usually did when things slowed down. He was still teed off about the way she kept shying away from Bill McHenry's house.

The elevator rose up from the basement. He strode inside, smiled at the tall blonde in short shorts and a snug knit top. Pimples for breasts, he noticed with a connoisseur's objectivity. Garment-center model – building up the income with some party-girl jobs, he surmised

The elevator pulled to a stop, the blonde slithered out with a faint backward look that was probably instinctive with her by now. Lord, the way he used to chase around! Never would he have thought he could stay faithful to any girl – even Holly. But why go looking elsewhere when you had what you wanted at home?

He slid the key into the lock with a pleasant sense of homecoming. God, he hated the job! If Holly hadn't got pregnant, he would have quit two years ago, bought an old jalopy, piled their stuff into it, and cleared out of New York.

He opened the door, felt himself enveloped in the warmth of parenthood. Holly sat on a corner of the sofa, feet tucked beneath her, folding the ever-present pile of freshly washed diapers. From the concentrated frown on her face, he guessed she was plotting the current piece of junk that would keep them out of hock. If she maintained this pace, he acknowledged with reluctant respect, they could swing the monthly payments on a car. They'd have to have a car if they bought Bill's place.

Wow, was he scared those last few weeks before the kid was born! Childbirth was as simple these days as having a tooth pulled, he'd kept telling himself – women didn't die any more, unless there was some rare complication. But he had paced that hospital corridor in a sweat – conscious of the other uneasy fathers who labored to conceal their own anxieties. The broad in the labor room next to Holly's had cussed like a stevedore – every filthy name in the book for her husband. And he'd promised himself, Al remembered with self-conscious humor, that if anything happened to Holly, he'd pack up and run. Leave the state.

'Hi.' In the low lamplight, her hair mussed that way, Holly still looked like a kid. 'Jonny just conked out. Finally.'

'So late?' Al lifted an eyebrow in surprise.

'He took a long afternoon nap.' She unwound herself from the sofa, rose to accept the brush of Al's mouth. 'Hungry?'

'Coffee,' he suggested, pulling off his jacket.

He walked to the bedroom, opened the door, walked inside to inspect Jonny in the muted shadows of the night light. Handsome little bastard, he thought for the thousandth time with non-diminishing complacency.

'Coffee's up,' Holly reported when he returned to the living room. 'Oh, I heard from Eric.'

'Coming tomorrow night?' He could never figure Eric out. How could a guy with Eric's brains and Eric's talent allow himself to get messed up the way he did? Not just the rotten breaks writing-wise – both Holly and he had encountered plenty of that. What writer worth his salt hadn't? But when it came to women and politics Eric was a loser. 'Or did Eric just sniff in disgust and make snide cracks about Ron's materialistic success?'

'He promised to be here,' Holly said, her eyes dark with incomprehension. 'But I can't get through to Eric any more. It's like talking to a stranger.'

'Nobody's been able to communicate with him for years,' Al reminded. 'Remember that creepy broad he got mixed up with?'

'Sara,' Holly supplied. 'I suppose that was the beginning of the end for Eric.'

'Don't go wallowing in sentiment,' Al warned. Twenty years ago Eric had been brimming over with promise. Fifteen years ago he was one step removed from a Broadway production. Now he lived in a secret, dark, ugly world that made him a stranger. 'Eric was bitter before he was out of the crib.'

It made Al uneasy to think about the incisive, sardonic comedy of which Eric had once been capable. Ron had looked at him in the store yesterday afternoon with the same shocked disbelief with which he might have looked at Eric ten years ago. What had Holly said? The beginning of the end. Was that what happened to *him*?

'Come sit down with me till the coffee's ready,' Holly urged, and he complied.

Talk to Holly. Have it out right now about the house. We won't even need a down-payment.

He should be able to sell Holly on this house deal. They never used to be afraid to tackle anything. Before Jonny, he amended – frustration pricking at him again. Now Holly was scared of her shadow.

'I wish to hell my folks could have lived to see Jonny. And what about my wife?' he drawled. 'They were so sure I was going to wind up with some glamorized floozy.'

'Some character tried to pick me up in the coffee shop yesterday,' Holly reported. 'With Jonny sitting right there. I was flattered to death.'

'I told you,' he reminded. 'As a call girl you would have made a mint.'

'Just missed my calling,' she flipped.

'I had a long talk with Bill McHenry again,' Al started cautiously. Damn, Holly was stiffening already. 'He made us one hell of a proposition. At first I thought he was kidding.'

'Let me turn down the coffee,' Holly interrupted. 'Before it boils over and messes up the whole range.'

Al followed her to the kitchenette.

'McHenry's willing to finance the deal himself. He'll let us take the place without a downpayment,' he announced with deceptive casualness. 'That's the break of a lifetime.'

'The house must be some dog. Why would any property owner do a thing like that?' But she was astonished, he told himself with a flicker of hope.

'Because McHenry's a character.' Al chuckled. 'He figures if he goes through a bank, gets the cash up front, he'll blow it. This way he'll have money coming in every month.'

'What about a sandwich?' Holly took refuge in an inspection of the refrigerator's contents. But she hadn't blown her stack.

'OK, so we'll only use it weekends,' he compromised. 'I'll keep the overtime to evenings, make sure I have Saturdays off. We'll—'

'Keep up the apartment *and* a house in the country?' Holly broke in. 'Rent here, mortgage payments, taxes, car expenses?'

'You'll be pulling in twelve thousand in the next twelve months. With overtime I'll—'

'*Maybe* I'll be pulling in twelve thousand!'

'So far you've been writing that shit for almost two years,' Al pointed out, 'with the money going up every six months. You said they want at least one book a month from you.'

'It's not a written commitment,' Holly threw back. 'It can stop any minute!'

'You know the field. If one source dries up,

176

you'll find another!'

'I don't know that. All I know is that I'm finishing up a book in maybe four days, and I'll get the other half of my advance within two weeks. How do I know there won't be a shift of editors and I'll be out and somebody else will be in?'

'Because, you dumb cluck, you're a good writer and they know it,' Al shot back. 'I admit it – I can't write that. You can – and some of the decent writing sneaks through to make it look good.'

'Al, the bonanza can dry up any time. How can we count on my checks?'

'Why can't you think of me?' Al's voice soared. 'I need that house in the country! I need it like a wounded man needs blood plasma!'

'What good would weekends do?' Holly challenged, her face stained with color. 'You'd just get rolling good – and we'd have to turn around and come back to the city. You'd be more frustrated than you are now.'

'Forget about the weekends,' Al shouted, suddenly reckless. 'On a full-time basis! Why do we have to stay here? You can work any place! Is there a law that says I have to sell shirts the rest of my life?'

From the bedroom a low querulous cry infiltrated. Not a just-awakened cry – the in-pain teething cry.

'Oh, thanks,' Holly said tightly. 'Now you've awakened Jonny!'

'I'll put up his bottle.' Defeat blending with bitterness in him. 'Go on – before the poor little bastard screeches his lungs out.'

Al pulled open the refrigerator door, reached for the bottle of milk. He wasn't through talking to Holly about the house, he vowed. It was all there – the whole book, he thought, sick with frustration. Just a matter of weeding out, building up, pulling together.

One lousy, rotten year! That's all I ask of Holly!

Nineteen

Wendy sat at the dinette table while Jerry poured a final round of coffee for the four of them. A quiver in an eyelid betrayed her unease. Tim's wife was sweet and charming – and fearful. Sitting there – with Tim's ring a glistening sliver of whiteness against the warm brown of her skin – Wilma was struggling not to betray her own anxieties. So young, so vulnerable, Wendy thought with a tightness in her throat.

'We really have to go,' Tim said self-consciously. His hand crept across the table to cover Wilma's.

'Take the car.' Jerry reached into his pocket for the keys.

'We won't need it,' Tim said. 'We'll check into a hotel for the weekend.'

'Check into a motel,' Jerry ordered. 'Get out of the city. Breathe some decent air. Bring the car back Sunday night.'

'You've been so sweet about everything, Wendy.' Wilma's eyes were eloquent with gratitude.

'Have a wonderful marriage,' Wendy said.

Wendy and Jerry walked to the car with Tim and Wilma. It was their wedding night. There should not be this air of defiance about them, Wendy told herself.

The car backed out of the driveway. Jerry had kept up a jovial front, yet Wendy was aware of his inner turmoil. Carol was in bed already – even though tomorrow was not a school day. Carol had not put up her usual resistance to an early curfew. For all Carol's nonchalance, she, too, was disturbed.

Involuntarily Wendy's eyes swept the unimaginative two-family brick houses which flanked their own. Nobody had seen Tim and Wilma take off in the car. Tim had been at the house often enough – alone. Now – with his wife – ugly speculations would arise, wind themselves about Jerry and Carol and her. If there was just Jerry and herself, Wendy reasoned, she could shrug a bored shoulder and ignore talk. Most of the neighbors figured her for a nut, anyhow – because she didn't sit around in kitchens gossiping over coffee. But there was Carol.

'Shit!' The dam that had controlled Jerry's fury collapsed like sand when Wendy and he were alone in the apartment again. 'What the hell's the matter with Tim? Why did he have to pull off something like this?'

'He got a kick in the teeth from the other girl.'

She tried to be matter-of-fact. 'Wilma's awfully sweet, Jerry—'

'How's it going to look for us when Tim and Wilma come visiting? What about when they have kids?' His voice was strident.

'You'll have to take the subway out to your mother's on Sunday, break the news to her.'

'I'd rather cut my throat than tell Mom.' Jerry shuddered.

'That would be the easy way,' Wendy tried for a touch of humor.

'Tim's not dumb!' Jerry flared with fresh frustration. He was silent a moment, driving one hand into the other, the way he did under stress. 'Hell, why didn't Tim think ahead? About how it's going to be? Look, Wendy, we'll just have to be frank.' He took a deep, agonized breath. 'We'll see them away from the house—'

'Jerry! How can we?'

But then, how differently was she behaving about the birthday party and Melinda? She'd promised herself she'd insist on switching to an all-girl luncheon – but how could she? She couldn't deny the kid a decent birthday party.

So it was a rotten world – they had to live by the rules. Melinda would *not* be invited to the party – and they would see Tim and Wilma away from the apartment. It was rotten – it turned her sick – but there was Carol to think about.

With an effort Wendy dragged herself back to the tirade spilling over from Jerry. All right, let him yell it out. He'd feel better. But she walked to Carol's room to make sure the door was shut.

'You phone up Mom and tell her,' Jerry threw

180

at her unexpectedly. 'You can tell her better than anybody else.'

Wendy stared in shock. 'Jerry, why me?'

'You can be calm about it.'

'All right,' Wendy accepted after a moment. 'I'll call her tomorrow instead of waiting till Sunday. That'll give her time to simmer down before Tim shows up at the apartment.'

'I'm out of cigarettes. I'll run down and get a pack.'

Wendy caught herself on the point of reminding him about the spare in their bedroom closet. No. Jerry wanted out of the apartment. OK, let him walk off some of that pent-up rage.

She waited until she heard the door slam before dialing Holly. It was late, but Holly and Al would be awake.

'Hello.' Holly's voice came to her with the familiar, cherished lilt.

'We've been through the fire with Tim and his bride,' Wendy reported, dropping on to a corner of the bed. 'Oh, Holly, I feel so sorry for those kids.' Because Tim passed – but Wilma couldn't.

'It was their decision to make, Wendy.'

'I know. But they're so damn young. Were we ever that young?'

She had been so frightened, so desperate at the way girls were dashing to the marriage-license bureau. She had grabbed at Jerry. But except for the money end of things – the wild battles Jerry and she had about spending – they had a solid marriage. It didn't matter that his grandmother had been Jamaican.

'How's Carol taking it?' Holly asked.

181

'I don't honestly know,' Wendy admitted. 'She's quiet. Too quiet. Maybe I can get her all involved in the birthday party the next few days.' She didn't tell Holly her decision about Melinda. Holly could be objective – *she* could not. It was her child being torn apart.

'Does Jerry's mother know yet?'

'I've been elected to tell her.' Wendy sighed. 'Jerry's a nervous wreck. He's sounding off about how we'll have to see the kids away from the house. You know the kind of neighborhood we live in, Holly. It bugs the hell out of me – but I know Jerry's right. This is where Carol will be growing up. She's dating already. She has to know, and the boy she marries will have to know – but we don't have to blast it out all over the Bronx.'

They talked a few minutes longer – until Jonny awoke and Holly had to go to him. Wendy changed into a nightgown, creamed her face, climbed into bed. She was exhausted, too keyed up to sleep. But when she heard Jerry's key in the door, she rolled over on her side – face to the wall – and feigned sleep.

She lay sleepless long after Jerry snored beside her. She squinted at the clock on the night table. Past four already. She had to be up in three hours.

'Ma?' Carol's voice, uncertain. From the vicinity of the doorway.

'Honey, what is it?' Wendy was at the edge of the bed fumbling for scuffs.

'Nothing—' Carol's small, troubled voice evoked a flow of maternal love. 'I woke up and

182

I couldn't get back to sleep.'

Wendy crossed the room quickly, gathered Carol to her.

'Let's go out into the kitchen, darling,' she soothed. 'I'll make us some hot cocoa.'

Whatever happens, Carol must not be hurt.

Twenty

The living room – converted to bedroom for the night – lay in darkness. Earlier what Holly whimsically considered their personal night light – the Empire State tower – had filtered a shaft of brightness into the room. It must be close to one – the tower had gone dark almost an hour ago, Holly surmised.

Why was she having such trouble falling asleep tonight? Too keyed up, of course – after the battle with Al about the house. Al had flung himself into bed, pulled the blankets over his shoulders, and ignored her. He hadn't said one word about the party. Technically it was his birthday – Saturday already.

In the bedroom Jonny erupted into a plaintive wail. Poor darling. That tooth trying to push its way through the gum. She raced across the room and into the bedroom.

'I know it hurts,' she crooned and reached to lift him from the crib. His arms tightening about her neck as she held him close. The warmth of him, the velvet softness of his face against hers, the baby scents, filled her with a fierce protectiveness.

With Jonny in tow she hurried to the kitchenette to put a bottle in hot water. With luck he would be asleep again in twenty minutes. Cuddling him, she walked back to the bedroom-by-night and crossed to the sweep of windows.

It was pleasant to stand here at the window – high above the street – and gaze out on to the Manhattan skyscape at night. She loved Manhattan, Holly admitted – with a faint guilt because Al was obsessive now about his love of the country. She, too, loved the country – in comfortable snatches. But she loved Manhattan with the dedicated, deep-rooted affection of the non-native.

Strolling through the village in the autumn, lounging in Washington Square, window-shopping along Fifth Avenue, walking through Rockefeller Plaza with no real destination. Winter snows before the city became bogged down in dirt-ugly slush. St George's Church on Stuyvesant Park – Christmas-lighted, snow-flecked, with the snow-encrusted park for its front yard.

She loved going to the theater, finding small gourmet restaurants, spending a purloined afternoon caught up in the wonder of the Metropolitan. Living on the East Side, she missed the spring of Riverside Drive – the greenness, the revitalization of the earth, the animated activity of city people welcoming the new season. With air-conditioning, she found even city summers acceptable.

The bottle was warm. She offered it to Jonny. He clutched avidly. She walked with him into his bedroom, settled into the rocker bought for such moments as this. How good it felt, to sit here in the night silence with Jonny in her arms. He was finding relief from his baby anguish – she found satisfaction in comforting him. These were the moments that made life worth living.

Tomorrow would be bedlam from the moment she woke in the morning. Her mind catalogued the endless small details with which she would have to cope. Al had told her to bring in a woman to help with the dinner and serving. She had recoiled from such pretentiousness – though it was normal enough these days. She didn't want a strange woman in the apartment, she thought in candor – not tomorrow. She rejected an outsider in that tight little circle tomorrow night.

Again, she thought about Al's anger at her because she insisted upon being realistic. Long ago she'd had it with television. Couldn't he understand that wasn't for her – any more than her market was for him?

Al had this thing that she could tackle any kind of writing. But there had to be an end purpose. With what she was doing now she *knew* there was a check at the end of the line. Precious security. Television was grasping at the brass ring.

But with nasty insistence a remark made by Sandra – on a recent chance encounter – gnawed at her mind. Sandra – a vital part of those early years in New York.

'When are you going to get out of the steno pool, sweetie?' Sandra had protested when she outlined her current activities. 'So it's a nice check and you turn out the stuff like a well-oiled computer. Where's it taking you?'

Al yelled at her for lack of ambition. Now Sandra. The two of them – locking arms – unnerved her. She had known Sandra for so long. Almost as long as Al. She'd been so young when she met Sandra. So full of dreams, bursting with ideas. And not afraid to take chances.

She'd met Sandra at the Genius Club, then at that play-reading group the night they were reading Eric's manuscript. Sandra walked in with that magnificent presence of hers – the ageless, ever-sparkling, strikingly attractive champagne blonde. Not till much later had she learned that Sandra had been on her way to Hollywood stardom when she was derailed by a car smash-up that kept her on her back for two years.

After the reading a bunch of them had gone with Sandra for coffee. In a burst of bravery she'd told Sandra she was trying to break into radio.

'Bring some material into my office,' Sandra invited with an encouraging smile.

That was how the relationship with Sandra had been born – over a casual cup of coffee in a midtown café...

Twenty-One

1944–45

Holly was enthralled by Sandra's acceptance of her as a potential client. It mattered little that she was writing 'on spec' – with the hope of a sale. Not isolated one-shot scripts – sample scripts plus outlines for a prospective series.

In the midst of fighting a war – via V-mail – Al had coaxed her into this. Al was sharp. She followed his advice. She was shooting for the moon – it was a gamble she could accept.

Not until she had been working with Sandra for weeks did Sandra realize that she was legally too young to sign her own contracts. Either her mother or father would have to sign.

'Don said you were a baby.' Don was an ad-agency man – married – who was currently big in her personal as well as business life. 'No matter. The brain and the talent are mature.' Sandra's eyes settled speculatively on Holly. 'How do you like your daytime job?'

'I hate it,' Holly acknowledged and shrugged. 'It's a way of paying the rent.' But something in Sandra's eyes alerted her.

'How would you like to be my assistant?' Sandra suggested with candid enthusiasm.

'We'd make a great team. I can't pay much. Twenty-five a week. But you'll get a raise when business picks up.'

Holly hesitated. Her heart pounding. That was a ten-dollar cut in salary. Her mother would be furious. But she'd give the same amount of money at home. She'd manage somehow. This was an important step upward.

'I'd love it,' Holly said. 'It'll be tough to manage on the salary—' Let Sandra know that she was taking a cut.

'As soon as I can, I'll up it,' Sandra promised. 'When can you start?'

She could handle the painful budgeting, Holly told herself. This was getting a foothold in the entertainment world. Sandra listed herself as a radio packager – with forays into the new television medium, worked as a theatrical casting agent through other agents' franchises. But most important – to both Sandra and Holly – were the audition scripts that Holly knocked out. From her own ideas, Sandra's ideas, and those contributed by Don Mitchell – who considered Sandra's office an extension of his own.

It was heady stuff – at her age – to be part of Sandra's and Don's lives. To go to the Fifth Avenue penthouse of a Hollywood star in New York to discuss a possible radio series. To be a sufficiently frequent visitor to a stage star's Fifth Avenue town house for the butler to know she drank only rum Cokes. To lunch with Sandra and some big name at the Le Pavillon. To spend weekends – with Wendy miraculously included – at Sandra's Fire Island cottage.

The months raced past. Holly was conscious of a growing restlessness. Sandra and Don talked a marvelous line – but *nothing was happening*. OK, look around. Make something happen.

She answered an ad for radio writers for a projected daytime series. After two interviews, the submission of sample material, she received a phone call.

'We'd like you to be part of the team,' the producer – Frank Hale – told her. 'Contracts are being drawn up. Three hundred a week. Deal?'

'Deal.' She struggled to hide her euphoria. Three hundred was a fortune! But two weeks later, the series was canceled. The government banned the sponsor's product because of war-time shortages.

Holly was crushed. But she was relieved that she had not written Al about it yet. She'd been waiting until the contracts were signed by both parties. On weekends she worked on a script to be submitted to the freelance radio market.

She woke this Saturday with the realization that as of yesterday she had just completed her fifth month in Sandra's office. Much laughter, much fun – but nothing accomplished career-wise. Except that she was wiser about the business than she had been five months ago.

Sunlight poured across the twin beds in the tiny bedroom. Wendy was fast asleep. Holly looked at the clock. Past ten. The mail would have arrived by now.

She hurried from bed, grabbed her robe, headed out of the apartment and down to the bank of mailboxes in the foyer. Her face brightened as she withdrew a V-mail from Al. And what was this? Her heart began to thump. She ripped open the envelope, pulled out the letter. It was an acceptance of a half-hour radio manuscript. On national radio. And there was a check. A hundred and fifty dollars!

Standing there in the tiny, drab foyer, staring at the check, Holly knew what she was going to do. Quit the job at Sandra's, settle down to try for a repeat of this deal. The check would buy her two months if she was very careful.

Sandra was unhappy but philosophical. 'We can still work together. On audition scripts. Don wants to do something on that night-time series you talked about for Laura Kendell. Why don't we have dinner together tomorrow night, try to work up something?'

'Great,' Holly accepted. Laura Kendell was an important star. If she liked a series, it would be a big asset in selling.

Months went by without any action on the projected Laura Kendell series. Holly had sold two low-paying – pioneering – television markets in the interim. With checks coming in – even small ones – she could manage without taking on a nine-to-five job.

Early in the new year – 1945 – Sandra called to report that Don had brought a radio account into the agency. Sandra was to be the packager.

'The series will be built around Clay Garner,' Sandra reported. Holly was impressed. An ageing Broadway leading man, Clay Garner was still a draw. 'Don and I want you to do an audition script to present to the agency.'

'Sure.' Holly was enthusiastic. So it was 'on spec'. It could be a break.

Each night Don, Sandra and she sat together in Sandra's office – sweating out possible formats that would please the agency, Garner, and the sponsor. Don was to produce and direct – provided the sponsor bought. Holly would be the writer.

Word came through that the presentation had been read, discussed. Both Garner and the sponsor felt the format was right. Holly was euphoric. But suddenly there was a blackout.

Sandra was evasive. Walking into Sandra's office unexpectedly one afternoon, she discovered that a name writer was working on the audition script. A platter was to be cut and presented to the sponsor. Sandra was casting. A recording studio had been set. Holly was out.

She swore she was through with Sandra and Don. She haunted the networks – striving for a staff writing job. Her age was a blatant deterrent. A local station seemed about to hire her – but the biggies were dubious about her age. Another depressing experience.

Later on an afternoon two weeks later, she stopped in a phone booth to call her message service. Sandra had been trying to reach her. She'd phoned three times. Holly called Sandra's office, learned she was at the ad agency, checked there.

'Holly, get into a cab and come right over,' Sandra ordered, a pressured quality in her voice. 'It's important.'

Fifteen minutes later Holly hurried from the

191

elevator into the lushly carpeted reception area of the agency.

'Go to conference Room A,' the receptionist instructed her. 'They want you there right away.'

She walked in – faintly breathless, taken aback by the presence of agency brass, Clay Garner, a pair of radio actors whom she knew from Sandra's office. The atmosphere hummed with dissension. Sandra gestured for silence. Don was about to start a playback of a platter. An underling barked a sharp order through the door that they were not to be disturbed.

Clay Garner starcd at her, scowled, swung about to face Don belligerently.

'Come on, Don, what is this?' Clay demanded.

'Take it easy, Clay,' Don soothed. 'OK, now let's listen again. Holly, when this is over, give us your honest opinion.'

Holly perched on the edge of a chair with an outward show of poise. She was conscious of the incongruity of the situation. These agency execs with their million-dollar accounts, Clay Garner with a name in the Broadway theater for thirty years, Sandra, seasoned radio actors – and they sat here waiting for *her* appraisal of an audition platter?

The platter finished in a loud display of dubbed-in music. The room was electric with unspoken recriminations. Clay Garner was a superb performer. The actors were highly competent. But the program had limped through to a dismal finish.

'OK, Holly,' Don said, a plotted note of challenge in his voice. 'What's wrong with this thing?'

'The script,' she said. 'No conflict, no feminine interest, no warmth. If I'd tuned in, I would have switched to another station in five minutes.' Not until that moment did she realize that the grim pair across the conference table were the original writer and his manager. Color flooded her face.

'Right on the nose!' Clay slammed a fist on the table, a diabolic gleam of triumph in his voice. He picked up the script in front of him, tossed it to Holly. 'Here, rewrite. Have it ready by tomorrow at eleven.'

'Sure thing.' *I'll work all night. Thank God, brownstone apartment walls are thick – nobody will complain about the typewriter being noisy.*

'Don, have somebody pick up the script at Holly's apartment. Give it to mimeo. Call a reading for four. Reserve a studio for the next morning – we'll re-record then.' Clay Garner rose to his feet and headed for the door. The meeting was over.

Holly worked till past 7 a.m., conked out for three hours' sleep. A young woman from the ad agency arrived on schedule. At 1 p.m., Holly caught up with Sandra – in Don's office. Sandra was enthusiastic about the rewrite.

'Clay's such a wolf. He was getting ideas about you.' Sandra chuckled. 'He asked Don how old you were, flinched when Don told him. You're jail bait – you won't have trouble with him.'

Everybody was pleased with the rewrite. The session was held on schedule, declared a success. Clay was happy. The sponsor was happy. The initial thirteen-week series was ostensibly in the bag. Holly and Wendy walked about in a cloud of joyous expectations.

The sponsor signed contracts. Air time was set with the network. But when it came time to sign a writer, Holly was ignored. Don hired a staff of two established radio writers. It was as though her whole world had collapsed.

'Holly, you did a sensational job,' Sandra soothed. 'But the sponsor feels they can't afford to gamble with a writer as young and inexperienced as you. Of course, I fought for you.' But Holly doubted that.

A week later, Holly received a twenty-five-dollar check from the agency for the rewrite. Her first rebellious instinct was to send it back. A month later – on a Saturday morning – Frank Hale called her.

'Holly, grab a cab and come right down to my office. I have a rush assignment.'

'I can make it around two,' she hedged – skeptical of this assignment.

'Make it in twenty minutes. There's a fast fifty for you – you can knock this out in three hours at the typewriter,' he wheedled. 'Come on, Holly, be a good kid.'

She dressed, swigged down coffee, and hurried downtown to Frank's office.

'Look, we want to do this script – it's an audience-participation show,' Frank explained, overly casual. 'Just rewrite the dialogue. Make it more casual. Put it in your words.'

It *was* casual. A smooth job. Why did he want

it in *her* words? Weird signals popped up in her mind.

She noted the name on the title page – they had not even bothered to mask that. The writer – a name in the field – was the husband of a client of Sandra's. He had a history of defeated suits in actions against program packagers.

Frank Hale figured her for being talented but green, Holly interpreted. He never suspected she'd realize this was a program being hijacked. How rotten!

She hesitated, reluctant to be part of this operation. But as Frank had said, this was a fast fifty – and she'd report this to Sandra afterwards.

She finished the rewrite in less time than even Frank Hale expected. She left Hale's office, found a drugstore phone booth, and called Sandra. She reported the thievery.

'Holly, it's useless.' Sandra surprised her with this cynicism. 'Nobody'll believe you – even if the case ever gets to court. Don't say anything to Nick or Eleanor – they'll just be upset.' She hesitated. 'You've heard Eleanor bitch about crooked packagers. She and Nick will just be more frustrated—'

Clay Garner's show went on the air amid much hoopla – but when the thirteen-week period was over, there was no renewal. Now Sandra and Don became engrossed in television. It was very experimental – but exciting.

It was inevitable that Sandra should try to bring her in on this when Don sold the agency on a thirteen-week trial television series. Sandra knew she'd sold three scripts to a television station up in Schenectady. For minuscule fees. Skeptical about the prospects, she went in to talk to Sandra about working on the series.

'Holly, television is going to be the biggest thing ever,' Sandra said persuasively while they lunched in a restaurant chosen for its status in radio circles. 'Now's the time to get in – while it's new. Don has this eight-week series set up, on a multiple sponsorship basis. This allows a bunch of clients to get their feet wet at small output. I'll give it to you straight, Holly. The money is stinking, but where can you walk into this kind of experience? You'll have a free hand on material, experiment all you like!'

'What about the money?' Holly still hurt from her past efforts with Sandra and Don.

'Ridiculous,' Sandra apologized with a beguiling smile. 'The cast works for ten dollars a performance. The best I could swing for the scripts was twenty dollars a shot.'

'That's insane!' She gazed at Sandra in shock.

'It can work into a fabulous situation, Holly. Do this deal with us.'

'Let me think about it.' She'd sold two radio scripts for a hundred and fifty each. It was galling to accept twenty for a television script. 'Give me a few days.'

But she knew the answer. She'd play ball with them. Because it was a new field – and she was intrigued. Until Iris Meredith – Don's assistant at the agency – called to suggest they have lunch together.

'Sounds like fun,' Holly accepted. Iris had been at the agency forever, Sandra had told her.

196

'Always be nice to Iris – she knows where all the bodies are buried.'

Over pastrami sandwiches at the Stage Deli – charged to Iris's expense account – Iris gave her the inside scoop on Don's new television project.

'I can't stand what they're doing to you,' she said with defiant candor. 'Don and Sandra have the deal worked out. He's buying from Sandra as a packager. Sandra is drawing up contracts for you to do the experimental series at twenty bucks a script.'

'I know—' Holly's heart was pounding. She sensed what Iris was about to tell her.

'Don's budget includes two thousand dollars for the writer of the series.' Iris's eyes were eloquent.

'And Sandra will pay me a total of one hundred and sixty dollars,' Holly computed.

'Look, honey, don't ever let on that I told you,' Iris ordered. 'But I couldn't just stand in the sidelines and see them screw you again.'

'Thanks, Iris. They'll never know.' Holly struggled for poise. 'But I won't be accepting the assignment.'

Twenty-Two

Holly swore under her breath as a tenant – ignoring the late hour – did battle with the incinerator. If that idiot woke up Jonny – asleep in her arms – she'd go out there and tear into him. But the banging ceased. Jonny emitted small, contented snores.

Cautiously, Holly eased him into the crib, pulled up the side. For a moment she stood there gazing at him with tenderness. She walked back into the living room. Al lay sprawled on his stomach across the sofa bed. Blankets kicked off. She slid in beside him, pulled the covers up, and drew the blanket across Al.

She felt a tightness in her throat. Was she failing Al? For him it was important to be recognized. For most creative people acceptance – approval – is a kind of love they need to exist. Was she as immune to this as she professed to be? The veneer, Holly acknowledged uneasily, was beginning to crack.

Holly came awake reluctantly. From the clatter in the kitchenette she deduced that Al was in the same foul mood as when he went to bed last night. She sighed, braced herself for his irritation. What a way to begin his birthday.

In her mind Holly inventoried the day's

activities. Pick up the cake, do some last-minute grocery shopping. Bring in the chairs, the table, and the dishes from Betty's apartment. And in a little while her mother would be arriving. The world would collapse, but her mother must be here on schedule.

She turned over, burrowed her face against the pillow. Staving off the day.

'Here's your coffee,' Al announced moments later. Coffee mug in one hand, bottle in the other – and that tight, angry look on his face. What had happened to the laughter in their lives?

Holly swung about, contrived a smile.

'Happy birthday, Daddy.'

Al ignored the birthday salutation. 'Jonny's still sleeping. I'd better put the bottle back in hot water.'

'You wouldn't want to phone in sick today?' Holly called after him.

'On a Saturday? Are you nuts?' Moments later he came out of the kitchen, ran a hand over his cheek. 'I'll shave tonight.' He was silent for a moment. Holly was aware of a debate raging in his mind. 'Look, we haven't got time to thrash things out today – but I've made up my mind what we have to do.'

'What?' She was wary.

'We're clearing out of this town. Heading for California!' He dug into a drawer for a shirt.

'What on earth for?' Memories of their experiences in California could still stir up sick feelings in her.

'If I have to settle for hack writing, let me at least do it where the possibilities are great. We still have contacts on the Coast. Like Ron. Let me try the screenwriting bit. I don't know if I can sell a line out there. But if I do, it won't be for nine hundred a clip. What have I got here? I can sell shirts in Los Angeles, too!'

'Al, stop talking such nonsense!' It was so easy for him to get her agitated this way. After all these years, why couldn't she cope?

'What the hell are we falling into here? You're always fighting to take a book in before the pay period closes so you'll have a goddamn check! Two hundred and a quarter a month for this apartment – that's already too small for us! The check to your mother every week – not that I'm complaining about that,' he said quickly because her back was already up. Ever since her father died eleven years ago, she supported her mother. 'You're days away from having to hire a nursemaid if you're going to keep on writing the shit – and you'll have to, to keep us above water.'

'Al—' She tried to interrupt – but he pushed ahead.

'Without a car you're dead in this town if you have a kid. Parking in the street is inviting an ulcer – we'll have a forty buck a month garage bill, high insurance fees if we do buy a car. We've got an octopus sitting on our heads, Holly! It's going to strangle us!'

'We can manage.' She fought for calm. In the past it had always been she who sought to keep their expenses low. But how could they live in a slum with Jonny? They didn't have to, as long as she was selling. *Don't think about the market*

200

drying up. About scrounging for another. 'Al, we can manage.'

'You don't want to take a crack at that house in the country. OK, we cut out for California. We've got enough ahead to buy a used car – one that's good enough to take us out to Los Angeles. You can write the shit out there as well as here. If I connect with a real deal, you drop the garbage.'

'What's the sudden love for California?' Holly flared. She left the sofa bed, reached for the empty coffee mug. *Al is out of his mind!*

'I might latch on to something with real money on the Coast. If I'm going to write shit, let me at least be well paid for it!'

'Jonny's awake.' She grasped at a chance to break away. 'I'll change him—'

She scurried into the bedroom, scooped Jonny from the crib. Oh, he was a happy baby, she thought tenderly while she deposited him on the bed for the morning change. But what was this insane business with Al? It turned her sick to think about leaving New York! What about her mother? How could they uproot her?

Moments later Al walked in with Jonny's bottle. Jonny crowed in approval. He'd established his own routine – bottle first, a brief rest, then his breakfast.

'I meant it, Holly. I'm getting out of the straitjacket. Monday morning I'm giving two weeks' notice at the store.'

'Al!' She stared in shock.

'I'll ask Ron for some letters. When we hit Los Angeles, I'll pick up contacts. We're not strangers at some of the studios.'

'Nobody on the Coast knows you as a writer! At the studio you were the Trio's personal manager!'

'I'm a writer!' Al yelled. 'I've been a writer all my life. It's time I made myself heard. I'll call you later,' he said abruptly. 'But we're leaving for the Coast, Holly – we've had it here.'

'Al, wait,' she called urgently because he was charging out of the room. 'Al, I'm not leaving New York—'

Al swung around to face her. He looked suddenly exhausted. His eyes were hostile.

'Think about it, Holly. You'll go.'

They stared at each other – strangers for the moment. Then Al was slamming out of the apartment. He hated California. He loathed the life-and-death struggles, the pressures, even the weather. He always said one week of California, and he'd had it!

He'd made up his mind that California was the answer for them. No! I won't go out there again. Can it end like this for us? Al in California, Jonny and me here in New York? After all these years can it end this way?

The California phase of their lives seemed a century behind them. But now her mind charged further into the past. To a Saturday morning some weeks after Al had come home from the war – when she was growing anxious because he seemed to be living in limbo, with no thought of the future. She had awakened early – perhaps because she was worried about Al.

Twenty-Three

December, 1945

Holly debated about staying in bed another hour, glanced across to the other bed. Wendy was sound asleep. The mail came early these days – go out and check the mailbox. She reached for the robe at the foot of the bed, pulled it on, hurried out to the cluster of mailboxes with a recurrent surge of anticipation. She had four scripts out making the rounds. That was the accepted freelance writer's routine – keep several scripts circulating, hope for a sale of one of them.

She unlocked their mailbox, pulled out a pair of ads, an envelope from an ad agency. All at once her heart was racing. A thick envelope. A contract? She ripped it open, withdrew the contents. Yes! A $300 check due on signing. She darted back into the house, up the stairs to Al's studio apartment. He was out.

Forty minutes later Al breezed into the apartment with a bag of hot rolls for breakfast – plus the announcement that on Monday morning he'd sign up for the 52–20 club.

'Hey, the government's ready to send out twenty bucks a week for fifty-two weeks to

203

unemployed GIs. I can use it.'

'It's like a writing grant.' Holly glowed. 'Your chance to settle down to write a serious play.' Al always said he needed an issue to write about – and the war was the biggest issue that had hit all of their lives.

Al squinted in thought. 'I don't know. Something's floating around in my head,' he admitted, 'but I'm not ready to tackle it yet. I guess I need to unwind. It's a war play – would cost a fortune to produce.'

'Al, don't worry about that end of it,' Holly urged. 'Just focus on getting it down on paper.'

'Once I can unwind,' he said again. 'Anyhow, I was talking to this guy at the bakery. His brother has a small office down in Times Square. He's ready to turn it over for a price. Maybe I can work out a deal with him. Let's face it,' he added after a moment. 'I can't go far on twenty bucks a week.'

Al managed to borrow enough money to clinch the takeover. It was an address. There was a telephone. A beat-up desk, a file cabinet, three chairs. Al would be in business again. An agent.

On this first day of the takeover Al and Holly tackled the tiny, dirt-encrusted office with enthusiasm. They went about painting with a frenzy. Late in the day Holly went down for hamburgers and coffee. They'd just polished off their food when the door swung open and a masculine voice blasted the quiet.

'I'll be damned! I thought I heard familiar voices!' Eric stood in the doorway – a grin on his lean, sardonic face.

'Where the hell have you been?' Al sat on the corner of his desk. 'We haven't seen you in weeks.'

'You know me.' Eric shrugged – an odd glint in his eyes. 'Going back into agenting?'

'I like to eat,' Al reminded. 'What's new with you?' Eric was known to wander from one menial job to another.

Eric dropped into a chair. An arresting air about him now. 'Just finished a new play. I think it's good. Want to handle it for me?'

'I'm not a literary agent,' Al pointed out.

'So be my personal manager,' Eric said. 'If the play's a hit, there's money enough for everybody. I've already got a Hollywood name interested in the female lead.' He grinned. 'How's that for a starter?'

Al nodded in approval. 'Bait for investors.' The atmosphere was suddenly electric.

Enthralled, Holly listened to the other two discuss what had developed in the weeks since they'd seen each other. This was a confident Eric. One of those fairy-tale chance encounters had brought him in touch with a fading Hollywood star – eager for a Broadway production.

For the next few weeks everything in their lives was thrust aside to push Eric's play ahead. Here was the big deal, the possible winning sweepstake ticket.

Al set up readings, chased prospective backers. Holly brought in Sandra to work with them on lining up people known to invest in plays. The Hollywood leading lady opened doors – but Al gave Eric credit.

'This is a solid, commercial script. No Pulitzer prizewinner – but it should do great at the box office.'

Eric seemed to stumble through each day in a euphoric daze. He had always been skeptical of success coming his way. He was honest. It wasn't only material rewards he was after – he had a festering need to see his name on a marquee, to thumb his nose at all the bastards who had crushed their heels on him.

With the furor over Eric's play Wendy saw little of Jerry – the new man in her life. It was Al and Holly, Eric and Wendy. Wendy rushed over to the office from work each day to help Holly type up promotional packages for prospective investors.

As Al had predicted, they had no difficulty acquiring actors eager to be part of their scheduled backers' auditions. Then, close to midnight after their second reading, Sandra returned to the rented studio with a towering white-haired, ruddy-faced man somewhere in his mid-seventies.

'Mr Henderson was at the audition with me,' Sandra explained. 'He loved the play. I thought he would enjoy meeting with you people.'

Sandra seated Henderson so that she was free to indicate through hand signals that the old boy liked to talk. He was a bored millionaire industrialist from Tennessee, who had been floating around New York for the past three years – searching for what entertainment his money could buy him.

The others sat listening in candid interest

while he told them – with the air of a small boy bragging about a conquest – how he had been taken in his three years in the city.

'Oh, I guess I've thrown about a hundred seventy thousand into plays, another seventy-eight thousand in some screwball movie. Then there was a record company and a dance troupe. But you kids aren't much like the folks I've been running around with lately,' he said, narrowing his eyes in speculation. 'You're young and full of ideas. Maybe I'm all wrong, but I have a feeling you're real – none of that phony stuff about you. So how about all of us piling over to Toots for something to eat? I'm a man with a healthy appetite.'

Al was smart. Not one bit of pressure anywhere along the line. Just a lot of honest enthusiasm, colored by the Al Rogers personality. Henderson didn't come out right away and say he was interested in investing. He'd pop in to drag Holly out for lunch or to pull Al downstairs for a drink. A couple of nights he took the four of them out to dinner and to a Broadway musical. Finally he came out with what simmered in his mind.

'I tell you what, kids. You come up with a name producer who'll lend himself to this thing, and I'll put up half the money. Sandra said you need something like fifty thousand to get it on, right?'

'That'll do with careful planning,' Al acknowledged.

'OK, if you dig up a name producer, I'll put up twenty thousand. You'll have no trouble raising the other twenty thousand with a name producer, a Hollywood star, and half the backing already up.' Henderson grinned, knowing the startled addition clicking in the minds of the others. 'Now, Al, you can shave that budget down ten thousand. We'll be in business.' He slammed his fist triumphantly on the table – as though he had personally saved that much cash.

Al kept warning that the forty thousand budget was too tight for comfort – but, somehow, they'd manage. That was part of the fun Henderson was buying – to see how they would wriggle through on his sharpened budget.

Al slaved away at lining up a producer. Finally he made a deal. In earlier days Jim Mattox had been a big-time producer. To Henderson he was still big.

'Holly, this is it!' Al chortled, and they dashed over to Henderson's hotel to tell him.

But Henderson had news of his own. Overnight he had gone cold on the play. He had just decided to put the money instead into a company manufacturing sugar-free jellies.

Later Al and Holly sat in the office with Eric and Wendy. The small room was stifling with the news Al had just aired.

'I don't believe it,' Holly protested. 'Henderson gave us his word. He told you, Al – go out and get a name producer – and we'll be in business.'

'He changed his mind. We had nothing in writing.' Eric's face was taut, his voice bitter. 'Old story around this town.'

'Henderson's not the only backer in this town.

We still have a name producer, a Hollywood star,' Holly began with a show of optimism.

'But no dough,' Eric shot back. 'The dough you and Sandra expected to come in was waiting for Henderson's twenty grand in the kitty. Anybody who might have been interested will run like a frightened sheep. I had one lousy chance in a million of ever landing a Broadway show – and it just blew up in my face.'

Twenty-Four

The sound of the door chimes brought Holly back to the present with a start. For a few moments she'd forgot her mother's imminent arrival. With her mother everything was timed to the minute. It was 8:30 a.m. sharp.

Al and her mother had an unspoken truce. Still, she was nervous if they came together without forewarning. Al was outspoken. Her mother would inevitably twist words to mean something entirely different from their intent. Al must have been going down in an elevator while her mother came up, she soothed herself. They didn't meet.

'Al's gone, isn't he?' Clara Woodridge asked. 'I watched the clock at the drugstore to make sure I wouldn't come in while you're in the morning rush.'

'He's gone.'

'Is Jonny awake?'

'He's having his bottle.'

'Then I won't go in to him yet. Are we going out this morning?' her mother asked.

'Yes.' She knew her mother hated sitting in the house. 'I have to pick up some things for the dinner.'

'I don't know why you didn't listen to me and call the whole thing off. Ridiculous to go to all that trouble.'

'It won't be that rough.' Mom knew this was Al's birthday, Holly thought – but she'd never acknowledge it. 'I've been marinating sauerbraten for two days. Everything else is simple.'

'You're going to be all worn out,' her mother persisted. 'And all that noise – they'll wake the baby for sure. But you never listen to me—'

'These are close friends.' Holly strived for patience. 'I look forward to having them here for dinner.'

'What time is Wendy coming over?' Her mother knew Wendy would arrive well before the others – to help out.

'Close to two, I think.'

'Then I'll leave at one thirty. I don't want to be in the way.' The familiar air of martyrdom.

The phone rang. Holly scurried to answer.

'Hello.'

'I'm about to go out of my mind,' Claire said, her voice muted to a whisper. 'I just can't take any more of this.'

'What happened?' Holly's voice held sympathy – she was accustomed to these dramatic declamations. 'Kids acting up?'

'Nothing like that.' Claire sighed. 'It's the old business starting all over again. I told Bernie – I can't go through that again.' In the background there was a jumble of voices.

'Where are you?' Holly asked. What old business did Claire mean? Claire's life was a series of crises.

'I'm in a drugstore around the corner from the house. The kids are at the soda fountain having hot chocolate. Bernie kept driving me crazy last night – dreaming up excuses to get me out of the house this morning. Finally he comes out with the truth. He has an appointment at the apartment this morning – with an FBI man.'

'What?' This was 1961 – the early fifties seemed a century away. 'Claire, what on earth for?'

'He doesn't know,' Claire said tiredly. 'He got this phone call at the office. The FBI man asked to see him outside of the office. They fixed up the date for this morning. I can't figure it out – after all these years. What do they want with Bernie now? He's been cleared for his job. For God's sake, he's been working at it for close to four years already. Why suddenly questions again?'

'Has he signed anything?' Holly questioned. 'Joined any organizations?'

'Are you kidding?' Claire scoffed impatiently. 'He thought a dozen times before we joined the Parents' Association. What the hell can it be about now?'

'When's the appointment for?'

'Right now. The man's up at the apartment this

minute. I've got orders to keep the kids out for another hour. We haven't heard from the FBI in ten years. All of a sudden visits again!'

'It's probably nothing at all. Go over to the fountain and have yourself a cup of coffee, then go to a supermarket and buy something. Just keep your mind off it until you can phone up Bernie and find out. There's no point in having a nervous breakdown when you haven't the faintest idea what it's about.'

'What could it be about?' Claire challenged. 'Didn't we have enough visits? Didn't Bernie walk out of a job he loved before he was thrown out?' Claire took a deep breath. 'I still remember Bernie's parents – burning books out in Jersey.'

'Claire, let me call you back,' Holly said, aware that her mother was tapping restlessly with one foot. 'My mother's here now.'

'Oh, hell, I forgot. Saturday morning. Anyhow, we'll see you tonight – if Bernie isn't en route to Leavenworth. I've got a babysitter lined up, so Bernie's clear.'

'Stop worrying,' Holly ordered. 'And buzz me back as soon as you know the score.'

She put the phone down. Her mother was always annoyed at phone calls when she was visiting. Her eyes traveled to her watch. So little time to get everything done.

'I have to run down to the laundry room with diapers,' Holly apologized. 'Shall I leave Jonny with you?'

'Oh, Jonny and his grammy get along just fine,' his grandmother crooned. 'Just too bad you can't afford diaper service.'

'I don't need diaper service at his age,' Holly pointed out. How many dozens of times had they gone through this routine?

'It's such a nice day you ought to get the baby out early – while the sun's strong. Of course, in my room I never know whether the sun's out or it's raining.'

'We'll run out as soon as I get the diapers in the dryer,' she promised.

How long had she swallowed that story about her mother's hotel room never seeing the sun? Six years? Until she went over one afternoon when her mother was staying in the hotel with a bad cold. The sunlight had streamed across the floor, across the bed. It wasn't a luxurious room. It was a small hotel room. That was what her mother wanted – a hotel room, with maid service, phone, no responsibilities.

She wished she could afford a large, front corner room in a swanky hotel, Holly thought grimly – but she couldn't. She had offered to pay another five dollars a week, but her mother refused that. How much better could she do with five dollars a week? Maybe she found a kind of pleasure in complaining. Maybe she would be lonely without complaints.

Holly lifted the diaper pail into the shopping cart, dropped in the box of soap flakes, groped in her change purse for quarters. This early on a Saturday morning there should be no problem about getting a washing machine. In forty minutes the diapers could go into the dryer – they could stay there for a while. She would put Jonny into the stroller, take her mother out of the apartment. Dear God, no battles today, please!

As Holly left her apartment, Betty's door swung open.

'Come on in and have coffee,' Betty invited.

'My mother's here,' Holly explained. 'But thanks.'

'I had a letter from Rolfe. He's going with a girl. He says they're talking about getting married.' Betty smiled, but there was apprehension in her eyes.

'An American girl or French?' Holly asked. How old was Rolfe? Nineteen, twenty? Betty had been nurturing hopes of his going to college.

'She's from California. Beyond that I don't know much.' The corners of her mouth lifted in wry humor. 'I wrote him an airmail last night and asked him if she goes to church, synagogue, or mosque.'

'They may be coming home earlier than you expected,' Holly encouraged. 'If Rolfe has found what he wants to do with his life.'

'I thought he wanted to be a painter. He's been so deadly earnest about it. Rolfe isn't like my sister's kids. They all take fliers at the arts, then settle down in middle-class domesticity.'

'I'll have my head chopped off if I don't get down to the laundry room and back—' Holly's smile was wry.

'What time do you want to collect the chairs and the table?'

'Whenever it's convenient for you. And the dishes you talked about – are they still available?'

'Sure – just sitting in a box, straight from the

214

dishwasher. One or the other of us is sure to be home until late afternoon,' Betty added. 'Come in whenever you're ready.'

'I shudder when I think of what I have to get done before tonight,' Holly confessed. 'It's been so long since we've had a party.'

'If Rolfe is serious,' Betty made an attempt at levity, 'I may soon be involved in a wedding. I'm glad the girl is an American. They'll return – eventually – to this country.'

Holly's thoughts shot to Mitch. The brief conversation with him yesterday had been disturbing. Would Mitch's marriage – Mitch's life – have worked out differently if Maria had been an American girl?

Mitch and Maria had been the first of their group to get married. Poor Mitch, he had been such a nervous wreck those months of waiting to cut through the army red tape, to bring Maria over from Italy. The tabloids had screamed about the staggering total of GIs who were returning with commitments to foreign girls.

So many American girls had been bitter at the influx of foreign brides. All the years of waiting for the war to be over, for the boys to return to resume their normal lives – and a shocking number came home with their lives already settled.

Some of the marriages were legitimate love matches – developed through the months and years of living in close association, born of loneliness and need. Others rooted in a determination on the part of cynical foreign girls to escape the war-torn countries and acquire

American citizenship, and destined to end – at the earliest practical moment – in the divorce courts. Mitch and Maria, it had seemed, were deeply in love.

Twenty-Five

August, 1946

Mitch and Maria were married on a Saturday afternoon in the living room of his mother's house out in New Jersey. Maria was lovely, enthralled with everything she saw. Mitch's family was warm, delighted that he was marrying. It appeared an auspicious union.

After the wedding, six of them piled into Jerry's car for the trip back into New York. Claire and Bernie were dropped off in mid-Manhattan, to meet Bernie's brother and sister-in-law for dinner. Wendy and Jerry were going to her parents' apartment for dinner.

Holly realized that Wendy had planned this day with canny desperation. First the wedding out in Jersey, then the evening with her parents – on their best behavior. Wendy was sure Jerry would ask her to marry him – but the delay was ripping at her nerves.

Jerry deposited Holly and Al at the stoop of their brownstone. Holly stared up at the door with distaste, brushed with restlessness, a reluctance to close herself in familiar surroundings now.

'Let's go out for dinner, Al.'

Al stared at her in astonishment. After the afternoon's festivities he would have been content to sit down to a quiet dinner in her and Wendy's apartment, Holly guessed. 'Where?'

'I don't know.' Holly squinted in thought. 'Down in the Village? Mitch told us about a place down there that's supposed to be great – and inexpensive,' she added quickly. 'I have the address somewhere—'

'Dig it out. If Mitch is wrong, we'll take it out of his hide.'

They found the place without much difficulty. It was small, unpretentious, with low-keyed lighting. The Saturday-evening crowd – if there was to be one – had not yet arrived. They were seated in a booth near the edge of the floor. Mitch had mentioned a male singer on weekend nights. Now, Holly recalled from the poster at the door, there was a girl trio appearing nightly.

'What are you in the mood for?' Al asked cajolingly. She sensed that Mitch had got on his nerves today – with his not-so-subtle cracks about people who took so long to get married. Aimed at him and at Jerry.

'Something mad.' Holly concentrated on the menu with a pixie grin.

After convivial debate with the waiter they ordered. Al's knee sought hers beneath the table and stayed with it. The food arrived, lived up to its press. By the time dessert and coffee were served they were both thoroughly relaxed. The

217

room was jammed with diners now.

The Trio came out for their first number. Their gowns were a disaster, Holly thought in a corner of her mind. Their hairstyles unflattering. They seemed to consider themselves a road-company Andrews Sisters. They even chose an Andrews Sisters' favorite for an opener. 'Don't Sit Under The Apple Tree With Anyone But Me'. Holly felt Al stiffen into alertness.

'They're good,' he whispered with an undercurrent of excitement. 'Raw as hell – but good.'

'They need to learn how to dress. How to wear their hair,' Holly summed up. 'Their make-up is too heavy.' But yes, there was something special about them.

Al gazed around at the other diners. They didn't appear spectacularly interested – but that didn't mean anything, Holly assessed. It was the usual Saturday-night scene. Diners were too involved in themselves, their personal campaigns of the moment, to pay attention to the low-paid entertainment provided.

The moment the Trio left the floor, Al ditched his cigarette. His face taut with purpose. Holly read his mind. This was the pre-war Al that Wendy and the others had talked about – the agent with an eye out for talent.

'I'm going to talk to those kids. Wait here.'

Ten minutes later Al returned to their table with an air of triumph. 'They're coming to see me at the office Monday morning,' he reported.

'What did you find out about them?' Holly pressed.

'Gloria and Bonnie are sisters, the other girl –

218

Marian – is their cousin. They've been knocking around town for six years – working at joints out in the boondocks, at a place like this when they're lucky. Another year of this,' he surmised, 'and they'll be running home to some small town in Missouri.'

At Al's insistence Holly went with him to the office at shortly before 11 a.m. on Monday. Minutes later the Trio arrived. Holly knew Al threw a terrific line when he was in the mood. She expected him to fascinate the three girls. He talked. They listened. Holly read their minds. He was the fairy godmother, and they were Cinderella in triplicate.

'Up till now,' Marian said with engaging honesty, 'we've wound up with two-bit agents with big talk and traveling hands. And lousy money when they did book us.'

'You've got a personal manager now, kids.' Al was in high gear. 'I talk to the agents. I make the deals.'

Now he brought out the contracts that Holly had insisted he prepare. In the past he'd had no contracts with those he booked – and when they moved upward because of his promotion, they'd walked out for a bigger name.

'You read the contracts before you sign,' he insisted. 'Anything you don't understand, you ask me.'

Watching the girls sign the contracts, Holly realized that she and Al were embarking on a whole new era. Now they plunged headlong into the task of building the Trio into an impressive act. Every cent they could raise went into arrangements, gowns chosen by Holly, reducing salons – whatever they felt necessary to add glamour to the Trio. They were a team now with one purpose. Young, dynamic, and bursting with optimism.

Lady luck was on their side, Holly told Al in soaring spirits when she sold another radio script as they were scrounging for money. Al had pushed aside all writing efforts. The Trio would be their passport to financial freedom. Then he would focus on his novel-in-work.

Al began to book jobs – nothing spectacular, but there was eating money in it for all of them. He borrowed money from a finance company – with Mitch as a co-signer – to finance a nose job for Gloria. When the doctor permitted her to inspect the results, Gloria devoured her new reflection in the mirror, cried in Holly's arms. Without Al and Holly, she swore she would never have dared the plastic job.

'My mother kept saying I was born with that kind of nose and I was stuck with it.' Brimming over with affection and gratitude, the Trio swore eternal loyalty to Al and Holly.

Wendy made a habit of hurrying over to their office – right after work each day. Now Holly realized Wendy wasn't seeing Jerry.

'What's with you and Jerry?' she demanded, shutting down on work for the day.

Wendy took a deep breath. 'I've been gearing myself to tell you. Jerry's married – but he's fighting for a divorce.'

'How long have you known this?' Holly was indignant.

'About a week. It was one of those wartime things,' Wendy explained dejectedly, 'where Jerry was expecting to be shipped out any minute, and she dreamt of an allotment check every month – or the ten thousand insurance if he didn't make it back home.'

'You mean they aren't living together?' Holly probed.

'Jerry wasn't back home two weeks before he found out she's the worst slut in the state – only for a New York divorce you need proof. She's smart. To Lola, it's a terrific joke.'

'Why does she hang on to him? Is Jerry giving her money?'

'Not on a regular basis, but she takes him for fifty or so every few weeks. Whatever she can drag out of the poor guy. He's praying she'll find a bigger sucker and let him off the leash.'

'He'll work it out,' Holly consoled. But she was upset. 'Give him time.'

'He can have all the time he wants.' Wendy was candid. 'Only he's made up his mind not to see me until he has Lola off his neck. All of a sudden he's developed a conscience – for *me*.' Wendy gestured dramatically. 'What about Al and you?' she prodded for the thousandth time. 'All it takes is two bucks and two minutes at City Hall.'

'Once we're set with the girls,' Holly evaded. Mitch had been on her back on the same score. 'Come on, let's go home. Al's with the Trio at the coach's studio. God knows when they'll break.'

Holly and Wendy had just walked into the

apartment when the phone rang. It was Mitch.

'Hi.' Holly's greeting was warm. She hadn't spoken to Mitch for almost a week. A long stretch for them. 'How's everything?'

'I'm worried about Linda,' he said. 'She's breaking up with Renée.'

'That's good.' Holly was startled by his reaction.

'She's chasing off to South America on some job,' he explained, his voice laced with anxiety. 'I don't like it.'

'Linda's over twenty-one, Mitch.' He wasn't still emotionally involved with Linda, was he?

'Oh, some good news,' Mitch said. 'Maria's pregnant.'

'Mitch, how wonderful!' Maybe their having a baby would settle Mitch into contentment.

'I'm going to have to go out and land a regular job. No more hit-and-miss income from arrangements or accompanying. The dough has to be there every week now.' Mitch sounded simultaneously apprehensive and pleased. 'Can you picture me with a kid?'

'I think it's marvelous.' The first baby in their tight little clique.

Two hours later Al came charging into the apartment. Glowing, he tossed a newspaper across the sofa, then dropped into his favored club chair.

'We got a nice shot on that children's ward bit,' he told Holly.

'What shot?' Wendy lunged for the paper, flipped through to the entertainment section.

'I planted an item about the Trio going into the

222

children's wards of the city hospitals once a week to sing lullabies. That was a smart gimmick, Holly.'

'The girls love it.' Holly chuckled. 'Nobody talks while they're singing.'

'Get hold of Mitch,' Al told Wendy. 'He has to play for the Trio at the record-company audition tomorrow.'

'What record company?' Holly demanded.

Al grinned. 'A little deal I cooked up this afternoon over a pastrami sandwich at the Stage Deli. Oh, you'd better call the Trio before Mitch. Let them know what's cooking.'

'What about this record-company audition?' Holly prodded. Wendy was already calling the Trio.

'It's not a big label,' Al warned. 'But if they like what they hear, we'll get a platter out of them. I can run with that.'

'It's exactly what we need.' Holly's eyes shone.

'Here's Marian,' Wendy chirped.

Al crossed to take the phone. 'Hi, Marian. Be at the rehearsal studio tomorrow by eleven sharp. You have an audition for this record company at one. I want you to work with Mitch for at least an hour before we go over. Now remember, this is a small company – their distribution's limited – their publicity budget stinks. But it'll be something for me to run with.'

Holly's heart pounded. They all knew nothing could push the Trio ahead so much as a good record. If this record turned out well, they'd be on their way.

The Trio's first record was a fair seller – nothing sensational. But it was a wedge that got Holly through to the disc-jockeys. Al was cautious about bookings, determined to be absolutely certain of the Trio's readiness before he high-pressured any solid spots.

The girls griped at regular intervals – but they always conceded Al was right. They were gaining assurance, style. They were learning how to handle themselves in promotional gimmicks. Time was racing past – but their standing was climbing upward. They celebrated their second anniversary with Al amid sensational vows of loyalty.

Through a fluke – chasing down a nebulous rumor – Holly arranged for the Trio to perform a number in a low-budget movie. A few weeks after the Trio returned from the Coast, Al set up an audition with a major record label. While it would be months before the movie was to be released, the film credit was a definite asset.

The Trio was great – neither Holly nor Al harbored any doubts. Right now – more than any one thing – they were hungry for a solid number on a major label – with the all-out promotion of a major company behind them. The most sensational record could get lost in the shuffle if the promotion wasn't there to shove it to the top.

The day of the audition with the major label arrived. Al and the Trio left for the recording studio. Holly paced the office – simultaneously exhilarated and fearful. Time went past with no phone call from Al. Had the audition gone badly? *Why hasn't Al called?*

Then Al burst into the office. Without the gals. For a moment Holly was terrified.

'Baby, we did it!' Al picked her up, set her on the corner of her desk. 'You should have seen Langley! Tried like hell not to let on how much he liked the kids, but it glowed from him like the Big Dipper. And the numbers they're recording.' He whistled expressively. 'If those kids don't make the Hit Parade this time, I quit the business.'

'It's definite?'

'Langley's having the contracts drawn up. We record on the twenty-ninth. Sol Berman's doing the arrangements – nobody can beat him.'

'Will we have them in time for the girls to work with Helen?'

'Berman's a speed demon. Langley's smart enough to know they need time with their coach. Helen's got a rep. Expensive as hell, the old bitch – but worth every cent.'

Holly frowned. 'Do you think Mitch is hurt because we don't call him to accompany any more?'

'Mitch is never free – with that stinking office job of his. He told you that himself.' Al sighed. 'Looks like poor Mitch is finished as far as music goes.'

'Don't say that!' Holly was startled at her sharpness.

'Why not? Between working ten hours a day six days a week – because they need the over-time – and listening to the baby cry half the night, when does Mitch have time for the music business?'

The baby – tiny Roseanne – was premature, heartbreakingly fragile, and Mitch was displaying an astonishing devotion.

'Al, that's temporary. It takes time to get back on a normal schedule after the siege they've been through.'

'Mitch won't be able to cut down on his overtime and keep paying doctors' bills – on top of everything else.' Al was blunt. 'Unless some great-uncle dies and leaves him a million.'

'If Mitch is going to write music, he'll write it, no matter what,' Holly insisted. Wanting to believe this.

'Holly, you can't divide yourself sixteen ways. Plus all of a sudden Mitch has a bug about writing fiction. Everybody we know is going to write the Great War Novel.' Unexpectedly bitterness crept into Al's voice. 'I'm out of cigarettes,' he discovered. right back.' Once a month he swore he'd quit smoking – but it wasn't happening.

Holly sat motionless – Al's death knell for Mitch's talent sounding alarms in her mind. What about Al and her? What about their writing? Publicity for the Trio – that was the sum total of her efforts. Their reading revolved around *Billboard*, *Variety*, and newspaper columns.

The phone rang, shattering her introspection.

'Hello, how's everybody?' Eric's voice at the other end was casual as though he had been away for a weekend instead of close to two years.

'Where have you been all this time?' Holly demanded.

'Hitch-hiked out to the Coast. Worked out there a year, came back. I've been home almost two months. Guess what? I'm getting married.'

'Eric!' She was dumbfounded.

She heard his cool, familiar chuckle. 'It's still being done.'

'When are you bringing the bride over?' Holly pursued. What kind of a girl could inspire permanency in Eric?

'When are we invited?' he countered.

'What about dinner tonight? Al's going to be tied up at an appointment, and Wendy has a date – but you two come over and keep me company.'

'Sure,' he accepted. 'What time?'

'How about seven?' By then Wendy would be dressed and out. Suddenly Jerry and she were seeing each other again.

'Fine. See you then.'

Holly was leaning absorbedly over the cake she had picked up at the bakery – struggling to affix the miniature bride and groom at the proper angle – when the doorbell rang. She thrust the cake into a cabinet above the stove, hid the bottle of wine behind breakfast cereal, then raced to open the door.

'Hi.' Eric stood there smiling.

'Eric, you character!' Holly kissed him, then turned to welcome the prospective bride.

'This is Sara.' Eric introduced her with a self-conscious air.

'Hello, Sara.' Holly contrived to conceal her

shock behind a warm smile.

'Hi.' Sara was nonchalant.

'Come on inside.' Holly prodded them into the living room.

Sara inspected the room in minute detail. At least nine years older than Eric – tall, stocky, devoid of any physical attraction, she wore jeans and a man's plaid shirt that appeared total strangers to soap and water. The coat that Holly was hanging away looked as though it had been slept in every night for six months.

Holly wasn't sure what was said in the next few minutes. Everything was mechanical on her part. Finally, she had Eric and Sara seated and was getting dinner on the table. What crazy quirk pushed someone as fastidious and sensitive as Eric to tie himself up with a misfit like Sara? Was Eric – through some confused obsession – deliberately dragging himself down to her level?

Most of the dinner conversation consisted of barbed questions from Eric and Sara about Al's current activities. She was just about to bring out the wedding cake when Sara – subtle as an Elsa Lanchester barmaid – dropped her small bombshell.

'I don't know why Eric has to go around saying we're getting married,' she cracked. 'He's just moving into my apartment. It'd be kind of impossible to get married – even if we wanted to bother.'

'A slight complication,' Eric explained. 'Sara has a husband, according to the laws of the state of New York. He's got the kid.'

'And I've got a cheap cold-water flat in the Village – so why should Eric live alone?' Sara sprawled against the sofa in sensuous satisfaction.

Holly managed to denude the cake of its wedding note. While they had cake and coffee, Eric held tightly to one of Sara's hands – as though to boast of his pleasure in this arrangement. Could this be what Eric wanted – this playing at having a wife and home without the attendant responsibilities of marriage? Knowing once he was weary of the situation he could pick up and walk out with no repercussions?

Holly was disturbed that Eric could settle for something so shoddy. Eric with a sensitive awareness of beauty that approached the painful. Eric with his passion for the philosophers and fine poetry.

'Eric's writing a new play. Did he tell you?' Sara was pouring cream into her coffee, sloshing the mixture into an ugly lake about the cup.

'That's great.' Holly tried to sound enthusiastic.

'I do freelance typing from my apartment,' Sara said. 'Regular office hours would drive me nuts,' she continued, pouring the spilled coffee back into the cup.

'So now I've got a secretary,' Eric flipped. 'Great deal, huh?'

Perhaps in her weird way Sara would be good for Eric, Holly tried to reason. He had real talent. Yet she'd long harbored a fear that this talent might be consumed by Eric's violent distrust of almost everything and everybody – even while his whole being cried out for affection.

The three of them pushed their way through an hour of small talk until Al arrived. Now the room came alive with backslapping and explanations. But Holly sensed Al's covert dislike for Sara.

Sara displayed every trait Al disliked in a woman. Not one iota of femininity or charm showed through. When she opened her mouth, it was like a breath of the gutter sweeping in through a door someone had carelessly left open.

Holly felt a surge of relief when Eric and Sara made overtures of departure. She guessed Eric wouldn't invade just any of his limited circle of friends' homes in Sara's custody. And custody it was.

'What the hell happened to Eric?' Al demanded, alone now with Holly.

'At least he's writing—' But Holly was troubled.

'The guy had genuine talent – now he's playing games with himself!' Al exploded.

But she was doing little writing because of the demands of the Trio – and Al was doing none. Did talent atrophy – like unused muscles?

Al and Holly tried to maintain a calm facade about the coming recording session, but both were keyed to fever pitch. Marian blossomed forth with a heavy cold three days before the date – which cleared up at the last moment. The session ran five hours to cut the four sides. Two hours over time, Holly realized uneasily. But with the way the session was going, the record-company executives didn't care.

As soon as the session broke, Holly cornered the company's promotion man to make sure she would not overlap with interviews she was working to set up. She could hear Al off in another corner coaxing for a fast release. The five of them – Al and Holly and the Trio – piled into the luncheonette downstairs for coffee. The atmosphere was electric.

'It's in the bag,' Al chortled. 'That "A"-side is Hit Parade for sure.' The Trio lit up like the Christmas tree at the Rockefeller Center on Christmas Eve.

'We won't know till the deejays start plugging,' Holly protested. She sensed the three girls were already counting royalty payments. 'We'll—'

'I know all that crap,' Al interrupted good-humoredly. 'What sounds tremendous in the control room can lay an egg when the first pressing comes through. But not this time, kids.'

Al was right. The minute the disc-jockeys started plugging, the radio-station switchboards were jammed with calls for repeats. In no time the Trio had a record riding the jukeboxes. The record jumped into thirty-second place and the following week shot straight up to number five. The weeks were racing so swiftly Holly could hardly believe the calendar.

She and Al were working at a frantic pace – so immersed in the business of the Trio there was time for nothing else. Wendy quit her job to come to work in their office. They scarcely knew what month it was until Holly sat down to pay bills.

They moved from their small office into a suite, bought smart new furniture to match. Their circle of acquaintances was ballooning. Mostly record-industry executives, musicians, arrangers. They rode a merry-go-round of cocktail parties, lunches at Toots and Sardi's, after midnight get-togethers at the Stage and Lindy's – with publicity people, disc-jockeys, contacts to be primed.

Holly shopped – with stabs of guilty pleasure – in Bergdorf's and Bonwit's. The excursions for bargains downtown – at Klein's or May's – had disappeared. No time for such frugalities. Time was money, Al pointed out.

Then – with bewildering suddenness – Holly remembered, they struck a snag. The Trio's new movie turned out to be a dog. Al had never been satisfied with the number assigned to them. The tremendous splash they had all expected never materialized. The next three record sessions netted only mediocre releases.

Night after night – all through the hot summer months and into the autumn – the lights in their office glowed past midnight while Al and Holly struggled for ideas to push the Trio forward. Every song-plugger that roamed into the office found himself with an audience. They were desperate for a hit to keep the girls hot.

'This is crazy!' Al slumped over his desk. 'Why can't we come up with a pair of decent sides? What's the matter with the company – throwing the Trio such crap?'

'Who knows what's a hit?' Holly sighed. 'We

232

all liked the two "A"-sides on the last session. Maybe they'll make it.'

'The Trio's been out of the jukeboxes for months now. You have the royalty statement for the last quarter.'

'Wait till the pressings come in with the new sides,' Holly consoled.

They waited for the reaction to the latest session. Al, surprisingly, had holed himself up a couple of nights to work on an idea for a play. Holly was reluctant to recall how long it had been since Al and she had written a line except for publicity.

She remembered the afternoon she had returned from a series of disc-jockey visits to find Wendy shining like a two-year-old at his first circus.

'What's with you?' Holly jibed.

'Good news. Jerry phoned. Lola's giving him an annulment.'

'Wendy, that's marvelous!'

'He couldn't talk much from the office, but he said there're only minor complications now. I'm meeting him after work to talk about it.'

'Holly?' Al yelled from inside.

'He's been bellyaching for the last hour about where you were,' Wendy reported.

Holly charged into the inner office. 'What's up?'

'Your buddy called.' Al exuded triumph. 'He'd just played that copy of the "A"-side you left with him this morning.'

'Which buddy?' Al loved to talk in riddles.

'Your favorite deejay, that's who,' he chortled.

'Said to tell you he thinks it's great. He'll plug it to death. Looks like we're back in the running, baby.'

That same evening Al finished off his final cup of coffee and headed upward to his own apartment with the usual outspoken reluctance. Holly decided to wait up for Wendy. She was anxious about the minor complications Jerry had mentioned.

In her rush to get inside, Wendy had trouble with the key. Holly hurried to the door to open it for her.

'Holly, look!' With a pixie glow in her eyes, Wendy displayed the new ring on her left ring finger.

'Wendy, I'm so glad!'

'We can't get married for a while,' Wendy explained. 'Naturally, Lola has to make it tough. She's promised that the minute Jerry can hand over a thousand bucks she'll go with him to his lawyer about signing an annulment. I want to pitch in on the money angle, but Jerry – the dumb jerk – refuses. He's got close to six hundred in the bank.' Wendy smiled tenderly. 'He's so sweet sometimes I can't believe it. He won't ever set the world on fire, but he's all the guy I want. Thank God for that wonderful sense of humor. If we're not going to be rich, we'll have that.'

'Tell me about tonight,' Holly prodded.

'Jerry borrowed a car, and we headed all the way up to Yonkers for dinner. He didn't say a word till we reached one of those spots along the parkway for emergency repairs – and he pulled

234

off and told me about Lola. And gave me my ring.' She giggled unexpectedly. 'It's a riot, me going conventional like this – but I'm mad about it.' She inspected the minute diamond with infinite tenderness.

'It's sweet,' Holly insisted, knowing what it represented to Wendy.

'Not what I'd ever pick out myself, natch – but if it makes Jerry happy, then I'll swear it's beautiful.' Wendy sat enveloped in silence for a moment. 'Maybe I did a wacky thing with Jerry—'

'What?'

'I couldn't go on letting him believe I'd never had a guy. Not somebody like Jerry. Maybe it was a gamble, but I had to tell him.'

'What did he say?' Holly searched Wendy's face.

'He just kissed me and said he hadn't expected anybody as passionate as me not to have had something.'

'How much did you tell him?'

'I sort of rolled everybody up into one. Hell, I wasn't involved with that many guys, was I?' Wendy grinned. 'I used Eric – I told Jerry we'd been engaged for two years, and then we broke up.'

'Oh, Lord!' Holly broke into laughter.

'Was I a louse?'

'No. You could have gone along without saying a thing. Like Al always says, a girl can fool a man. But I'm proud of you.' Smiling encouragement, she went over to the kitchen. 'Coffee?'

'Sure, since we're fresh out of champagne.' Wendy followed Holly. 'With most guys it's great for them to play around all they want. You know that gorgeous line – why shouldn't a girl have her fling? After all it's normal, so what's so terrible? But when they get married, they've got this wistful hope that it's virgin territory.'

'I'm glad you told Jerry.'

'Holly, he was the sweetest thing. After I told him, he kissed me, and I could see he was getting passionate as the devil. I thought, after all, we're engaged – but he said he'd waited this long, he could wait another few months. Isn't he something?' Tears shone in her eyes, matching the sparkle on her finger. 'This is going to be a good marriage.'

Four weeks later the Trio was riding high again. The trade papers predicted their new record would hit the million mark. This knowledge showed itself in the confidence in Al's walk, the way he held his shoulders. Even the way he handled the papers, Holly was thinking as they sprawled across the sofa on Saturday night with the early edition of the Sunday *Times*.

Al thrust the paper aside now. 'Holly, we've got to get out of this hole. It gives me the creeps. What do you say we start looking for a house?'

'What do you mean?' The unexpectedness of it threw her into confusion.

'You pay rent, it's down the drain. With a house you have something to show.' This was fast becoming the national anthem.

'You need a car to search for a house.' Holly struggled to push down the tattoo of excitement beating in her brain.

'I don't want to spend next summer in this hole. And it wouldn't bother me if we got out right now. You don't want to stay in this dive, do you?' Al challenged. 'It's a joke, our living in this hovel.'

'No,' Holly said slowly. She glanced about the shabby living room. Those millions of years ago – when Wendy and she had first acquired the apartment – it had seemed sumptuous. But she understood what Al felt. In the humid summer months – like most city apartments – it was unbearably hot. Al complained that the fan only blew the hot air around. Most sweltering nights they sought relief on the Drive, with flocks of other cliff dwellers – sitting on the benches or walking along the river until three or four in the morning.

In the winter the heat was meagerly piped into the icy apartments only at the most conventional of hours. In the spring and autumn – the kindest of seasons – she and Wendy dashed for the Drive again – grateful to trudge along its paths, which led to the edge of the river.

Al refused to share these excursions. This city version of enjoying nature held no charm for him. He sat closeted within the apartment walls.

In the winter, city snow was an utter waste, Holly thought with a wisp of sadness – imagining the pristine whiteness of snow in the country. In the city, snow was too quickly dirty slush.

'Let's see what happens with the record deal first,' Holly hedged. 'Then we can talk about a house.' But could she accept a live-in arrangement without a marriage license?

Four days later Al bought a car. He purposely waited until Sunday morning to surprise her. Wendy had gone out to Jerry's mother's house on the Island for the weekend – Al was staying in the apartment with her. He had arisen at an unconscionably early hour – for him – on Sunday, prepared breakfast, then pulled her out of bed to eat.

She'd showered and dressed – then he rushed her out to the street. The car sat there – sleekly beautiful and alarmingly expensive. And Holly was wild about it.

'Really like it, huh?'

'Al, it's gorgeous.' And theirs!

He flung open the door. 'Look at the slip-covers. Custom job, the best.' Here sat tangible evidence of their success – something to flaunt before the world. 'I paid two-thirds cash – the rest we pay off monthly.' Al urged her inside. 'Let's move.'

'I'm not dressed!'

'Where we're headed slacks are great,' he assured her. 'Ride in the country to look at houses. Just looking,' he insisted, feeling objections rising within her.

Al started the motor with a sigh of pleasure. Holly sat next to him – tense with intrusive doubts. Of course, she had realized that any day Al would want to buy a car. If they hadn't run into that setback during the summer he would have bought it then. But shouldn't they have selected a less expensive car – to keep something in the bank for emergencies?

Every Saturday night Al grabbed for the Real Estate section, and Wendy waited impatiently for him to finish. She and Jerry, too, harbored fantasies about buying a house. Only a small down-payment, the balance like rent, the copywriters proclaimed – like modest benefactors of mankind.

'Under the GI Bill you can't be stuck,' Al pointed out. 'They inspect everything to be sure it's on the level. Besides, one good year and we'll pay off our mortgage. Who's going to carry a house for twenty-five years?'

Now Al and Holly moved along the ramp and on to the Henry Hudson Parkway in cozy silence. They were just past the first toll station when Al reached into his pocket to verify its contents.

'How'd you like to have a ring, baby?'

'What kind of a ring?' Unexpected skepticism crept into her voice.

Al chuckled. 'On the right finger, or you don't get it. Cost me fourteen hundred bucks, pulling strings.'

'What's the right finger?' she persisted.

'Engagement finger, you ninny.' He swung his eyes to hers for an instant – laughing.

'I suppose it could be managed,' she conceded, not thoroughly able to maintain the attempted flippancy.

'Here.' He tossed the box into her lap, then turned on the radio. 'I've got the other ring all picked out.'

Holly opened the box, inspected the resplendent diamond in its smart setting, slipped it on her finger.

'Like it?' His voice wore a satisfied lilt.

'Exquisite.' She slid her hand into the one he placed on the seat between them. 'It's a little big – but I'll take care of that.'

They were married – a month after Wendy and Jerry – at City Hall – late on a Friday afternoon, with Wendy and Gloria standing up for them. Her mother, Holly recalled, was on one of her safaris to Florida – that began after Dad died. Al called his sister out in Cleveland, but she was much too involved with her own family to fly in for the wedding. Holly was briefly hurt – for Al.

There was no time for any splash – even if they had been so inclined. The Trio was on a rat-race of dates. She and Al considered themselves in luck to be able to drive up to Westchester for two nights at a motel. Anyhow, she'd conceded humorously – the honeymoon was long since past.

Twenty-Six

The diapers in the washing machine, Holly hurried back to the apartment. Her mother held Jonny in her arms.

'Holly, he feels a little hot to me,' her mother fretted.

She checked, deposited a gentle kiss on one

cheek. 'He's fine. We'll go out as soon as I can switch the diapers into the dryer,' she promised. There were several dryers – nobody would bother that the diapers would sit for a while.

Her mother was talking on in that endless, rambling fashion that was part of her. The phone rang. Holly rushed to answer – aware that her mother was annoyed at this fresh intrusion.

'Hello—' She wouldn't let this be a lingering conversation.

'It's all right.' Claire's voice came to her with the richness of relief. 'I was worrying for nothing. The FBI is doing a check on some teenager in a family Bernie is working with now. They wanted to talk to him away from the office.'

'You see? You were worrying for nothing.' But she shared Claire's relief. Al and she had gone through their own private hell during the McCarthy period.

'OK, we'll see you tonight,' Claire ended. 'Bernie and me.' The babysitter situation had been handled. And Claire was impatient to see Ron after all these years.

Around 1 p.m. her mother left – with the expected quota of pique. Jonny had been fed, was drifting off for an early nap. Now she'd concentrate on party preparations. Polish the silver – remnants from more prosperous days. She was finishing this chore when the door chimes tinkled. A smile lit Holly's face. Wendy was here.

'Lord, I thought I'd never get away,' Wendy effervesced. 'I went out this morning to buy bagels and lox—' She grinned. 'To coax Jerry

241

into a good mood.' The effervescence ebbed away. 'What can we do? We have to live with things.'

'You talk to your mother-in-law?' Holly asked, heading into the kitchenette to put up coffee.

'No,' Wendy admitted. 'I chickened out. I'll call her in the morning. I need time to work up the strength. But a funny thing's happening all of a sudden. You know how I'm dying to get out of the Bronx into a house on the Island. Jerry's always so scared we won't be able to swing the payments and all – even if I drive myself into a steady job. Now he's talking about maybe we ought to start looking around.'

'Think you'll like it?' Holly was skeptical. 'Being stuck so far from the city?'

'We don't have to go more than forty-five minutes or an hour out. It takes me almost that long to come down from the Bronx. I'm dying for space. And the neighborhood's getting so creepy. Our block's OK, but a bad element's moving in all around. There've been a few incidents already. A girl in Carol's class was beat up last week by a gang of teenage girls. A ten-year-old was raped in the elevator in her house – five blocks from us.'

'Suburbia's far from Utopia,' Holly reminded.

Al hadn't been yelling for suburbia. They'd been through that. He wanted a spread of land in the country. 'A year,' he said. But it would be one year, and then another and another. How could she go along with that? How did she know her market wouldn't dry up? Now this California kick. It was absurd. He couldn't drag them out to the Coast that way.

'We're not buying right away, anyhow.' Wendy shrugged. 'There's still that ugly little matter of down-payment and closing costs.' A note of defeat clouded her voice. 'But it's something to think about and hope for. Without hope you might as well be dead.'

The phone rang. Wendy raced to answer. Al had not called her yet, Holly realized. Either he was awfully busy, or he was still in a foul mood over their battle this morning.

'What happened?' Wendy demanded, her voice laced with horror. Holly turned down the light under the percolator, hurried from the kitchenette to eavesdrop. Wendy sounded so disturbed.

'Look, I'll take a train right up – it'll be faster than a cab.' Wendy's face mirrored her distress as she listened to Jerry. 'Jerry, what's going on there?' She sighed impatiently, shaking her head.

'What's happened?' Holly hovered anxiously.

'That stupid playground behind the school! Carol and some of the neighborhood kids were playing there when a gang invaded with broken bottles and God knows what!' Her voice rose heatedly. 'It's not the kids in our own section, though they're no angels – but they don't go around swinging broken bottles. Jerry says that Carol has a cut on her arm that needs stitches. They're in the emergency room at the hospital.' Wendy's face suddenly softened as she focused again on the phone. 'Honey, how do you feel?' Wendy listened, eyes dark with concern. 'You're sure you're all right? Did the doctor say any-thing about X-rays?' Apprehension still hovered about her. 'Good, sweetie. Now let me talk to Daddy again.' She put a hand over the phone. 'Carol can be so sweet and down-to-earth some-times it's unbelievable. She says it's ridiculous for me to come chasing back home. She tried to keep Jerry from calling me. It's only the cut, and the doctor stitched it already. Now they're waiting for her girlfriend Dottie to be treated.'

'If Carol feels all right, she's not going to be sitting around the house all day. No need for you to be there.'

'The poor kid, what a thing to happen!' Wendy returned to the phone. 'Jerry, Carol says I should stay. Is it all right? I feel like such a stinking mother.'

Holly returned to the kitchenette to pour the coffee. Relieved that Carol was all right. But after this Wendy was going to be all the more determined to move to suburbia.

Wendy put down the phone, crossed to join Holly at the table. 'Everything's settled. I'm staying. Jerry won't go back to work today – he'll call up and explain. He'll take Carol and Dottie out for an early dinner and to a movie – to get their minds off what happened.' She lean-ed back tiredly. 'There's never one real calm period in our lives.'

'Stop worrying about Carol,' Holly coaxed gently. 'If she wasn't all right, Jerry would have told you to come straight home.'

'I keep thinking about how the hell we can get out of the city,' Wendy admitted.

'By the way I didn't tell the others this was a birthday dinner,' Holly warned. 'I didn't want everybody to come trooping in with presents. I said it was a reunion with Ron. I'll bring the cake in at the end of dinner.' Her mind focused on this morning's battle. 'Al's on a wild new tear – about our leaving New York and going out to California. First, it was the house in the country. Now it's California.'

'What can Al find in California that he can't find here?' Wendy challenged in disbelief.

'It's the rotten job. His never having time to write.'

'How many people do you know who're happy in their jobs? Little handfuls here and there – in professions. People work,' Wendy said bluntly, 'because it's the only way they can live. If they make a few dollars more, maybe they can grab in some of the goodies. You tell yourself life's going to be great with a new washing machine or a new vacuum cleaner or maybe an air-conditioner. Unless you're a nut, you settle for what's within your reach.'

'Al's never learned to compromise.'

'Too bad nothing came of that Off-Broadway production he had. When was it? Four years ago?' Holly nodded. 'I thought it was a terrific play.'

'That whole thing made me sick.' Holly shuddered. 'It was miscast because the money man had a girlfriend. You've heard enough about that. Plus there was no time for revisions, when Al was bursting to build up scenes. He swore he'd never do another play Off-Broadway unless we could finance it ourselves – but you know how costs have skyrocketed these last two years. It did one thing for Al, though. It switched him – fully – into the novel form.'

'He could get out of the stinking store if he'd get into hack writing,' Wendy reminded.

'He's had this book bugging him now for years—' Holly stared somberly into space. She could understand how he felt.

'It's going to be great to see the old crowd tonight. I can't believe how long it's been since I've seen Ron. Wow, he's really done well.'

'I should have picked up some autumn flowers. Maybe I'll pick up some 'mums when I go down for the cake.'

'Yeah, 'mums are all over the place, yelling, "Hey, what do you know? It's autumn." '

Holly visualized other autumns. The house in Westchester, the autumnal art show that was outdoors. The pungent aroma of leaves burning on weekends – which was the only time they were at the house except to sleep. She remembered the winter nights when snow blanketed the landscape – transforming the grounds about the house into a Currier and Ives print.

Sometimes it seemed as though that house had never existed

Twenty-Seven

December, 1949

Holly was alone in the office – on the phone with a record-company publicist – when the second phone jangled insistently. It was a broker calling from northern Westchester. Holly promised to buzz him back in ten minutes, returned to the publicist.

When she got back to the real-estate broker, he was ebullient about a new listing – positive it was exactly what Al and she wanted. So far enchanting descriptions conjured up by high-pressure brokers had dwindled down into disillusioning actualities. But Holly promised they'd drive out next day. Al was so keyed up about a house in Westchester.

Eleven the next morning she was sitting between the broker and Al on the front seat of the broker's car.

'I knew the minute I saw the house,' the broker was saying, 'that this was right for you.' He swung off the main road on to a secondary one. 'It's just a piece down here.'

The car made a sharp left, headed up a steep incline. Al and Holly looked eagerly out at the wooded area, rich in autumn colors. Al was beaming even before he pushed open the car door. The house was a sprawling ranch, set in a rustic background. On a tiny plateau to the left of the house was a swimming pool.

Al grinned, reached for her hand. Wariness crept over Holly – this wasn't their cup of tea financially. They went up the flagstone walk and into the house.

The living room was huge, with wide expanses of glass, a floor-to-ceiling fireplace faced in cut stone. The kitchen was straight out of *House Beautiful*. The dining room, the den, the three bedrooms, the two baths, showed expertise, sophistication. The broker was out of his mind showing them a house like this!

'What are the owners asking?' Al asked, and Holly's eyes widened in shock. His hand pressured hers, ordering her to play it casual. Al was out of his mind to consider this!

'Fifty-two thousand,' the broker said expansively, 'with the pool and three acres.'

Holly's stomach churned when Al began bargaining. The broker knew this was a sale. She read this in his eyes. Both Al and the broker knew. Half an hour later she reached into her purse for the checkbook to write a binder.

The closing went through in record time – though they wouldn't move in right away. The former owners cajoled for an extra thirty days' time in the house. After that the painters would come in. Al was impatient to take over, surging with proprietary pride.

Holly came back from the closing to find Wendy impatient to talk with her. Wendy hadn't told her she had a lunchtime appointment with an obstetrician.

'It was the nuttiest thing,' Wendy said exuberantly when they were closeted in Holly's small office. 'I went to see him, and he said – with this mad twinkle in his eyes—"Are you pregnant?" – and I said, "You're supposed to tell me!" '

'And he did – and you are,' Holly said, and Wendy nodded. 'You phone Jerry yet?'

'I practically ran to a phone booth. He's acting as though this was the first baby ever to be born. He's talking already about my quitting work the fourth month. I screeched, "No!" I ought to be able to work right up through the seventh.'

'I'll miss you like crazy.' Holly laughed nostalgically. 'Like when Al and I came back from your wedding. I walked about, looking at the empty closet space and the drawers – and felt so lonely!'

'I know. I felt almost like it was a divorce.'

'Your mother'll be thrilled to death about the baby—' It would be so strange not to be seeing Wendy in the office every day. 'Her first grandchild.'

'Oh, Lord, can't you hear her?'

'How do you feel?'

'Marvelous,' Wendy crowed. 'And the doctor says I can sleep with Jerry right up through the seventh month. This kid will have to get used to the fact that he has passionate parents!'

The baby – Carol – was almost five months old by the time she was able to persuade Wendy to come up to the house for a weekend. Jerry was working overtime – Saturdays and Sundays.

'Oh, do we need the money!' At the last moment Wendy reported she'd be coming up alone. Jerry had to work. His mother would sit with Carol.

Holly invited Mitch and Maria to come up, also. Only he could make it, Mitch reported at the last minute. Maria was afraid to take Roseanne out so soon after a bad cold. Holly sensed Mitch's pleasure in escaping for a weekend. He seemed to be chafing under the responsibilities of family life. Maria appeared sweet, bewildered, and unhappy.

On Friday evening Wendy and Mitch drove up with Holly and Al. Holly leaned back with a sense of well-being as Al turned the car on to the parkway. Mitch and Wendy sat in the back, holding hands like old times, singing all the old songs while they drove along in the cozy warmth of the car. This was like turning the calendar back to those early years.

By the time they pulled into the garage, the first faint snowfall had begun.

'From the looks of that sky,' Al prophesied, 'it's going to snow the whole weekend.'

'I hope it does,' Wendy said blithely. 'We don't have to worry about getting out until Sunday night.'

This would be the most relaxing period any of them had spent in years, Holly thought next afternoon as they watched the huge, seemingly endless flakes drop down to the lush white blanket that was the ground. It was as though time was suspended. Even Al's restlessness subsided.

They lounged before the living-room fireplace, piled high with birch logs – the radio providing soft background music. Now Wendy and Mitch rose to dance to an old Glenn Miller record some nostalgic disk-jockey had pulled out of his files. Al was heading for the kitchen. In a little while they would be summoned to partake in whatever small feast he was inspired to prepare.

Mitch was changing over from the radio to the record player. He bent over to scrutinize a pile of records Wendy had collected for his choosing. Mitch's too slender frame rested against Wendy's full ripeness. There was an extra fifteen pounds since the baby that Wendy couldn't seem to shed.

Holly wandered over to gaze out the wide picture window into the night. The crisp cool whiteness of falling snow whispered an invitation. She went into the master bedroom for boots and a coat, then slipped outside.

The sky was a dusky pink, heavy still with unreleased snow. As she walked, she found her feet sinking into the crunchy wetness until the snow was above her ankles, threatening to reach up past the protective range of the fur-trimmed boots. But the view was worth the risk. Only one house stood in sight of theirs, and this was at least three hundred feet beyond. In the silence of the night it appeared miles.

The rows of evergreens flanking the driveway were sprightly reminders of Christmas – like small replicas of the proud, tall trees that rose all around, as far as Holly could see, with fresh snow piled inches high on their winter-dark limbs. The air was brisk – exhilarating. Holly walked along, so lost in the beauty of the night that she jumped when Mitch's hand touched her.

'I didn't mean to scare you to death.' His smile was apologetic.

'I was a million miles away.'

'Anything special?' Mitch slipped an arm through hers as they walked along.

'Not really. I was thinking how wonderfully peaceful it is out here.'

'I'd give ten years of my life for one year of living free from the world. Maybe a cabin up in the Maine woods – driving into town for supplies once a month. I'd come out with some decent work then. I'd be able to think again.'

'Problems?' Holly asked gently.

'I don't know what's the matter with me, Holly. I'm lousy to Maria. I yell at her for no good reason. I'm sleeping on the sofa these days – I can't stand feeling her next to me in bed. You know me – I was never like that.'

'You've been working so hard, Mitch. You're letting things get all mixed up.'

'I don't know. The human body's such a crazy mechanism. Nothing seems to satisfy me any more. Did Maria tell you I was drinking like a lush for a couple of months? It's a miracle they didn't fire me. Then I snapped out of it – because I couldn't find what I was looking for in a bottle, either.'

'Could you take a couple weeks off, come up here and just rest up? We're hardly at home at all – you'd have the place to yourself.'

Mitch stopped, brushed off the snow from a

tree trunk, and sat down.

'Holly, all that stuff about Linda and Renée – there was never any truth in it, was there?'

'Yes,' Holly said, with all the gentleness she could muster.

'It happened after that flier crashed, right?'

'Yes,' Holly agreed – guessing it was important for Mitch to rationalize.

'OK.' Mitch's face tightened. 'You've told me and I know. Now do me a favor. Forget I asked.'

'Sure, Mitch.' She waited, sensing he wanted to talk.

'There was a while – not long – when I began to wonder about myself. There was a fellow – just a kid, really. We were taking some classes together – that year when everything was wild with the baby. You know how tired I was all the time, never getting enough sleep. I was taking that course in writing the novel – and I met him. It didn't last long. I knew it was all wrong.'

'Things just – happen sometimes, Mitch.' She tried to keep the shock out of her voice. Both Al and Wendy, as well as she, had nurtured uneasy suspicions about Mitch's traveling the homosexual road – yet his painful admission startled her.

'Holly?' Al's voice cut through the crisp winter night. 'Come on inside. I've got dinner ready.' On rare occasions Al cooked – and he expected appreciation,

Despite their success with the Trio, Holly was uneasy in that era because of the way their expenses seemed to outpace their income. When the bills piled in at the first of the month, she

253

was invariably stunned. Her task to deal with them.

Both she and Al were signing tabs at the most expensive restaurants – this was part of the Big Front. She wined, dined, and gifted disc-jockeys, radio and television people who might be useful. Al entertained record execs and talent-buyers. It was exciting and hectic. According to the books they should have been wallowing in happiness.

Al was trying – at odd moments – to get rolling on the novel. It was not going well. He was disgusted, angry – but determinedly kept trying.

For a while Al began to fill the house with guests every weekend. The guests were acquain-tances he convinced himself he should know better. This was the deal, he harped regularly – entertain, build up the right contacts, be smart. Al reigning over his minor kingdom, Holly thought – and was disturbed. Where Al belonged was behind a typewriter, pounding out a book.

Holly longed for a weekend of solitude now – with only Al and herself in the house. It wasn't the labor involved, she rationalized. They had been lucky about finding competent help in the village, though most of their neighbors griped about the domestics problem. It was the need for silence, for no intrusion of strange voices, for an opportunity to relax.

She kept silent about the assaults of loneliness in unguarded moments. The knowledge that this race for a bigger house and a finer car and all the accouterments filled only a surface need. Always, too, there was the glaring knowledge that their indebtedness far outweighed their material assets. Yet this soaring recognition of consumer credit, she conceded, was part of their age. Happiness came with payment books.

Like Al, she was plagued with the drive to write – but there was no time for personal side roads. Everything revolved around the Trio.

Their second spring in the house arrived in a rush. All at once everything was green. As usual, she and Al were maintaining their crazy hours. Chasing up and down the parkways at one or two in the morning, rushing back down again the next day at nine. They were old-timers now to the toll-gate attendants, who dubbed suburbanites 'liverwurst millionaires'. After meeting mortgage payments, suburbanites had money for little else, the gossip mocked.

She breathed a sigh of relief when the snow and ice were safely behind them. Al loved driving in any weather – it was a challenge to him to maneuver a car over rough terrain. She dreaded those nights when they crept up the hills on thin sheets of ice.

Once in a while now, she would steal a day for herself – away from the office – to wallow in solitude like a rapturous drunk. Now, with spring singing about them, she felt a rebellious desire to forget the city existed. To erase from her mind such things as recording dates, disk-jockeys, selling charts.

Al held court in the office every afternoon. There were the camp-followers, all eager that he do for them what he had accomplished for the Trio. There were the girls with too-tight dresses, perilous necklines, and rape in their eyes. They bothered her not at all. Al loved people and loved attention.

The spring days were suffusing Holly with fresh reverence for the earth's recurrent reassertion of its powers. She dropped to her haunches to inspect each fresh crocus, daffodil, each hyacinth. She clipped masses of forsythia, to fill the house with butter-rich yellowness. These mornings she joined Al in the car with candid reluctance.

'Want to stay home today?' Al asked good-humoredly when Holly pushed back her break-fast chair and began to load the dishwasher – her eyes fastened wistfully on the spring view through the wide window.

'I have no definite appointments today. Think it's all right?' If the day stayed sunny and warm like this, maybe she could put up the typewriter out on the terrace and take a stab at some writing. There were half a dozen ideas simmer-ing in her mind.

'Sure,' Al persuaded. 'Stay home and relax.'

Ten minutes later, he kissed her, hurried – whistling – out to the garage. With a sense of exhilaration, Holly carried the typewriter out on to the terrace, gathered together supplies, collected herself a warm sweater because – even with the sunlight splashing down upon the terrace – there was a chill in the air.

She frowned – two hours later – when the tele-phone shattered the pristine quietness, marred previously only by the clatter of the typewriter keys. She pushed back her chair and headed for the kitchen extension. It was probably Al. Everybody expected her to be downtown at this hour of the day.

'Hello,' she said with a lilt in her voice.

'Holly, I just got a crazy call.' Al cleared his throat in that nervous way of his when he was disturbed.

'What is it?' Alarm streaked her voice.

'Everything's going to be OK,' he said quickly. 'I got a call from the Psychiatric Division of Bellevue Hospital.' He emphasized 'Psychiatric'. 'They were trying to reach you. Eric gave your name as next of kin.'

'Eric?' Astonishment deepened her voice.

'He's not critical,' Al rushed to reassure her.

'What happened?' They had not seen Eric for over a year, Holly recalled. *God, where does the time go?* 'What's the matter with him?'

'They refused to tell me. They just said that you're the one person who'll be permitted to see him until the regular visiting day – on the next-of-kin basis. What weird stunt did Eric pull to land him in Bellevue Psycho?'

Holly's mind was jumping on a dozen tracks. Damn Al for always managing not to let her get a car for her own use. She felt so cut off from the world at the house like this. But Al was a nervous wreck every time she was behind a wheel.

'Al, how can I get there?'

'Call the village for a cab, then take the next train in. Want me to meet you?'

'Never mind, I'll go straight to the hospital from Grand Central.'

'Good, then I won't be late for my appointment. Hold it a sec – I'll give you the ward number and the doctor to ask for.'

Holly toyed with the phone cord until Al got back with the information. She said a hurried goodbye and rushed to dress. Not until she phoned the village for a cab did she realize she was trembling. Should she call Wendy? Better not. The thing to do was to get right over to Eric. Poor Eric. He had called for her. It touched her that he considered her that close.

She was lucky. There was only a five-minute wait at the station before a train was due in. She boarded the train, tried to concentrate on the morning paper – but this was futile. What was Eric doing in Bellevue Psycho? The question ricocheted through her mind. Would the train never pull into Grand Central?

Holly was at the exit when the commuter train completed its underground Manhattan crawl to come to a complete stop. She hurried along the platform, up the stairs, debated about the exit most likely to yield a cab.

In ten minutes she was walking into the gaunt building that was Bellevue Hospital's Psychiatric Division. She followed the signs to the reception area. Caught up in a web of unreality, she sat down to wait her turn to talk with the resident physician and to receive permission to go up to see Eric. Across the room a distraught couple waited with an elderly man who appeared completely disoriented from life. In a corner Holly noticed a policeman in quiet conversation with a young woman – red-eyed and self-reproachful.

258

'Mrs. Rogers,' the nurse called and beckoned her inside.

The doctor behind the desk was quite young. 'Have you been informed of what has happened to Mr Lodge?' he asked gently.

'No.' Holly waited, her pulse racing.

'A neighbor went to the apartment to borrow a cigarette. He discovered Lodge on the bathroom floor with both wrists slashed.'

'Oh God!' Holly gasped, eyes dilated in shock. What had she expected? She didn't really know.

'I have the report here.' The doctor opened a folder. 'The police interviewed neighbors. He was battling with a woman in his apartment last night. I gather she left. The neighbor saw the door open, walked inside. If he had not been skilled in first aid, Mr Lodge would have died.'

'I can't believe it!' Holly's voice was husky.

'Has he ever to your knowledge attempted suicide before?' The doctor's dark eyes were sympathetic as he probed, pen in hand.

'Never.'

There was always that edge of witty sarcasm in Eric, but never this. There was the much-circulated opinion – presumably basic psychiatry – that most people who attempted suicide were actually crying for help. How had they failed Eric? How did you know what to do? At the same time, doubt took root in her that Eric had expected anything except success in his attempt. The doctor said he would have died if the neighbor hadn't been trained in life-saving.

'I must warn you,' the doctor said, 'that another such attempt is not beyond possibility.

What we need right now is any information you can supply about his background. Family, habits, employment and so on.'

'I'll tell you what I can.' Holly searched her mind – anxious to fill him in as fully as possible.

The doctor listened to Holly, made notes. 'I'll give you a pass to go up and see him,' he said when she had finished. 'We've had to place him in the Disturbed Ward, since he became quite violent when he realized his whereabouts.'

'Oh, no! Eric is one of the gentlest people in the world! He's terribly sensitive, a talented writer. Can't he be transferred?'

The doctor sighed. He must encounter dozens of such cases every day, she guessed – yet his compassion had not dried up.

'We'll see what we can do tomorrow,' he promised. 'If he's quiet when he's examined, I'll have him moved from the Disturbed Ward.' The doctor studied Eric's chart again. 'Physically there was little damage, thanks to the neighbor.'

'Then he'll be released soon?' *What happens in cases like this? Is there a criminal charge involved?*

'That depends upon a great many things,' the doctor hedged.

'Is there any way of speeding it up?'

'Yes,' he said, surprising her. 'A patient can be signed out by an outside psychiatrist who takes on the case.'

'I'll look into that right away.' Holly was relieved to clutch at some concrete action. As short-staffed as they were in the city hospitals, the doctors must be relieved when patients were signed over to private psychiatrists.

'Here's your pass.' The doctor signed a slip of paper, slid it across the desk to her. 'We'll try to move him tomorrow,' he repeated.

Holly stood at the elevator – waiting for it to descend to her floor. Unnerved by the session with the doctor, she battled against tears. The elevator stopped, disgorged hospital personnel. She entered, gave her floor to the operator.

On the designated floor a double set of doors had to be unlocked. She relinquished her pass. An orderly led her inside the closed off area. Her throat tightened as she followed him.

'Visitor for Lodge! Visitor for Eric Lodge—' The announcement was passed down the long corridor ahead of the orderly and her. How quickly they got to know each other – as though members of a special fraternity!

The ward was overcrowded, with beds set up out in the corridors. It was like moving through a nightmare to gaze at the sick faces, Holly thought – anguish in her heart. A boy – a child, actually – came over and tried to wheedle a cigarette from her. An old man fell off the bed in his efforts to turn over. Two patients yelled a warning at Holly.

'Let him be. They'll say you pushed him if you try to help!'

Then a young-old face rushed to inspect her – its owner grasped her arm, startling her for an instant. A patient who wanted to reassure himself there were such beings as girls, who suffered an uncontrollable impulse to feel the softness of her coat, to touch her hair. At last, she stood in the doorway of the tiny room where Eric lay alone, his face to the wall. She moved hesitantly into the room.

'Eric.'

Holly spoke in a soft whisper that did what nothing had done since Eric had been brought into the hospital. He turned his face to her, and she took him in her arms while he cried against her shoulder.

When Eric was quiet, he tried to apologize. Holly rushed in with rash promises of future miracles – anything that might ease his mind. Eric held her so tightly her ribs ached – but she made no effort to free herself. She remembered his childhood, his father. How desperately he must have needed love.

She called Al from a phone booth. She could sense the shock engulfing him as she poured forth the full story.

'Look, we'll take him up to the house the minute he gets out of the hospital. When do you think that'll be?'

'We can have him signed out by a private psychiatrist,' she began.

'Call up the Psychiatric Association right now,' Al ordered. 'Ask them to recommend a man. Get the poor kid out of there before he goes really nuts.'

'I'll get on it this minute.' She was already reaching into her change purse for more dimes. She wouldn't even wait to get back to the office where people might pop in and cause delays.

It was almost an hour before Holly was able to contact a psychiatrist who was willing to have her come over immediately to discuss the situation. She brushed aside offers of appointments two weeks hence. She grabbed a cab, fifteen minutes later was sitting in the psychiatrist's office.

He had been in residence in a state mental institution for many years, he explained, and was thoroughly conversant with regulations. After a brief phone consultation with the Bellevue psychiatrist, he arranged to meet Holly at the hospital the next afternoon.

Holly was to write out a check for fifty dollars and promise to finance one visit weekly for an indefinite period. Twenty dollars a week was little enough to help set Eric on his feet again. The doctor refused to commit himself on the extent of improvement one visit a week might provide – but right now her concern was to remove Eric from the confining walls of Bellevue.

When Al drove Eric and her up to the house the next afternoon, Eric lifted one eyebrow in respectful amazement as the car pulled to a stop in the impressive driveway. He slid out of the car, sauntered about the grounds, inspecting while Al unloaded the boxes of groceries they had picked up on the way home.

'Hell, I left the meat down in the village.' Al grunted in annoyance, returned to the car.

Holly slipped a hand through Eric's arm, led him into the house. 'We can afford this like a hole in the head,' she said, 'but you know Al. He swore we could swing it. So far we've been squeezing by.'

She kept up a steady flow of conversation –

with a hope that Eric would lose that bitter, self-conscious air.

'All right, you can relax.' Unexpectedly Eric smiled. 'I'm OK except for food. What's in the refrigerator? I'll bet it's more interesting than spaghetti.'

'How about a chunk of porterhouse, this thick?' she gestured invitingly, going back mentally with him to the spaghetti days. In retrospect, they hadn't honestly minded.

'Sounds tremendous.' Eric flung himself on the long, low sofa before the fireplace. 'This thing work?'

'Sure. Not like that one back in the apartment. Remember?' Holly regretted it the moment the words were out.

'Yeah.' He was silent for a moment. 'I was cracked. Should have married Wendy years ago – instead of stuffing myself full of pipe-dreams. Know what happened to the great Sara?' he flung at her derisively. It was the first time he had talked about this. 'She threw me over for the television-repair man. Said he drove her crazy in bed.'

Holly hovered uncertainly, wanting to lead him into less painful channels. At the same time, she thought, perhaps it might be the best thing for him to talk it out.

'Throw a couple of logs on and see how much talent you have for building a fire while I start cooking,' she coaxed – uncertain about what to say that might be comforting. 'It's turning chilly.' She headed for the kitchen. 'Eric, I have a Royal portable here, in case you feel like working,' she called back to him. 'It's in your room.'

'Yeah—' Eric's voice was muffled as he leaned over the fireplace, but the bitterness was unmistakable. Whatever work he had been producing was clearly not to his liking.

Later – sitting before the fire, listening to records – Holly became conscious of the way Eric's eyes roved constantly about, inspecting everything with wise cynicism. Suddenly she realized the house was a barrier between Al and her and Eric.

It had been a mistake to bring Eric here. He craved material success, people fawning over him, his name on theater marquees. To Eric, what Al and she had achieved spelled success. Couldn't he see how utterly without roots this was?

They'd been opportunists – seizing on the Trio, to exploit them to the point where money was coming in comfortably fast. That was the unimpressive sum total. Neither Al nor she was writing. Only when that happened would they be truly content with life.

In less than a week Eric announced his desire to return to the city.

'I'll drive in with you two in the morning.' He avoided eye contact, offered no explanation. 'OK?'

'Sure—' She pantomimed to Al not to press him.

He'd be able to find a job through one of the temporary agencies, she reassured herself. And she'd paid a month's rent on his basement studio in the West Seventies. He'd refused to see the psychiatrist. They'd done all they could.

Al had embarked on a fast campaign to 'get Eric back on his feet'. This meant stuffing him with every delicacy available in the grocery stores, piling up magazines for him to read, driving home each night with new clothes for him.

Eric – Holly surmised – was snowed under by this avalanche of fine intentions. They only served to salt the wound of his own bitterness. The wall she had felt rising between them that first day remained in position. A week later unable to reach Eric by phone – Holly went to his apartment. He'd moved.

Sitting over a cup of coffee in a drugstore around the corner, Holly pondered over the whole situation. Had they been wise in bailing him out of the hospital? Had it been a terrible mistake to expose him to their own personal comfort in his state of mind? The house, the car, all the accoutrements of material success – which to him were tremendously desirable. She drained her coffee cup and went to the phone booth to call Wendy.

Wendy was frank. 'I can't let myself become emotionally involved in Eric's problems. I have my own family to worry about now. Besides, what's the point? He's determined to hide himself away until he's ready to emerge again. We know the pattern, Holly.'

Twenty-Eight

The phone rang, jarring Holly out of her introspection. She rushed to pick up before Jonny was awakened.

'Where were you?' Wendy joshed affectionately. 'You seemed light years away.'

'In our hectic past,' Holly admitted, scooping up the phone. 'Hello—'

'Holly, what about Eric?' It was Mitch, oddly abrupt. 'Is he coming tonight?'

'Yes, didn't I tell you I was able to reach him?' At one time – millions of years ago – she had suspected Mitch resented Eric. Resented his talent – real where his own was minuscule. She was conscious of that same undercurrent in his voice now.

'Do you think it's smart having Eric in your apartment?' Mitch demanded, irritation showing through.

'He's one of the old clique.' Holly was defensive. 'Why shouldn't I invite Eric?'

'You know what Eric's fallen into.' Mitch's tone was ominous. 'That hardbitten, rabid Commie mob!'

'He's not going to try to bring us over to his side.' *This is just a dinner party for a few people who were terribly close years ago. What's the matter with Mitch?* 'Al said Ron and Eric shared an apartment once – I figured Eric would enjoy seeing Ron again.'

'Oh, come off it, Holly! Stop playing Polly-anna.' Mitch's voice rose unnaturally high. Was he drinking? Holly was uneasy. 'Didn't you have enough trouble because of Eric?'

Holly felt her face grow hot. 'Things are different these days. We're not living in that insane era any more.'

'Eric may not have been a Commie then, but he is now,' Mitch said with unfamiliar vindictiveness. 'Every now and then I run into somebody who knows him. He's in so deep it would make your hair stand on end!'

'This is a gathering of old friends, Mitch.' Holly struggled to remain casual. 'If Eric gets political, we all know how to cut him off.'

'Is Wendy coming tonight?'

'Oh, sure.' Holly was relieved to be off the subject of Eric.

'How's the kid?' Mitch asked with a more normal warmth. 'Yours and Wendy's,' he expanded.

'They're both fine. What about Roseanne?'

'I missed seeing her last weekend – she had some school affair. I'll spend tomorrow afternoon with her, though. You won't mind if I leave early tonight, will you? No matter what happens, I make sure I put in two hours a night on the book.'

'Leave whenever you have to, Mitch.' Again, she heard an unsettling sound of agitation in his voice. Mitch was rewriting for the third time.

She was grateful that he hadn't asked her to read his novel. After years of ignoring the truth, she faced up now to the fact that Mitch would never be a writing success.

'I'll try to be early,' Mitch promised, and hung up.

'Mitch sounded so strange,' Holly told Wendy.

'What did you expect?' Wendy shrugged. 'He's popping out of his skin because Ron's flirting with full-blown success.' Wendy eyed her watch speculatively. 'I'll wait another half-hour and then try Jerry to see if they've got back home.' All at once she grimaced. 'Oh, damn! I think I left a soaking skillet on the range. Jerry's going to be ticked off. There are times when I think all men ought to be roped in and thrown together on a desert isle.' She chuckled. 'Too bad the biological urge makes them essential. Now he's on this kick about women being lousy housekeepers because they're basically absent-minded.'

'How can he believe that, with all the upturned toilet seats across the nation every day?'

'No matter how civilization progresses, the male animal will forever consider himself superior.'

'Maybe I ought to run over now and pick up the birthday cake,' Holly decided. 'If Jonny awakes, he won't mind as long as you're here.'

'Oh, we have a mad love affair going. Go get your birthday cake – I'll call up my character husband.' Wendy's eyes were restless despite the light tone of her voice.

'Stop worrying about Carol,' Holly exhorted

tenderly. 'She told you she's OK.'

'Until the next time that gang decides to go on a rampage.' Wendy was still upset. 'I know it scares the hell out of Jerry to take on a big financial responsibility like a house – but when are you really ever safe in this world? What guarantee have we got that we'll be alive tomorrow?'

'You're not supposed to get dramatic until after the cocktails,' Holly joshed.

'Remember when I used to get high and climb up on the piano to sing "The Man I Love"?' Her eyes were nostalgic. 'I wasn't too bad in those days. What rotten luck I didn't have the drive to push for a career.'

'You were good,' Holly agreed.

'I guess you know you're getting older,' Wendy said, 'when you look back and you realize the dreams are over. You try to settle for little things – but a piece of you is dead.'

'Let's not get morbid.' But Holly recoiled from this. 'Not on the night of Al's forty-sixth-birthday party.'

For all Al's cynicism, his bitterness about not yet doing what he wanted to do, he had not put dreams to bed, Holly thought. He yelled and griped – but deep inside was a deep-rooted belief in what waited for him.

Holly walked with small, swift steps towards the nearby bakery. Children skated past in shrieking exuberance. A jewel-collared black toy poodle charged in her direction because they had a long-standing friendship. She halted briefly to exchange affection with it. When Jonny was a little older, they must get him a dog.

At First Avenue she made a left. Her eyes swung to the large complex of apartments that flanked the east side of the avenue. If you were realistic, there lay the finest bargain in housing in the city of New York. Almost impossible to get in – certainly with a two-bedroom demand – without pulling strings. Wry amusement lit her eyes. With a child, in those buildings the management decreed you must have two bedrooms.

With a second bedroom they could utilize one as a den. Maybe with a place to work where he could close the door, Al would be less frustrated. That was why he wanted the country house. He had so much he wanted to say in the only way he knew how – in novels. Like herself.

Al could be so jug-headed sometimes, she remembered apprehensively. How could he be serious about their going to California? *But he is.*

Holly was aware of the woman walking towards her with a beaming smile of recognition. Who on earth was she?

'You're Holly Rogers, aren't you?'

'Yes,' Holly acknowledged uncertainly, and then recognition flooded her. Wow, the past was flying in her face this weekend. 'Mrs Edison.' She identified the pleasant, late-fifties woman. 'You lived across the road from us in Westchester.'

'That's right.' Mrs Edison beamed. 'We sold just a few months after you people bought. Back in New York again?'

'Yes, for quite a while,' Holly said without

271

elaborating. 'We have a little boy now. He's fourteen months old.' Tenderness crept into her voice. 'I guess we're doing things backwards, coming back into the city and then having children.'

'When are you having the next one?' Mrs Edison pursued, her eyes skimming Holly's figure. 'Keep them close together.'

'Not for a while.' Both Al and she wanted another – in the vague future. *Will there be a future for us? Will Al walk out on Jonny and me if I refuse to go to the Coast?* 'This one's keeping me busy.'

'Do you live around here?' Mrs Edison was inspecting her watch.

'Two blocks to the west,' Holly told her. 'We'll probably stay there – since we're so near to a good school. Though it sounds ridiculous to worry when Jonny's just fourteen months old.' She had said that about staying, Holly thought, to reassure herself. Suddenly nothing was certain in their lives. Not with Al carrying on this way. *But I meant it about not going to California.* 'We're in one of the new buildings.'

'I hear the rents in those new houses are wild,' Mrs Edison said. 'But I suppose it's elevating to live in those surroundings.'

'There's little elevating except the rents.' Holly's smile was ironic.

'The model apartments were so nice.' Mrs Edison was faintly wistful.

'How's your daughter?' Holly searched her mind for the daughter's name.

'Donna's married, has a three-year-old daughter, and teaches in the neighborhood here. Sometimes I can't believe the way the years race by. Donna had just started college when we lived in Westchester.'

'Does Donna like teaching here?' Claire had congratulated her, Holly recalled, for moving into this school district. She said it was the closest thing to private school in the city – if the Board of Education didn't louse it up.

'In some respects Donna likes it.' Mrs Edison's eyes went opaque for a moment. 'Oh, well, there's a disagreeable period in any job, isn't there? This year Donna's plagued with a clique of middle-class, education-obsessed mothers who expect their kids to be PhDs at seven. Maybe she'll have better luck next year.' She glanced at her watch again. 'I'm afraid I have to run. I'm picking up Donna's little one at her nursery school. I'll probably run into you again soon. Give my best to your husband.'

By the time Holly returned to the apartment with the white-boxed birthday cake, Jonny was awake and romping with Wendy.

'I feel better,' Wendy announced with a grin that poked fun at herself. 'I spoke to Jerry and Carol. They're home. She feels OK. Jerry's taking Carol and her friend out for an early dinner and then to a neighborhood movie.'

'Great. Now relax.'

Holly brought out the jumbo bowl that held the future sauerbraten, tried to concentrate on the details of preparation while Wendy and she carried on good-humored banter with Jonny. She loathed housework, but cooking was satisfying –

when it was for a festive occasion. Today the satisfaction was missing.

It was insane of her to be so nerved up over Al's stubbornness. Wasn't it? She was *not* going to California. This time he had to be reasonable. He couldn't disrupt their lives this way. She wasn't going to let him drag her away from New York. Yet a coldness clutched at her because she knew how immovable Al could be.

If Al insists, goes on out to the Coast without Jonny and me – it'll be the end. She'd thought they'd safely passed that hurdle – the near-divorce that practically every couple stumbles into somewhere along the way.

The phone rang. Wendy sprinted to pick up.

'It's probably for you this time,' Wendy guess-ed, reaching for the receiver. 'I've had my quota for the hour.'

It was Al. Holly crossed to the phone. What kind of a mood was he in now? What happened this morning had been triggered by Ron's arrival in town, but it had been there – underneath – all the time. The unrest, the rebellion, the bitterness. Ron threw a spotlight on the festering sore.

'How's everything?' Al's voice was without its usual lilt.

'We'll be rolling by the time everybody starts to arrive,' Holly promised.

Al cleared his throat – putting Holly on warn-ing. 'I was talking to a fellow at the store. He's moving in from suburbia, wants to sell his car. He figures in the city he won't need it. He's ask-ing eight hundred. It's in top-notch condition.'

'Al, we don't need a car.' *Don't think about the*

274

California absurdity.

'We need it,' Al shot back. 'He's driving it in on Monday so I can get a look. I've got to go. Talk to you later.'

Al refused to believe she meant what she said. In his mind they were already en route to California. How could he be so unrealistic when – for the first time in years – they were latching on to a certain security? California again? She shuddered in retrospect. Hadn't they had enough of the Coast – those years when their world was crashing down about them?

Twenty-Nine

1953–1954

Al and she were riding in triumph. He had swung a deal with a major film company for a three-picture contract for the Trio. The girls were slated for a preliminary test before signing the contract, but nobody was worried. These would be high-budget films – with heavy promotion behind them. The Trio had a hit riding the jukes again. Everything seemed right.

Al flew out to the Coast with the girls, phoned her nightly – with no hint of disaster until his fourth night out there.

'Holly, pick up a reservation for the next flight out,' Al ordered brusquely. 'Do it right away –

no stalling.'

'What's wrong?' Anxiety shot through her.

'I don't want to talk on the phone—' His reticence unnerved her further. 'Wire me when you'll arrive. I'll meet you.'

A dozen questions ricocheted through her mind. No, don't press Al. It would be futile. He was in a bad state, wouldn't talk until they were face to face. What had driven him into this tailspin?

A series of phone calls secured her a seat on the morning flight. All the way out to Idlewild her mind churned with unanswerable questions. She was exhausted after a night of insomnia. What happened that made Al send for her this way?

She sighed with relief – hours later – when the plane circled for a landing. She should have been fascinated by the newness of the trip west, she derided herself. She stirred only with restlessness.

Al was waiting for her at the gate. His eyes were bloodshot, puffy. That always happened when he missed a night's rest, she remembered.

'Let's get out of here.' His face was a taut mask.

'Al—' she began, anxiety spilling over in her.

'Later,' he said.

He refused to discuss anything except the weather and her flight until he had herded her into a restaurant and they were seated in a secluded booth, with their orders given.

She leaned forward urgently. 'Al, what's this all about?'

'The studio refused to sign the contract.' His eyes met hers in pained frustration. 'They've nixed the whole deal.'

She was dizzy with shock. 'Why? Was the test that bad?'

'The test was great. Everybody was drooling. Only all of a sudden, kaput.' He slammed a fist on the table. 'I don't get it!'

'What was their excuse?'

'They didn't offer any. It isn't because they're postponing the picture. They're set to start shooting right on schedule. Only without the Trio.' He reached for a cigarette. Holly noticed that his hand trembled.

'Al, this doesn't make any sense,' she said after a moment of baffled silence. 'They dragged you all the way out here – they owe us an explanation.'

'I told you it was nuts.' His eyes narrowed in concentration. 'Myers did say something to Marian I can't figure out. He asked her how much longer their contract with me has to run. He didn't know I was standing close enough to hear.'

'What'd she say?' Holly's throat tightened. Everything they had built up was riding on the Trio.

'She said it was running as long as we wanted to handle them – what do you suppose she'd say? That finished off the whole deal.' He gestured eloquently.

They sat absorbed in thought. Al's contract still had another year to run. There was no question in anybody's mind of its not being

277

renewed. People in the trade were saying the girls wouldn't wash their hands without asking Al.

'Who the hell's out for me?' Al broke the silence.

'That's absurd!'

'Is it?' he challenged, a nerve twitching in one eyelid. 'How else can you explain this mess?'

'We've got to do something about it.' How? Where did you begin in a situation like this? And the Coast was unfamiliar territory.

Al clenched and unclenched one hand. 'If this studio won't touch the girls with me in on the deal, you can bet your bottom dollar that's the story all over Hollywood. Somebody's after me. Somebody big.'

'Who'd want to knife you?' Holly searched her mind, came up with no answers. It was ridiculous!

'I've had plenty of battles,' Al admitted. 'I blow up when I'm sore – you know me. But ten minutes later it's all over.' He sat back, shook his head. 'Where do we go from here?'

'Back to the studio and demand they quit this double-talk. We have a right to some answers.'

'You try it – I can't talk to them.' Al exuded defeat.

'Did you have a fight over there?'

'When Goldberg gave me the heave-ho, we both got a little excited and yelled – but what did he expect? It's not that.' Al shrugged this off.

Holly could envision Al's 'getting a little excited' – and Goldberg's temper was notorious. They probably could have been heard all the way to San Francisco.

'Ross Lane handles publicity out here now, doesn't he?' Holly was groping for an approach. Al nodded. She had worked with Lane when he was in the studio's New York office a couple of years ago. 'OK,' she decided. 'I'll tackle Ross tomorrow.'

'Let's eat and get out of here. And the sooner we clear out of this fucking town, the better I'll feel.'

At eleven next morning Holly sat in the impressive offices of Ross Lane. A knot was tightening in her stomach as she listened to him. He hated telling her this – but he was being honest. For that she was grateful.

'Look, Holly, I know it's a low punch,' Ross said uncomfortably, 'but I don't want you to keep knocking your heads against the wall. Go back to New York. Forget this deal. Maybe in a couple of years things will blow over—'

'Why?' she tried again. 'Because Al fought with Goldberg?'

'It's a bad break, Holly.' He continued to be evasive. 'Forget the picture deal for the Trio.'

Baffled – frustrated, she returned to the hotel to report to Al. He paced – anger surging in him.

'I figured they'd give you the run-around, too. All right, screw them. I reserved a table at the Troc for dinner – for the five of us.'

He prowled about the room while Holly dressed, outlined his itinerary to show off the Trio in some of the 'in' spots – where a columnist or a columnist's stooge might be around to pick up items.

'Let's make a show of celebrating,' he ordered – though they both knew the truth was buzzing through the Hollywood grapevine by now.

Sitting at their table in the Trocadero – keeping up her end of the synthetically bright chatter – she sensed the undercurrent of unrest shuttling among the three girls. They had argued the matter, arrived at a decision – but the results were not to be divulged. Not yet.

The secretiveness of their eyes telegraphed a message. The Trio on one side, Holly and Al on the other. That earlier avowal of loyalty had come up for sharp revision.

'Know what we decided?' Marian threw into the ring with flip gaiety. 'As long as we're out here and there's nothing madly important waiting in New York for the next two weeks, we might as well stay on a little longer.'

'Sure.' Al gazed from one to the other of the girls with taut cynicism.

'There are some sensational parties we don't want to miss.' Gloria shivered with exaggerated anticipation. 'And there's this gorgeous hunk of man!' Her eyes drew Marian and Bonnie into the conspiracy.

In ordinary circumstances she and Al would have swallowed this. Gloria had an affinity for 'gorgeous hunks of men'. Ever since the nose job – though now Gloria was insulted if anybody even suspected plastic surgery. Of the three girls, Gloria was the one who had to be cut down to size from time to time.

'See you back in town,' Bonnie babbled at the end of dinner. Then the three girls made an ostentatious display of kissing Holly and Al goodbye.

They were back home less than ten days when they realized something was amiss in New York as well as on the Coast. Evidence piled up with shocking speed and clarity. For some impenetrable reason, they were high on everybody's 'Don't Touch' list.

People who had flung down the velvet carpet were now too busy to see them. Disc-jockeys who had treated Holly like a little Queen Bee – many of whom had been treated in the manner they liked best, via the checkbook – couldn't salvage a couple of free moments to say hello.

Al clung to the belief that he and Holly were getting the brush because they had lost out on the Hollywood contract. Holly refused to accept this simple explanation. This was a deeper, far more insidious wound.

The weeks slipped into months. They watched helplessly, sick with the havoc being wrought. The Trio's record royalties kept coming in – but nothing else. Every radio and television appearance Al had been working to set up was nixed. The record company was evasive about the Trio's contract – up for renewal in two months.

'This is the damnedest thing I ever saw.' Al paced up and down the office till Holly ached to scream at him. 'Those kids are the hottest thing on platters! They've had three records already that hit the million mark! All at once the freeze. Why?'

'Stop it, Al!' She closed her eyes in defeat.

She had puzzled over the situation till she was

281

dizzy with it. Night after night, lying awake, searching her mind for a reason, coming up with nothing – conscious that Al, too, lay sleepless. How could you fight when you didn't know what you were fighting?

'Did I tell you Marian sailed in this afternoon again, while you were out?' He sat down exhaustedly. 'Complaining like hell because the guys aren't plugging their platters.'

'Not because the stations aren't getting plenty of requests,' Holly said with a surge of rebellion. 'I've bought that information from switchboard operators and office boys! This is a definite campaign to cut off the Trio.'

'Them or us?' Al snapped back.

'It's the same thing – while you're managing them.'

'They were crying on my shoulder every day last week about how sales have slid down. Suddenly they're CPAs.' Before this they had never looked at sales charts, Holly realized. Now they searched for means to rub in their displeasure.

Everybody knew why sales were off – everybody in the industry. The disc-jockeys make the hits. Somebody in the upper echelon was nixing plays of any records put out by the Manners Trio. There were desultory plays of lesser releases – just enough so it was impossible to prove they were entirely cut out.

Their own record company was in on whatever was top secret. When she attempted to pump their promotion man, he merely shrugged and muttered something about tastes changing. Even a top record – without promotion – was lost in the shuffle. Now the clan she and Al had nurtured and pampered was handing out the ice treatment. Intuition told her everybody was waiting for Al's contract to expire.

'For God's sake, Holly, can't you break them down? You used to handle those characters like butter. What's the matter with you now?'

'Try talking to them yourself!' She was sick of his harangues.

'That's your job, not mine,' he flung at her, and slammed out of the office. This was the way most of their arguments were concluding lately.

When time for contract renewal with the record company came up, there was absolute silence. The girls didn't even bother asking about it. The trade papers heralded the news in bold type. The Trio was not being re-signed.

The word sped around town like wildfire. Nobody else was interested in signing up this potential gold mine. Not with Al Rogers doing the asking.

The girls – who had been so lavish with their cries of loyalty and affection – were not so warm. Where once they had flung their expensively dressed selves into Al's arms, they now managed a cool hello.

Holly recalled the tedious, tiring days she had spent shopping with the Trio – and they were forever shopping – so that when they appeared in public they might avoid resembling tenth-rate chorus girls on a binge. The dull nights she and Al labored with them so they might handle themselves creditably on interview shows. The multitude of hours they had listened sympathetically while Gloria poured forth tales of woe over her current love.

She remembered the messy gossip items Al killed, when Marian had fallen for a married stage star whose wife was out for blood. How did Marian suppose she felt when Al raced over to the hotel room Marian was sharing with her stage star, just in time to shove the actor into the bathroom and do a fast semi-strip so the wife's detectives caught Al in dishabille with Marian rather than her husband? But these things were now forgotten.

The office no longer spilled over with good fellows anxious to pass time yakking with Al. The entourage of butter-uppers was fast dissolving. When the time rolled around for the renewal of Al's contract with the Trio, the girls were down in Bermuda soaking up sun. Al was too proud, too hurt, to press them.

Three days after the expiration of Al's contract, Holly picked up that week's *Variety*. There – emblazoned for the entire trade to see – was the news that the Trio had just signed a new movie contract plus a solid recording deal with a major label – both handled by a top agency. Holly avoided showing it to Al until they were back in the house for the weekend.

'Great!' he approved bitterly. 'I'm thrilled to death for them.'

He ripped the paper into shreds, then reached into the bar for a bottle of Scotch and retired with it into the den. When he had slept it off, Al had arrived at a conclusion. The world was out to screw him.

Al went back to booking two-bit joints. *'At least they still speak to me.'* Holly fought a losing battle over expenses. She argued that they must stop hanging on to the expensive suite of offices, cut down on overhead. The overdue bills were piling up. They had almost nothing coming in. Al had grown accustomed to high living. It wasn't easy for him to switch.

When Holly walked into the office and saw Al poring over their loan books – the mortgage on the house, the furniture at home, the office equipment – plus the heap of past-due bills, she guessed on what road his mind was traveling.

'Only one way out,' he decided. 'We'll take a second mortgage. On the house.'

'Nobody will give us a second mortgage – not with our current income. We have—'

'All right, you tell me – how do we keep going?' Al broke in.

'Move out of this office, first of all – we're strangling ourselves with this high rent. We don't need four phones – one's enough.'

'Sure,' he broke in derisively. 'Advertise to the world we're through!'

'We've got to retrench!'

This was almost like being in the room with a stranger, she thought. If she stayed a moment longer – with the two of them facing each other like antagonists in the boxing ring – each would say things that couldn't be retracted. She wheeled about, hurried out into the reception room.

Al took a bank loan on the car. They paid off a few of the most pressing items. Yet he clung to the office as though his existence depended on it. When three months' back rent stared them in the face, he had no choice. He relinquished his futile hold and moved to a much less ostentatious address. He swung a personal loan – Holly never knew from whom – that kept them eating.

With time on her hands, Holly struggled to get back into writing. Al yelled at her to concentrate on television again.

'You did it when TV paid peanuts. Now it's a lush green field. You can do it – I can't.'

With the need for money beating at her shoulders, she knocked out a script, dropped it off at Sandra's office. Sandra was delighted to get the material, scolded Holly for staying away so long. Ten days later Holly received a phone call from Sandra.

'Drop by the office as soon as you can,' Sandra said. 'We need to talk.'

Waiting in the reception room for Sandra to finish up with an appointment, Holly explored her mind. In ten days Sandra could not possibly have had the script around much. What did they need to talk about? Had Sandra disliked the script?

Five minutes later Holly sat in Sandra's inner office, struggled to assimilate the facts that Sandra – stricken but honest – was ladling out.

'I don't understand—' Holly stared in shocked disbelief.

'Holly, the networks and agencies are scared to touch you,' Sandra reiterated. 'The minute they paste on the red label, you're finished.'

'I'm no more red than Eisenhower!' Holly was charged with indignation. She and Al knew about the red-baiting, thought it outrageous. 'That script I gave you deals with just that kind of mud-slinging.' And in back of her mind – though she had insisted on ignoring it – had been the knowledge that this might be playing dangerously.

'It was so good. I was stupid enough to show it. I was out of my mind,' Sandra admitted.

'It's not un-American to preach tolerance.'

Sandra fumbled with the disarray on her desk to avoid a direct confrontation with the protest in Holly's eyes. 'Look, we knew it was controversial material – but we blocked that out of our minds. We all know what's been going on the last three years or so with that creep McCarthy. Look what's happened in Hollywood, for God's sake.' It had happened to *them* in Hollywood, Holly acknowledged – but Al and she had not recognized it.

'It's all so crazy.'

'You could have written the Bible and they wouldn't touch you,' Sandra said gently. 'They have got a file on you that says Hands Off.'

'You mean I'm blacklisted?'

'That's the story, Holly.'

'I don't get it,' Holly said after a painful silence. 'So Al's talked out for freedom of speech – lots of people have done as much. We signed peace petitions – but so did millions of others.'

'Millions of others haven't bailed Commies out of Bellevue Psycho and taken them into their homes.' Sandra was blunt.

Everything danced wildly out of proportion.

'Eric? That's ridiculous – he's no Commie.' Holly experienced a weird sensation of being on the outside, listening to two strangers. 'Besides, Eric's nobody.' How did Sandra even know about Eric? How did anybody know? And if they did know, what did it matter?

'Everybody's somebody now. That dirty mob is digging up stuff about people their own families never suspected. I shouldn't be repeating this much.' Sandra was uneasy now. 'That character you nursemaided is living with some babe who's a card-carrying Commie – and in addition, she works for the Commie newspaper!'

But what does Eric's private life have to do with me and Al? While she sat there – silently laboring to puzzle out the whole picture – Sandra tried to make it clear she was out of sympathy with the whole smear campaign, yet unable to buck the situation. Listening, Holly saw the whole Hollywood deal – the disc-jockey freeze, all the rest – falling into focus. Everything stemmed from their friendship with Eric. Guilt by association, don't bother to ask questions.

She returned to the office, heard herself – with a sense of unreality – relating everything that Sandra had said to her. Al gazed at her as though she were speaking some foreign dialect.

'Al, it can't last – it's just a matter of time,' she fumbled. But in the meantime – havoc. Coming to the office each day now would be a grim joke.

They weren't alone in the storm of witch-hunting that infested the country. Every day new names were dragged into the limelight of this twentieth-century Inquisition. The most frightening part, Holly thought, was to see everyday average people – *good* people – being swept up into this phony hysteria.

The clerk in the grocery store in the village, the woman in the post office with whom she always chatted when she bought stamps were fearful. These people looked in their closets and under their beds each night – expecting to discover Communists. Careers built on agonizing years of struggle were annihilated with one whisper of gossip.

Holly sat at her desk, placed bills in a neat pile – as though order might diminish her panic. At home – as here in the office – everything was months past due. Furniture, electricity, the milkman, the grocery – this morning a letter from the bank pointing out that mortgage payments were sixty days late. No longer the polite little 'Past due' reminders – ultimatums now.

'Are you going to sit there all night?' Al demanded. 'We may as well hit the trail.'

'Al—' Holly was hesitant. 'What do you think we ought to do?'

'What do you mean?' His voice was hostile.

'The bank isn't going to wait more than another thirty days – you know that. They won't increase our mortgage – we went through that last month—'

'So?' He jingled the change in his pocket – watching her.

'It might be smart to put the house up for sale. Before we get dragged under altogether.'

'Like hell! I listened to you and got out of a decent office. You've pulled me down into this crummy hole. I'm not going to let anybody take away my house!'

With a sense of shock, Holly recognized the depth of Al's pride in the house. To him his home was a tangible symbol of his accomplishment in the world, his rebuttal to his mother's morbid prediction he would die a bum – because to her it had been unmanly to sit at a typewriter and build fantasies.

'I'm going out after a second mortgage – the banks aren't the only ones,' he said with a bravura air. 'I've got a solid lead already.'

'A loan shark?' A knot tightened in her stomach.

'So what? The bank isn't doing anything for us! I'm not talking about the kind of loan sharks you read about in the papers, that lend out ten bucks and collect five bucks a week interest. These characters run a legitimate business.'

'Yes?' Holly was skeptical.

'They loan the money to the business. At legitimate commercial interest rates. We put up the house as security.'

'And we miss one month's interest payment and they take over the house!'

'We've got to have cash, don't we? OK, I'm getting it.'

A week later she walked with Al into the real-estate office-front of a thriving loan-shark operation. Sam Hartman sat beside his lawyer's executive-size desk with a cigar in hand as he inspected a sheaf of legal-sized papers. She had met Sam once before, hated him on sight.

'This won't take long at all,' Sam said with a smile. 'You two look over these papers. It's the routine bit.'

She shook her head when Al offered to pass the papers over to her. Her body was required at this meeting. More than that they would not have.

Sam and his attorney were intent upon having everything 'legitimate' – to protect their unctuous hides from the reaches of the district attorney, she interpreted. It was like sitting at the deathbed of an era in their lives.

They walked out of Sam Hartman's presence with considerably less than they'd anticipated – because of all the additional 'charges' deductible in advance. Back at their own office – after a stop to deposit the check – Al scooped out the payment books, the bills. They brought the first mortgage up to date, paid a month ahead, sent out checks for the most pressing bills.

Al began to spend like a maniac – in a life-and-death assault to get them back on their feet. To no avail. In four months they were back where they had been before the second mortgage – plus now they faced the scandalous interest charges.

When she walked into the hock shop with her engagement ring, Holly knew this would be one of a series of trips. By the middle of the year nothing remained to hock. Al had annexed another loan shark – with both Shylocks ready to close in.

It was a matter now of the bank's catching up with them to repossess the car. They were scrounging even for dimes to take them past the toll gates into the city each day. A town garage for the car was a relic of the past.

They were afraid to answer the phone – in the office or at home. A hundred to one, it was another creditor screaming for blood. Nothing remained now but to sell the house, pay off everybody – before they lost the house to the loan sharks altogether.

She phoned up the brokers, put the house on the market. In Al's mind, everything was her fault, Holly thought tiredly. His whole attitude shrieked this.

Each time a broker pulled up before the house with prospective buyers, he would disappear into the woods behind the property. Few candidates showed up – the price bracket was high. And there was a real-estate slump.

When people arrived on a Sunday afternoon at the end of the second month, Holly suspected from their avid glances about the grounds that here was a live prospect. Al and she had looked about with that same appreciation.

Two hours later – after much private inspection and discussion with the broker – they made an offer. So low, Holly conceded – but how could they not grab at it? The loan sharks were aching to clamp their teeth into the property. This way, at least, they could salvage a thousand or two for themselves.

She was fighting for tomorrow, Al drowning himself in a morass of regret for yesterday. They were two strangers.

* * *

'Holly—' Wendy brought her back to the present. 'Why don't I take my boyfriend over to the park for an hour? That'll give you a chance to get the apartment ready for tonight without interruption.'

'Would you?' Holly felt a surge of relief.

'Of course I would,' Wendy said ebulliently. 'I'll even go to hell with my diet and have an ice cream with Jonny!'

It was almost two thirty, Holly noted as she jogged the vacuum cleaner free from the jumble in the utility closet. In five hours the living room would be full of the sounds of people who had been close for many years – and the knowledge that one of them – a stranger only to her – had pulled himself to the top of the heap.

Why should that make *her* feel defensive?

Thirty

Al punched out at the time clock, dropped his card into the proper slot, and sauntered towards the doors that led to the street. Two thirty, he noted with momentary complacency. How could he push off going to lunch any later than that? This way, the afternoon was sure to race past.

God, this was a creepy day. The way the past kept sneaking up, clobbering him over the head. Why in the world, for instance, was he thinking about Jake Saunders right now? He hadn't seen

Jake since right after Holly and he moved back into the city. Before that, when? It must have been ten years!

Al pushed through the Saturday afternoon crowd moving along the sidewalk. *Ron* made him think about Jake – because Jake was out in Los Angeles, doing something in public relations. Ron called Los Angeles his permanent headquarters. But if the play was a hit, Ron would make the New York scene. He would bask in playing the literary lion.

Al crossed with the traffic light, headed south to a cafeteria where the food was good and the customers would be at a low ebb this time of day. Eat lightly – Holly would be offering a feast tonight.

Unease filtered through him. Sure, Holly was all burnt up, the way he had thrown the California decision at her. But he wasn't going to sit back and rot! He'd had it up to his gullet with this way of living.

She didn't mean it – about not going out with him. Holly flared up, but she was bright. She'd see that this was important to him. Hell, his whole life was at stake.

Suppose she insists on staying here with Jonny? What then? I can't play games any more. Time is running out on me. Can I go out there, leave Holly and the baby behind? Holly can manage financially. She doesn't need me. I'm fighting for my life – why can't Holly see that?

Holly had such drive when she was a kid. What happened to that drive? God, she was still young. Maybe that was the real trouble between them now. Holly could afford to wait. *I can't. Why can't she understand that?*

Tonight at the party he'd sit down and talk to Ron. Not just about himself. About Holly, too. She could work as well out there as she could here – she was established with those people. They wanted what she gave them. She could do that shit any place.

But if she wouldn't see it his way – and she could be so damn stubborn when she was sure she was right – then he'd have to go out alone. This time no compromising. He'd buy a heap, drive out. With Holly and the baby – or alone.

He'd look up Jake out there. Jake would have contacts, steer him around. What a hell of a six years since he'd seen Jake last! They were back in the city, and Holly had gone into that foul-paying job, writing a house organ. Her mother fell, was in the hospital. Evenings Holly went to see her mother.

He'd been alone at the apartment – watching television – when the doorbell rang. He went to open the door – and there stood Jake. Same brash good looks, same professional charm. It was as though the calendar had double-backed and they were in uniform again – bitching about the war, boasting about what they were going to do if they got out of the war in one piece...

Thirty-One

October, 1955

'Jake! You old bastard!' Al stared at him with a mixture of disbelief and pleasure. 'What are you doing in New York?' He drew Jake into the apartment, slammed the door behind them. He caught the look of swift appraisal Jake was shooting about the living room. The apartment advertised – loud and clear – that Holly and he were not in the chips. 'Business or pleasure?'

'I'm running out on my alimony claim,' Jake explained with the candor that was part of his charm. 'Third divorce. This one's lawyer hit me like I was co-owner of Fort Knox. I figure I stay away long enough, she'll get married again – and I'm off the hook. Worked that way with the others.' He fumbled in his pocket for a cigarette. Al supplied one. 'Besides, you know me, Al. I got restless – all those years in one place. What arc *you* doing? I read in the trade papers about your tie-in with the Manners Trio. That go sour?'

'Blew up in my face,' Al conceded. 'Now I'm looking for fresh angles.'

'I've got some things cooking in television films,' Jake said leisurely. 'Nothing firm but lots of promise.' He squinted in thought. 'What are you doing tonight?'

'Holly's visiting her mother at the hospital – the old lady fractured a rib. I'm doing nothing.' A nerve in his eyelid jumped again, and he frowned in annoyance.

The dark, bewildered looks Holly covertly shot in his direction these months since they had come back into the city were growing less bewildered, more reproachful. He knew what she was thinking – when was he going to stop sitting on his ass and go out and do something? Guilt touched him because he knew the way he hammered out his frustrations on Holly. *Why do I do that? She's my Rock of Gibraltar.*

'Get on a tie and let's go over to this brawl I'm supposed to show my face at tonight,' Jake ordered. 'It's more your speed than mine. Mostly writers, a few television production people.'

'Writers?' Al recoiled from encountering people he might know. But how many writers did he know these days?

'Writers who're beginning to make it in television,' Jake amplified with relish. 'Writing used to be your beat, didn't it?'

'I sold a few short stories.' Al was brusque. What had he written since the war – in those years of building the Trio? A handful of short stories, a couple of which sold to low-paying literary magazines – plasma for his ego and guilt. The rough draft of two plays – neither of which satisfied him, a chunk of the novel that had nagged at him for years. 'I never went in for TV. Holly knocked around in it for a while. In the early years.'

Jake and Holly met once, Al recalled. Holly had liked Jake – though she was frank in labeling him a bull-throwing con artist. Holly was accustomed – lately – to his walking out of the house and not showing until two or three in the morning. Trying to walk off his frustrations. So go to this bash with Jake.

The first time he came home around 3 a.m. she sat up – waiting, scared, furious in her relief when he walked in. That was Holly – getting scared at the stupid, inconsequential things. She could accept the way they were thrown back on the junk pile – but she had been in an uproar when he stayed out till three without phoning her.

Holly would never walk out on him, would she? Lately they'd been sharing a bed – but little else. By the time he was ready to call it a night, knock off the television – his Big Escape – she was asleep. Sometimes, she pretended to be asleep. A year ago, he would have reached for her in the darkness. How long was it since he had made love to his wife? The realization tightened a knot in his stomach.

'I'll leave a note for Holly.' He thrashed about in a desk drawer for a piece of paper.

With the note conspicuously displayed, he strode into the bedroom – which accommodated only the double bed and night table. It was as lousy as that first apartment Holly and Wendy had shared years ago, he thought with disgust. But the rent was double – in deference to the rising costs of living.

298

On impulse he decided to change into the one decent suit that had not made the trek to the hock shop. He was glad Jake had popped in this way. Jake was a quick man with the promotions. Maybe together they could wrap up something big. He was beginning to think like Holly. Maybe she was satisfied to live on that crummy pay check she pulled in each week. Not he.

Jake talked the whole way across town to the eighteenth-floor over-furnished penthouse apartment – belonging to a host they were not destined to meet. Al was restless the moment the door closed behind him and he caught the cruising glint in the eyes of guests. Everybody there looking for something. Everybody with an axe to grind.

Across the clutter of people he spied Oren Williams, whom he had not encountered since – God, the late 1930s, he realized in disbelief. Seeing Oren this way shot him back to the days when he was breaking his back, knocking out one play after another – before he became a two-bit agent.

Oren had fed him many a dinner when meals were hard to come by – because he was too proud to write home for money and too stubborn to settle down into the straitjacket of a job. If anybody could find a job in those Depression days.

'Somebody you know?' Jake asked, momentarily distracted from his own searching.

'I doubt if he'll remember me.'

'Go find out,' Jake prodded. 'See you later.'

Jake strode off towards a small clique surrounding a heavily made-up, much be-diamonded matron. Al made his way towards Oren – engrossed in conversation with a slender attentive woman in her late fifties.

Oren had changed little in all these years. But then he had always looked older than he was. But the same pixie charm, Al thought, watching the woman lean forward to catch Oren's every word.

Though Oren was barely five foot four when he stood up straight and possessed little of the physical attributes calculated to evoke sensual reactions in attractive women, Oren always managed to have someone bright and attractive in his stable.

'Oren?' Al said carefully.

The balding, Hollywood-tanned man turned in Al's direction, for a moment was caught off-balance.

'Al,' Oren said joyously after that fleeting doubt. 'Al Rogers. My God, where in hell have you been all these years?'

'New York, mostly,' Al said, reluctant to mention his years with the Trio. 'In personal management for a while.'

'What happened with the writing?' Oren demanded. 'You talked great theater in those days.' His eyes narrowed in thought. 'Say, weren't you involved with a singing group? I thought I saw your name in the columns fairly regularly for a while.'

'The Manners Trio, honey,' the woman beside Oren told him.

'We broke up. Remember the great Red

Scare?' Al asked with an attempt at sardonic humor.

'We're out of it now,' Oren said – ghosts in his own eyes. 'At least, that's what everybody keeps telling me. Oh, Al, I forgot. You don't know my wife, do you? Laura, Al. Don't know how I ever lived without her. Six years now. I stole her from my agent out in Hollywood.' He chuckled. 'Lost myself the best agent I ever had but collected one hell of a wife.'

'You were out there writing for pictures, right?' Al asked. Oren probably knew Ron.

'The pressure's wild out there.' Oren grimaced. 'I'm getting old enough now to want an easier pitch. I've got some hot chestnuts in the fire. Keeping my fingers crossed on a possible TV series. We're working on the pilot now.'

In the back of his mind Al thought of the myriad of times he had heard this same opiate expressed, in endless variations – the elusive winning sweepstake ticket, the run of luck at a Vegas gambling table. He used to believe in that luck for himself. What had happened to him?

'Oren, we promised Maggie we'd meet her for dinner,' Laura reminded after a long interval of exchanged reminiscences.

'Oren, I've been looking all over for you.' A tall, almost gaunt redhead swooped down accusingly. 'Laura, you look marvelous!' The gaunt redhead kissed Laura, then puckered up for a mock-passionate kiss shared with Oren.

'Peg Landis is the queen of the confessions.' Oren dropped an arm about the redhead. 'Does she look like she has two husky boys tucked away at home? Al Rogers,' Oren said without elaborating on the category in which Al labored. 'Queen Peg Landis.'

'Not the queen,' Peg corrected with infectious humor, 'but I've got my fingers in the fudge pot.'

What was Holly doing – knocking her brains out on a house organ for a shitty weekly salary? She was so damn versatile – she'd do well in any hack field she tackled. But she was satisfied to hang on to any little patch of security. She'd made up her mind to lock up the past.

'Maggie's going to be waiting,' Laura reminded. Her eyes swept the other two. 'Why don't we all have dinner together?'

'Hell, wish I could,' Al improvised. 'I just remembered – I have to meet my wife in twenty minutes.'

He made a swift departure, pausing for a brief exchange with Jake – all involved with his be-diamonded matron. Holly would have left the hospital by now. They needed to talk.

She didn't say anything, but he knew she was burnt up over the way he was hanging around the house – doing nothing. She was *young*. She could bounce back faster than he could. Holly had some naive idea – in the first couple of months – that he would sit down and pound away at the typewriter ten hours a day. How could he, with their whole world shot to hell?

Holly had left a small lamp on in the living room. He walked into the tiny bedroom. She lay motionless at one edge of the bed. Something about the stiffness of her body told him she was awake.

'Holly,' he whispered. 'Holly—'

He sighed, went back into the living room to switch off the lamp, debated about flaking out on the sofa. No, he told himself with a tightening in his throat. He moved quietly back into the bedroom, sat at the edge of the bed, pulled off his shoes.

'Holly?' She remained motionless. Too motionless. She didn't want him to touch her. It was a painful realization.

All right, he considered as he stood beside the bed and stripped. This was his *wife*. He still had the inside track. He had to make up his mind where he was going, stop sealing himself up in this rotten vacuum. Begin to live. What did he want? How was he to get it?

Sleep was elusive. He lay huddled in loneliness until the day broke full and strong. Finally, he fell into a heavy drugged sleep, awoke at noon. The apartment was quiet.

He threw off the blanket, sat up on the edge of the bed. Shower, dress, go over to pick up Holly for lunch. She always went out very late – it made the day less long.

He was whistling as he showered. The trouble with him, he had been too busy feeling sorry for himself. First and foremost, he had to break through this wall between Holly and himself. He knew when Holly and he got married that it was for always. Not everybody went through the divorce mill – despite the statistics. Holly was part of him. How could he live without her?

He was swinging on to Madison Avenue when

he saw her emerge from her building. He was about to call to her when he realized she was not alone. A tall, thirtyish man walked beside her, obviously attentive. He swung about, walked away from Holly and her companion.

He spent the afternoon roaming about Manhattan – seeing nothing, thinking much. All right, what did he want? He wanted his wife. More than anything in this world, he wanted Holly. The way it had always been between them.

At five he hung about the entrance to the building where Holly worked. Staying off to one side – where she would not be likely to spot him when the crowds began to shove through the doors on to the avenue.

He stiffened when he spied her – engrossed in conversation with the same young man with whom he'd seen her at lunchtime. *Who's the creep? What does he mean to Holly?*

Holly was shaking her head, rejecting some suggestion. Dinner? Sack? He waited until she had walked down into the subway, checked his watch to make sure she'd be inside a train before he descended the same stairs. He knew what he must have to be a man. His wife and his work. Holly beside him and the typewriter in front of him.

Time was running out. He was a writer. Having Jake pop up that way – with his usual supply of bull, running into Oren after all these years, had forced him to look upon the future with clear vision.

Oren – spilling over with rich enthusiasm

304

about that nebulous TV series. Jake searching for the perennial broad to take first to bed, then to the bank. The savor of the rat race had fizzled away.

The next morning he stood at the employment office of the department store – waiting for it to open. Self-conscious. Faintly defensive. He was the first one inside. The girl stared at him when he hovered there at the stand-up desk – concentrating on the application form. He was offbeat, he guessed, for this sweatshop salaried job.

He finished up the forms, sat down to wait for his interview. To his astonishment, he was hired. There must be an acute shortage of salesmen!

OK, starting tomorrow, he had a job. The salary was stinking – a messenger boy did as well. But there would be that salary each week. It was a starting point. He had to show good intent.

And this daytime job would take nothing from him. His creativity would belong to the after-hours – away from the paycheck job. That had always been the trouble in the past – for both Holly and himself. How could either of them work to their full capabilities when so much was siphoned off to the Trio? Now was his time.

OK, go home, prepare a celebration dinner. Have it on the table when Holly came home from the salt mines. His taking the job would say a lot to her. Wouldn't it?

He bussed back to Third Avenue, sauntered into the supermarket to shop for supplies – checking the contents of his wallet first. A pair of club steaks – extravagant but this was an occasion. Idahos, the trappings for a tossed salad.

He was singing as he moved about the kitchenette. A bottle of champagne chilling on its side in the refrigerator. *Domestic* champagne out of deference to their budget.

He waited expectantly when he heard Holly's key in the door. He grinned at the startled look on her face when she spied the table, set with festive cloth – a hangover from the house – and silver. Chuckling, he brought forth the bottle of champagne from the refrigerator.

'So I've already spent my first week's salary,' Al exaggerated good-humoredly. 'I figure we rated one splurge before I settle down to the salt mines.'

So he'd be a working stiff. This wasn't the end of the road.

Thirty-Two

Holly poured herself a cup of coffee, walked into the living room to sit down with it. The sauerbraten simmered in its pot, sent forth tantalizing spices-and-wine aromas. Wendy had taken Jonny off to the park. This would be an oasis of quiet if she was not so upset over Al's ultimatum.

Is this the way separations happen? Out of nowhere? Leading to divorce.

A coldness closed in about her. She used to think that divorce was something that happened to other people.

Don't think about it tonight. Tonight they were having a party. Oh, it had been so *long* since they had filled the apartment with people.

It wouldn't be a crowd. She hated large parties paired off in couples. Al and she both enjoyed the company of people in small numbers – people with whom they had much in common. The way it was possible in urban areas. Not necessarily people in theater or writing – but their kind, who thought in their vein.

She swung her feet atop the coffee table in a gesture of libertine comfort. The living room appeared strange with the playpen banished to the bedroom for the night. Distaste invaded her as she glanced about the room. A replica of thousands of such rooms in apartments throughout the city. No individuality in these new buildings.

Her eyes swung to the wall clock. The moment of respite was shot. Time to borrow the table, extra chairs, and dishes from Betty. Cup in hand, she headed for the door. The phone rang.

'I'm about to burst right out of my skin,' Claire announced joyously. 'First, that crazy business this morning – and now I go shopping in the supermarket and run into this woman I knew back in graduate school. She's a big wheel with the Board of Ed. I haven't received official word yet – but Holly, my appointment came through!'

'Claire, that's marvelous!' Her mind shot back to the years when Claire had been teaching – and had spilled over with discontent and frustrations.

'The money's shitty, of course,' Claire sighed. 'The years I taught before don't count. I resigned – I didn't take leave. But at least this will get me out of the apartment. It'll pay for some domestic help.'

'I have to get steady help, too,' Holly acknowledged. 'I can't work this way – just calling in someone from a temporary agency when I'm climbing the walls.' *Here I sit talking to Claire as though everything is normal. How can Al do this to me – to us?*

'You'll have to wait until Jonny's three for nursery school,' Claire reminded. 'Though I had two kids who were two and eight months when I was running the nursery school up in upstate New York.'

'I remember,' Holly said with involuntary sharpness.

'We were crazy to go tearing off upstate the way we did,' Claire said with a flash of resentment. 'Bernie, the book lover. Opening a bookshop in farm country. The most popular literature in the area was the Sears, Roebuck catalogue!'

'I'm not worrying about nursery schools,' Holly backtracked. 'Not yet.' But the prospect of soaring nursery-school fees was unnerving.

'You don't expect anybody before eight, do you?'

'No, but if you're going to be downtown earlier, come on up,' Holly encouraged.

'I'd like to stop in to look at that furniture again. It'll be a chance to take Bernie in without the madness of the kids. We won't be late, though,' Claire promised. 'I'm dying to see Ron again – after twenty years!' Claire emitted a sudden shriek, triggered by activities at her end of the phone. 'Oh God, what now? Holly, see you later—'

Claire slammed down the phone. Holly headed again for her earlier destination.

'I'm being deluged with mail,' Betty greeted her – holding up an airmail special with foreign stamps. 'Things are happening so fast I can't keep pace. They're both coming home in two weeks. The plans now are for a Christmas wedding.' Betty's usually serene eyes wore a baffled unease. 'Rolfe talks about a job in advertising.'

'Practical,' Holly pointed out while Betty dug bridge chairs out of the depths of the closet. Why did she feel self-conscious about judging something practical?

'Maybe Marty and I both hoped Rolfe would not be completely practical,' Betty admitted. 'Sure, we wanted him to go to college, have that to fall back on. But deep inside, we both wanted him to fly.'

'He's still very young, Betty.' But she understood. Betty – and especially Marty – nurtured hopes for their child to accomplish, whereas they had only dreamt.

'I worry.' Betty was somber. 'I look for some signs of stability. I remember the three years when Marty was in and out of sanitariums – trying to find his place in the world – and I have to know this doesn't happen to Rolfe.' At best, Marty had achieved a tasteless compromise.

'You have to give Rolfe a chance to find his

309

own way,' Holly pointed out. 'At least he knows you're always there to help.'

'I'm glad I didn't mail out that last package of shirts and sweaters I bought for him. I'd been fairly good for almost three weeks.' Betty chuckled. 'And then I went on this last shopping spree. Every now and then Marty gets nervous – he asked me to cut down on the buying for a while. I don't know what he worries about,' she shrugged. 'There're always two more checks coming in at the next pay period. So we don't have much cash piled up in the bank. We have our pensions funds. We won't have to worry about living expenses for the rest of our lives.' But Marty was wistful because he had not served his talents well, and Betty – like Wendy – was a compulsive spender.

Betty helped Holly cart the extra chairs, the table, and the two cartons of dishes into her apartment. While they lingered in talk, Wendy and Jonny returned from the park.

'You look pooped,' Wendy commiserated when Betty was gone. 'Conk out on the sofa for a while.'

'Five minutes,' Holly agreed. 'And I'll soak in a tub for ten minutes instead of showering.'

'Soak for half an hour,' Wendy commanded. 'Live dangerously.'

Holly collapsed on the sofa with a sigh of relief. She was tired – but more because of tension than anything else. If she weren't so upset about Al, this could be such a cozy few moments – with Jonny toddling about good-humoredly, Wendy close at hand. The late-afternoon heat tinkling in the radiators and dinner aromas infiltrating the air.

But our marriage is at a crisis. How do I handle this?

Holly fed Jonny, bathed him, tucked him into his sleeper, and allowed him to roam about in smug freedom. Not until he was safely in the crib would ashtrays – lethal weapons in Jonny's hands – be brought down from on high, the dinner table set, cocktail glasses and shaker arranged at the bar – which was a relic from the house.

'Go on, soak,' Wendy ordered, settling down to a romance with Jonny.

Wendy was right. It was good to lie back in the warm, scented water, close her eyes – and almost forget that her life was about to be shattered. She lay there until restlessness propelled her from the tub into the routine of dressing.

She stood before the full-length bathroom mirror – concentrating at length on her make-up. This wasn't the sitting-at-the-typewriter Holly – nor the sitting-in-the-park Holly. Al enjoyed her pulling out the glamour tricks on social occasions. They had few enough social occasions in their lives these days. Would Al even notice how she looked tonight?

She reached for the turquoise wool crêpe shift on a hanger on the wall hook, slid it carefully over her head. She heard the raised voices in the living room, the excited squeals from Jonny that told her Al had arrived.

Running a brush over her hair, she heard

Wendy at the phone. Calling Carol probably, to soothe her sense of guilt at having a night out.

'Honey, we'll go shopping Monday evening.' Wendy was soothing Carol. 'We'll pick up some new skirts and sweaters for school.' Wendy trying to buy happiness for her child, Holly thought with tenderness for both. Wendy, the giving mother and the giving child. The last year of her mother's life had been horrendous. Wendy had shouldered the care her mother required with a stoic philosophy.

Holly hurried from the bathroom to greet Al. Nobody – not even Wendy – knew about the ultimatum Al had flung at her. Wendy knew, of course, that Al was throwing about this California bit, didn't know he was determined to go – with or without her.

'Hi.' Holly's smile was determinedly casual. Her eyes skidded past Al, concentrated on Jonny. 'It's late, you'd better shower and dress.' It wasn't that late, actually. He had plenty of time. 'Oh, want some coffee first?'

'Bring it in while I shave,' Al said. But his eyes were opaque. *What is he thinking?*

She put a light under the percolator, Jonny's bedtime bottle in a pot of hot water, and began dumping out ice cubes. Wendy was off the phone now, came into the kitchenette.

'What's with the coffee?' Al yelled a few minutes later.

'Coming, master,' Wendy called back and reached for the percolator to pour.

In a matter of twenty minutes Jonny was deposited in his crib in the bedroom with his bottle, the improvised dining-room table was set up, with early autumn leaves for a centerpiece. Wendy did some last minute touch-ups to her make-up. Al showered in the bathroom.

The doorbell rang. Holly scurried to answer. It was Claire, a festive glow about her. Alone.

'Bernie's circling around trying to find a parking space. The way he figures, in the time we've each spent looking for parking space through the years, we could have earned our doctorates. But he'd die before paying the high garage rentals.'

'Claire, you look terrific,' Holly approved.

'All-out effort.' A defensive note in Claire's voice. 'After all, we'll have a celebrity in our midst.' She spied Wendy, waved ebulliently, wriggled out of her coat. 'Oh, guess what I did this afternoon? Rented a piano.' Her voice dropped. 'I can't tell Bernie yet, but the rental applies towards the purchase price.'

'You're buying it?' Holly was startled.

'Eleven hundred dollars,' Claire said with satisfaction. 'Once I'm on the job, I can swing a loan with no trouble at all. Teachers are great risks at the banks.'

'Eleven hundred for a piano for a child to practice on?' Holly's smile was wry.

'Look, I want the best I can swing. Not just for the kid. To lend graciousness to the living room. I told you, Holly, we have to start entertaining. It's important for both Bernie and me, career-wise. You can't stand still if you want to get anywhere.'

'There was a while when Carol talked about

313

playing the piano,' Wendy reminisced. 'Thank God, she switched to the guitar. That we could afford.'

'I'm going to have to take it easy with Bernie – you know he's the cautious type when it comes to laying out a buck. But our living room is absolutely shot. How long can we live with furniture that's so beat up?'

'It'll be more beat up before the kids are in a human stage,' Holly warned.

'The kids will have to learn to stay out of the living room,' Claire said, an unfamiliar tightness about her mouth. 'We have a right to one elegant room in the apartment. Bernie and I have to live, too.'

'Holly?' Al yelled from the bathroom.

'He probably wants fresh underwear,' Holly guessed aloud, and dug into the bachelor chest for a supply before she headed for the bathroom.

'Who was that?' Al asked, emerging from behind the shower curtain.

'Claire.' It pained her, the way Al and she looked at each other this evening – with screens over their eyes.

'Where's Bernie?' Al had a special fondness for Bernie's quiet, offbeat humor.

'Looking for a parking space. On a weekend night, you know what that's like.' Holly placed the underwear in a corner safe from the spray. She hesitated. Wanting to say something to Al. Scared of unleashing a dam. 'I'd better go check on Jonny.'

Jonny was asleep, still clutching the drained bottle. Gently, she released the bottle, covered

314

him. He would sleep through the noise – nothing bothered him, thank God. She switched off the lamps, tiptoed out, closed the door behind her.

Bernie was at the door. She hurried over to welcome him, then went into the kitchenette to check the sauerbraten – which didn't need to be checked. Tonight – for tonight at least – let her forget the threats. Let this just be a birthday party for Al. He saw fifty staring him in the face – and he was scared. Did everybody have to be raving successes? *Was that necessary?*

In the living room, Wendy and Claire were talking animatedly with Bernie. He had his usual store of stories – humorous on the surface, poignant beneath. Al joined the group – with no outward signs of his inner turmoil.

'I don't know how I'm going to settle down among all these writers.' Bernie grinned. 'I once had ideas myself. So twenty years ago I bought myself a typewriter.'

'With your sources of material, you ought to turn out volumes,' Holly joshed.

'Oh, sure, I'll make the next bestseller list,' Bernie derided himself.

Was it because she was particularly sensitive to frustrations, or was there a self-reproach lurking behind Bernie's customary banter? Hadn't Claire said once – years ago – that Bernie wrote poetry in childhood? On the one occasion when they met Bernie's younger sister – the one who wrote songs for the Freedom Riders – the sister spoke resentfully of Bernie's relinquishment of writing. Where was there time, when Bernie held down a demanding day job as school

315

psychologist plus a part-time evening job as well? They could never manage without that second job, Claire insisted.

'Oh, I bumped into your neighbor next door as I came up,' Claire recalled.

'Betty?' Holly asked.

'Her husband. He walks around with such a sour look. Must be a real crank,' Claire guessed.

'Marty?' Holly stared in astonishment. 'He's the sweetest, most gentle person alive.' That wistful, lost look of Marty's must often be misinterpreted, she suddenly realized.

'Let's get some liquids flowing around here.' Al was brisk. 'Bernie, what are you having? I know the broads around here,' he jibed in a show of high spirits. 'For them you have to dilute good liquor with garbage.'

'Be gentle,' Bernie drawled. 'My wife's a potential breadwinner. Claire tell you?'

'With the younger kid so small?' Al turned to Claire, lifted an eyebrow. 'You'll spend half your salary on help and taxes.'

'I'll escape from the house.' Claire was blunt. 'And the raises come regularly,' she reminded with pride. 'Once I earn my doctorate, I can swing into college teaching.' Overnight it was no longer 'if' but 'when', Holly recognized with sharpened sensitivity. How many years had they heard Bernie mention an ebbing resolve to work for his doctorate? 'I've no yen to tangle with fifth-graders forever.'

'Remember,' Bernie kidded, 'for two years you tangled with three-year-olds. You're progressing.'

316

'God, when I think of those years!' Claire shuddered. 'A lousy thirty bucks a month they paid, and I had to go chasing up to parents half a dozen times a month to collect my money. And don't forget, I had the elite of the town. A nursery school was newfangled nonsense in that farm belt. They threw the kid out of the car, en route to work, and yelled, "How's Patsy doing?" But if you wanted to hang on to the nursery's clientele, you couldn't scream back, "Patsy's masturbating because she feels insecure at home." You had to wait for your once-a-year conference and delicately get the message across.'

'What about Jonny?' Bernie's face lit up with satanic amusement. 'You doing anything about lining him up with a good analyst?'

Al chuckled. 'We'll line him up with a good paddle across his rear, when the need arises.'

The doorbell rang. Everybody reacted, Holly noted. Everybody curious about seeing Ron Andrews after all these years. Al pulled the door open, and Linda threw herself into his arms.

'Al, how wonderful! You know, it's at least eight years since I've seen you and Holly?' Linda pulled herself away from Al to engulf Holly. 'Mitch told me about the beautiful baby. Do I get to see him?'

'He's apt to join us when we least expect it,' Holly told her.

'Wendy – and Claire—' Linda effervesced in a burst of self-conscious greeting. 'I haven't seen you two in fifteen years!' Linda's eyes went opaque. She was thinking about the Renée inter-

317

lude, Holly guessed. Mitch saw her, on her brief returns to New York. 'I shouldn't say that, should I?' Linda chastised herself humorously. 'I still don't admit to a day over thirty.'

'Do you remember Bernie?' Claire asked, a flicker of annoyance in her eyes.

'I remember Linda,' Bernie said. 'You haven't changed a bit, except for the hair.'

'I went blonde about two years ago.' Linda giggled. 'I had this sensational job in Paris – with afternoons off lots of times – so I went in one day and made the switch-over.' Linda swung around to Holly. 'I should have phoned you to let you know I'd be coming alone, but we didn't find out till the last minute—' She gestured in apology.

'Don't worry about that. All we do is remove a plate from the table.'

'What are you drinking?' Al piloted Linda towards the bar.

'Anything wet.' Linda's smile was synthetic. 'Living away from the States so long it's a wonder I'm not a confirmed lush. I spent three years in France, then went down to South America for a while—'

Holly went into the kitchenette to check on the pots on the range. She heard Linda spouting off as though she had memorized a travel folder. Wherever she was, Linda probably lived in her own tight little circle, Holly guessed. Being on the scene without being part of it.

'Say, Holly—' Linda began with a fixed smile, a glass in hand as Holly returned to the living room. 'Did you talk to Mitch this afternoon?'

'Yes.' Holly looked up. Warning signals shot up in her mind. Why did she feel apprehensive about Mitch? 'Just for a few minutes.'

'Oh, I thought maybe you were on a long gab fest with him.' There was that opaque look again. 'I tried to reach him for almost two hours, and the line was busy,' Linda said. 'I was going to pick him up with the car and drive him over. I have a Citroën.' Linda's French pronunciation carried a schoolgirl note.

'That sounds like Holly,' Al joshed. 'When she and Mitch get on the phone, consider the day tied up.'

'That's my social life,' Holly tossed back as the three of them returned to the group in the living room. 'But Mitch takes the phone off the hook when he's at the typewriter – so he won't be interrupted.'

'Doing what?' Claire was curious.

'Didn't I ever mention it to you?' She must have – Claire forgot. 'He's soft-pedaled the music for quite a while now. He's been working on a novel for the past two years.'

Claire lifted an eyebrow. 'Mitch?'

'Mitch did all right as a music copyist,' Wendy recalled. 'He didn't make a mint, but it was a living. Why did he go off on those temporary office jobs?'

'Mitch is looking for something creative,' Linda said sharply. 'When he works for temporary agencies, he can cut out any time he likes. He was all tied up when he was in the music field.'

'Look, how many people get to be creative –

except in bed?' Claire was impatient. 'We live in a push-button age. Let the computer be creative.'

'Mitch feels differently.' Linda's voice was ice-coated. 'He's started to paint, too. Did you know? Serious about it.'

'At his age?' Claire was derisive.

'Look at Grandma Moses,' Wendy pointed out. A twinkle in her eyes that didn't reach out to Linda.

'Mitch has a lot of talent. It's just a shame that the right people have never recognized it. Some people are all wrapped up in themselves.' Linda's glance about at the others was loaded with superiority. 'I've been everywhere these last years – I know talent when I see it.'

'We have some sensational records Holly picked up last week.' Al dived in with a determination to shatter the moment, pregnant with antagonism. 'Where're those albums, Holly?'

'I thought records was a dirty word around here,' Bernie kidded.

'We've learned to cope.' Holly shrugged this away with a faint smile.

The records – hilarious material well executed – were a marvelous idea, Holly decided. Everybody relaxed into comfortable positions about the room. Only Linda sat there, too erect, too watchful. Linda looked great, Holly thought – not drained, sloppy about her appearance, the way she had been for a while. This was almost that Linda she had first met all those years ago – except for the blonde hair and the faint lines.

The doorbell buzzed. Ron? Again, Holly was

aware of an electric excitement in the room as Al went to the door. Eric stood framed in the doorway for a long moment, with the well-remembered cynical smile.

'What are you trying to do, make an entrance?' Al slapped him across the shoulder with a joviality that Holly sensed was forced. 'Come on in!'

They had not seen Eric in several years. Now and then Eric's name infiltrated their conversation. But to see Eric face to face this way – *today* – was like being kicked into the past.

'Eric!' Holly shot forward to kiss him, was aware of an unfamiliar reserve.

There was a foreign note of superiority about Eric – or was it merely that he was ill-at-ease? Was it true – all those things that Mitch and others had said about Eric? The Commie cells, the hard-core Communist bit?

Looking at him now – as Wendy swept forward with sentimental exuberance – Holly was conscious of a new cynicism about Eric's motives. Why had he come tonight? Out of an omnivorous curiosity – to see Ron Andrews, the success figure among them? Eric looked at all of them – even Wendy – with the eyes of a stranger.

When the convivial greetings were done and Eric had been supplied with a drink, he positioned himself on the sofa between Wendy and Linda. After a moment of consideration he dropped an arm about Linda's shoulder. Linda was the one in their small clique with whom Eric had been the least close. In some odd way, he felt more at ease with her than the rest of them.

Holly remembered the sensitive, ascetic quality of Eric – all those years ago – that had set him apart from the everyday faces. Beneath the cynicism there had been humor – and tenderness. Time had drained away both humor and tenderness, she guessed – or left a harsh ersatz humor that saw everything out of focus. Now the fineness of his face had given way to flabbiness. The lines about his mouth were deep. The erect bearing sagged. She remembered the Eric of twenty-two and felt a painful desolation.

'Where's the famous guest of honor?' Eric mocked. 'Too busy to show?'

'Actually, Al's the guest of honor,' Holly said – too quickly. It was growing late. Dinner should be on the table this minute. Had Ron lost the address? He could phone – they were listed. Where was Mitch? 'It's Al's birthday.' Holly strived for an air of festivity. 'I was going to keep it as a surprise until I dragged out the birthday cake.'

Holly withdrew from the backslapping, slightly ribald birthday wishes being tossed about to check with dinner preparations. Why couldn't people be on time? She took away the place setting put out for Linda's absent friend. Linda had not even mentioned him by name. Or her.

Holly put up the oversized percolator of coffee, adjusted the jet beneath. She would *not* hold off serving dinner more than another twenty minutes.

'Should I try Mitch?' Linda asked with an air of unease when Holly walked back into the living room.

Holly nodded. 'Good idea.'

Linda dialed, waited, frowned. 'Now there's no answer at all.'

'Maybe he's on his way over,' Wendy said. 'It's only a ten-minute walk.'

'We'll wait ten minutes,' Holly decided. 'Then dinner goes on the table. Mitch and Ron can join us when they arrive.' Ron was probably at some cocktail brawl and tonight's dinner had evaporated from his mind. What was it with Mitch? He had taken an almost morbid interest in tonight's small party.

'This is the first *normal* party I've run into in years,' Eric said with sly sarcasm. He was watching them for reactions. 'Usually there's pot or LSD – or it's gay and before the night's over a pair of bull dykes are belting one another around.'

Holly's eyes widened in shock. Linda had gone white – her eyes frightened. How rotten could Eric be?

'To the dinner party out in Scarsdale or Brooklyn, we might not be exactly normal, either,' Al objected. 'Don't be upset, old boy – you're running true to form. We don't fit the slick magazine family picture, either.'

'What are you writing these days?' Claire asked Eric. But the undertone was skepticism rather than honest interest.

'I hocked my typewriter eight years ago,' Eric said. 'I haven't taken it out. Sometimes I *had* the money.'

'We both had "almosts" on Broadway,' Al reminded Eric. The somber glow of his eyes ill-matched the joshing quality of his voice. 'What's the use of living if you can't hope for something better?'

'You give up the Cinderella story,' Eric taunted. 'Settle for reality. What chance have we got in this dog-eat-dog world with Washington playing into the hands of the money guys all along the way?'

'No politics,' Holly injected. 'This is a party.'

'I'm not talking politics – I'm talking about humanity,' Eric said with unexpected heat. 'Who gives a rotten damn about people in this country? All that matters is the profit, the dividend!'

He was looking at them as enemies, Holly thought in sick dismay. Everybody here belonged to the 'they' of his indictment.

'Eric, you're living back in the thirties,' Al protested. 'Catch up with civilization.'

'This country hasn't,' Eric challenged, sinking back into contempt. 'Everything's geared to the dollar.'

'How would you plan on changing that?' Linda demanded, but didn't wait for a reply. 'Holly, you don't mind if I try Mitch once more? Maybe he fell asleep—'

'OK, so we need to do some educating.' Bernie refused to react to Eric's hostility. 'The schools need to teach kids our basic philosophy along with math and reading and the other elementary subjects.'

'We have no philosophy.' Eric's cynicism took refuge in contempt. 'We produce machines to go out and specialize and earn the buck. We produce people who hide in a corner while a neighbor is being murdered and calling for help.'

'You're talking about isolated instances that make the headlines. Not just in this country – all over the world. If they weren't shocking to most people, they wouldn't *be* headlines,' Bernie rationalized. 'It's the schools' responsibility to teach the kids the American philosophy.'

'Bernie, please,' Claire protested. 'Don't we have enough with the new math and the new reading and the other hogwash? What have kids got parents for?'

'It's nice to feel you're able to accomplish something,' Bernie said quietly. 'Like what I run into. A kid needs counseling like crazy – maybe a hundred hours of it – but I have to see the kid, the mother, the rest of the family, and bring about a miracle in a maximum of five hours. The office says they can't afford to allot more time to this kid. But in ten years he may be committing rape or murder because I wasn't allowed the time to follow through with him. That's what takes the heart out of a job.'

'Mitch still doesn't answer,' Linda broke in with an air of bafflement. 'I can't understand it.'

Holly rose to her feet. 'We'll have dinner now. No point in the rest of us starving because Mitch and Ron are delayed somewhere along the line.'

Despite the missing guests, the party acquired a festive air as they gathered about the table. Holly and Wendy brought in platters and bowls of food. Al poured wine. And then – a sharp reminder of the two untenanted place settings – the phone rang.

325

'I'll get it—' Al pushed back his chair.

He went to the phone. Stubbornly, Holly pursued conversation with Linda about a current play. The attention of the others was riveted on Al at the telephone.

'Oh, sure, Ron.' Al was casual, but Holly was aware of an undercurrent of anger. 'We understand.' He frowned, pantomimed his scorn of the conversation from the other end. 'Of course, drop over later if you can get away.'

'He's not coming,' Claire said derisively. 'I didn't really expect him to show.'

'Why not?' Holly's cheekbones were touched with color. 'What's so holy about Ron Andrews that he can't spend an evening with old friends?'

Everybody here knew Ron in some special way – except for Bernie and herself. He had shared an apartment with Al, had borrowed Eric's typewriter and Eric's clothes, had written a one-act play for Claire as a workshop project – and made a pass at her. Linda? Linda and Ron had been caught in bed together one New Year's Eve – when their hostess was arranging sleeping space for the hangers-on.

'Ron's hung up at some production meeting,' Al reported, heading back to the dinner table. 'He doesn't know how long it'll run.'

'You didn't honestly think Ron would waste an evening with us?' Eric drawled. 'I suppose you expect him to save house seats for us at opening night, too?'

'We'll buy seats,' Holly said, 'for four weeks after the opening. If it's a flop, it'll close by then and we don't waste our money on a lousy show.

If it's a hit, we'll have tickets – who needs Ron?'

Everybody knew the party had been planned at the last moment *because* Ron Andrews had walked into Al that way and – for a few minutes – had spilled over with auld lang syne. They had all been conscious, of course, of Ron's arrival in town – and its purpose. The Sunday drama pages had emblazoned the news.

'He won't show up later,' Eric decided with a sly smile. 'Ron hasn't needed any of us for a long time.'

'I'm glad he popped into the store that way,' Holly declared with soft defiance – triggered by Eric's smugness. 'He brought the rest of us together for an evening.'

'I'll have some more of that,' Bernie announced with an air of satisfaction – pointing to the sauerbraten. Dismissing Ron Andrews from their lives. But for Al and her, it wasn't that easy, Holly reminded herself.

Claire dug into the contents of her plate with a loss of enthusiasm. She was annoyed that Ron hadn't showed up. Perhaps she'd mentioned to someone about having dinner with an old friend – 'Ron Andrews, the playwright, you know.' Even if the reviews were lukewarm, having dinner with a Broadway playwright was a status symbol. Holly glanced about the table. *Does it really matter that Ron isn't coming?*

For a little while – when the birthday cake was brought in and cut and coffee poured – it was almost as though Ron had not been expected. No one had any illusions about Ron's coming later.

'What's with you, Al?' There was a snide

casualness in Eric's voice that brought Holly's back up. 'I heard around town that you aren't handling the Manners Trio any more.'

'I haven't been handling them for seven years,' Al said brusquely. 'I sell shirts instead of talent these days.' His face was taut. 'Not much longer, though. I'm quitting, going out to the Coast.' He made a point of avoiding Holly's eyes. 'We should be out there before Thanksgiving.'

'You're going to California?' Linda squealed with an exaggerated show of interest. 'I've never lived there. All over Europe and South America, of course.'

Claire spoke in an undertone, but her eyes mirrored astonishment. 'When did this pop up?'

'Al's been working up to quitting for quite a while. The California part just happened.' Holly took a deep breath. 'I'm not going.' She was conscious of Wendy's frozen disbelief.

Claire frowned, gazed from Holly to Al, back to Holly.

'Ron scared him,' Claire said. 'He'll get over it.'

'No,' Holly guessed.

'You know what you're doing?' Claire probed, while Eric concentrated on baiting Al. Nobody tuned in to the private conversation between Holly and Claire. 'Holly, Al and you have been through an awful lot together.'

'I can't run, Claire. Not with Jonny.' Holly gestured futilely.

'Reason with him,' Claire urged.

'When could anybody reason with Al?'

Enough of this. 'We're ready for more coffee. I'll bring in the percolator.'

While Holly was in the kitchenette, she heard the phone ring – shrill above the table talk. Al was picking up.

'Hello—'

Holly returned to the table – percolator in tow. A quality in Al's voice as he talked snapped her into watchfulness.

'Mitch, it's OK,' Al said for the half-dozenth time – with a surface quietness she didn't believe. 'Just relax, will you? I'll be right over.' Holl sensed an urgency in Al. 'Stay where you are. Read a magazine. I'm coming.' There was silence about the table now – an aura of apprehension as they waited for Al to be off the phone.

'Al, what is it?' Anxiety lent sharpness to Holly's voice.

Linda pushed back her chair. 'What's the matter with Mitch? I'm going with you.'

'No!' Al rejected. 'Bernie, you'd better come along—' His eyes were worried.

'Al, tell us,' Holly ordered with controlled firmness.

'It sounds like Mitch is going into some kind of a breakdown,' Al explained. 'He kept asking me to come over and get him. He – he's talking irrationally—'

'Let's go.' Bernie pushed back his chair, rose to his feet. The two men were in an unspoken truce to carry this off calmly.

'We'll be back as soon as we can,' Al promised, hesitating at the door. He frowned in thought for an instant. 'Holly, you've met Mitch's sisters a few times – try to reach them. Have them call over at the apartment.'

'I've got his sisters' phone numbers,' Linda said, white beneath her make-up. 'We were going to have lunch with them one day next week.'

Holly waited while Linda fumbled through her purse for the phone numbers. What had happened to Mitch to throw him off this way? Ron's appearance with a possible Broadway hit on his hands? No, she decided tiredly – Ron was the final, fingertip push that shoved Mitch off the precipice. This had been a long time in building up.

How can you ever know – completely – what went on behind the civilized facades convention demanded? How could you know what was the end of any one person's endurance? All those years ago, Eric tried suicide. Marty was in and out of sanitariums. How many people they knew supported analysts! Now Mitch – which they should have seen and didn't. But nothing like this for Al, Holly insisted with a sudden inner fear. Al was too strong!

But how can you know what's the end of any one person's endurance?

Thirty-Three

The door closed behind Al and Bernie. Linda silently held out her phone book. Caught up in unreality, Holly took the small leather book, walked to the telephone. She was remembering the anxious trip to Bellevue to see Eric. But that was another Eric, she thought as she dialed Mitch's older sister's phone number. The phone was busy. While the others about the table waited in somber silence, Holly tried the younger sister. There was no answer.

'No answer at Dorothy's,' Holly reported. 'Fay's phone is busy.'

'I'll have another piece of birthday cake,' Eric announced.

Seeming to enjoy the shock of the others, Eric helped himself to another slice of the cake. He was deliberately baiting them, Holly realized with anger – and guessed this thought echoed in the others.

Eric was lost. She wished he could be saved – but the battle had been lost before any of them had ever met Eric. She doubted that they would ever see Eric again – except by accident.

'We couldn't call Mitch's mother, could we?' Linda's voice was high-keyed.

'It would be awful to upset her,' Claire objected. 'When we don't really know what's going on.'

'She's a wonderful old lady,' Holly remembered with a tightness in her throat. 'When Mitch took this last apartment, she insisted on coming down to clean it herself before he moved in. She even hemmed dust cloths for him—'

'Couldn't you try Dorothy again?' Linda prodded. 'Maybe she just went out to the incinerator.'

Holly went over to the phone again, dialed Dorothy's number. No answer. She tried Fay's number again. Not busy this time – nobody there. By now Al and Bernie must have reached Mitch's apartment. Nothing for them to do here – just wait.

They contrived to carry on light conversation – mostly about subjects in the news. The construction of a concrete and barbed-wire barrier to seal off Berlin. The high unemployment rate. The ineffectual civil-rights bill passed by Congress. Holly was relieved – as they all were – when Eric decided to leave. Their Eric was dead. This was a stranger.

Holly closed the door behind Eric, walked back to the table.

'Did you ever encounter such a creep as Eric?' Claire burst out. 'Let him crawl back into that dirty sewer where he lives. Who needs to waste time with that?'

'It seems a sacrilege,' Holly said unhappily. 'When there was such potential in him.'

'The world's full of people with potential,' Claire scoffed.

'He might have waited till Al and Bernie came back,' Wendy said – her voice deep with hurt. 'He didn't have to make such a point of letting us know he doesn't give a damn about Mitch.'

'He's always taken pleasure in making people uncomfortable,' Linda said, her eyes contemptuous. 'I never knew what you all saw in Eric.'

'How was Mitch the last time you saw him?' Wendy asked Linda, who focused on breaking a small piece of cake into endless crumbs on her plate. 'Did he seem more upset than usual?'

'He was fine,' Linda insisted, her eyes fastened to the tablecloth. 'He kept talking about old times.' She frowned, fighting some inner uncertainty. 'He sort of hinted about our getting together – like marriage.' Linda took a deep breath. 'I told him that was impossible.'

Linda did not try to elaborate. It was unnecessary. The other three had watched her move into that other world – all those years ago. That was Linda's life now. Linda's choice. But Mitch had reached a drowning hand to Linda, anyway.

'The coffee's like ice.' Holly rose to her feet. 'Let me put up a fresh pot.'

When they heard a key in the door half an hour later, the four women swung compulsively in that direction. Al walked in.

'Bernie'll be right up,' he explained. 'He's looking for a parking spot.'

'What's with Mitch?' Holly asked.

'A complete breakdown,' Al reported. 'When we got over there, he was shouting irrationally into the phone. Obscene stuff – to his sister Fay. He'd called Dorothy earlier – before us. She

333

drove right over. She's with him now.'

'Where?' Linda demanded.

'The Veterans' Hospital,' Al explained. 'Fay got the drift right away. The ambulance arrived minutes after we did. It was kind of grim.' He sighed. 'We told Fay what little we knew. She headed over to the hospital with him. There was nothing else we could do.'

'What does it mean?' Wendy's voice was shaky.

'It means he needs professional care,' Al said. 'There's nothing we can do for Mitch now but wait until he comes out of this breakdown.'

'It's so awful,' Linda whispered. 'I can't believe this could happen to Mitch.'

Jonny woke with a querulous teething cry. Al went into the bedroom to pick him up.

'I'll call home and see if everything's OK,' Claire decided. 'I've used this sitter a couple of times before, so there shouldn't be any problems.'

'Can't you sleep over?' Holly prodded Wendy as they stacked dishes in the dishwasher. 'It seems such a shame to make that long trip out at night like this.'

'I'll have to, honey.' Wendy's smile was wry. 'Especially after Carol's awful experience today.'

Bernie returned with an amusing story to report on his parking escapades, but the atmosphere remained somber. Inside the darkened bedroom, Jonny fell asleep again. Al came out and started bar activities. Claire completed her low-keyed telephone conversation, rejoined the others with a glow of satisfaction.

'Mom was at the apartment,' Claire said, exchanging smug looks with Bernie. 'She was out in the kitchen when I called. The sitter's probably livid.' But Claire was pleased that her mother had made the effort.

Linda had become a heavy drinker, Holly noticed. They'd better have more coffee later – with both Linda and Bernie driving. She eavesdropped on the spirited conversation between Claire and Al.

'Look, why shouldn't women do important things in this world?' Claire said to Al. 'Is there a fundamental law that says we have to settle for the short end of the stick?' Claire's eyes were supercharged. Bernie sat back, with a glass of Haig and Haig in one hand and a copy of Max Lerner's latest in the other.

Holly and Wendy carried on an impersonal conversation with Linda. Part of Holly's mind remained tuned in to the discussion between Claire and Al. Al was all keyed up over what happened to Mitch. From the restless movements of his hands, the giveaway gestures, she knew he was disturbed. And there sat Claire, spinning her facile ode to ambition.

But ambition was open to a multitude of interpretations. To Claire, ambition centered around material rewards. With Al it was not a race for the great material achievements. It had been for a while – they had grown past that, along with their hold on the Trio. Al's was another kind of ambition – more a desperate need. Al had been a long time coming to terms with himself – but now he knew where he wanted to go. What was it Marty had said? He had never been used to his real potential. How many of the travelers to the psychiatrists' couch echoed that same plaintive lament?

Am I cheating Al? Does Al look at me and see a selfish, insensitive monster who blocks his way to fulfillment? But what about reality? Responsibilities? There's Jonny to consider. His future.

Al thought she was satisfied to compromise with the hack work. He felt she had no respect for her capabilities. But she was too realistic to fight for freedom when security was at stake. It all came down to one basic fact. Al was a gambler – she was not. They weren't free to go running with the wind.

'I should be going soon,' Linda said, checking her watch. 'I have to be up early tomorrow morning.' She moistened her lower lip with the tip of her tongue. 'Do you mind if I make one phone call?'

'Of course not. I'll put up fresh coffee – have a cup before you go.' Holly rose to her feet.

'Do you have a phone in the bedroom?' Linda asked, her eyes evasive. 'I'll talk very low – I won't wake the baby.'

'No extension,' Holly apologized. 'We live primitively.' She tried to make it light.

Linda debated for a moment, then headed for the phone. Wendy had joined in the conversation between Al and Claire, with Bernie an amused observer. How did Bernie feel, deep inside? Every now and then – on the rare occasions when Bernie and she came together – she sensed

336

an underground store of explosives in him, with the lid always just held in place.

Linda was speaking in muted tones, yet some semblance of desperation crept through.

'I haven't been drinking that much,' Linda's voice billowed in volume for one unwary moment. 'Anyhow, we're having coffee.'

Holly went into the kitchenette, then detoured into the bedroom to check on Jonny. The blanket kicked off as usual. She tucked it about him again, fought down an urge to pick him up and cuddle the fragrant baby warmth of him.

When she returned to the living room, she noted Linda was standing at the window – staring out into the night. The tenseness of Linda's shoulders, her immobility, spoke of inner turmoil. They would never reach through to Linda again. Had they ever?

Bernie intercepted Holly's look, smiled faintly, conscious of her mood. He sat in the lounge chair as though a spectator at a stage performance. For a little while, Holly guessed, he was relieved to be just a spectator.

'I know there's only one way out for us,' Wendy was saying with surface calmness – yet Holly knew the cross-currents of anxiety beneath that facade. 'There's no place in the city for people like Jerry and me. We can't afford a luxury apartment. The slums are closing in all around us. In the suburbs we've got a chance.'

'You think that, Wendy,' Claire scoffed. 'You get out there, and it's a vacuum. They don't live with the rest of the world.'

Bernie chuckled. 'Like my kid sister. She and

her husband went out to my older sister's house in Westchester for the weekend. They took along this couple with whom they're close. He's working for his PhD and his wife's a practicing psychiatrist. But my suburban nephews thought their aunt was bringing along her domestic help. The only blacks they know are servants.'

'One of these days we'll have to buy a brownstone,' Claire said with matter-of-fact finality. 'Maybe with another couple. How else can you ever afford six or seven rooms in Manhattan?'

'Why does it have to be Manhattan?' Al challenged.

'Because this is where we want to live,' Claire threw back. 'This – with a country place for an escape hatch.'

'OK, go out and make the money,' Bernie ordered. 'Then we buy a brownstone.' He focused on Al. 'What about you and Holly? Go along with us on a deal?'

'I told you – we're going to the Coast.' Al's face tightened. Holly stared into space – her face hot. Claire turned to her with a questioning look. 'If I hit on something substantial on the Coast, make a bundle, maybe in five years we'll be ready for a Manhattan brownstone.'

'So we'll discuss it in five years,' Bernie accepted.

The evening was disintegrating. Everybody was unnerved tonight. Particularly Linda – anxious to break away.

'We'll have to leave in a few minutes, too,' Claire said, when Linda had taken off with a sudden burst of vivaciousness. 'Mom's going to stay there until we get home. No point in keeping her up half the night.' She turned to Wendy. 'We'll drop you off at your subway station.'

The apartment seemed astonishingly quiet when everybody had left. Holly was alone – except for Jonny, asleep in the bedroom. Al had gone down with the others – to buy the Sunday *Times*, waiting in fat, folded piles for the Saturday night parade.

Holly stacked the dishwasher – rearranging to accommodate the extra load. It was too late to run it. The dishes would have to sit until the morning. The ones that couldn't go in would soak in the sink.

She walked back into the living room, kicked off her shoes, settled in a corner of the sofa. Mitch kept infiltrating her thoughts. What a nightmarish conclusion for what should have been a festive evening.

She closed her eyes – fighting off the visions of a confrontation with Al. The door opened. Al came in with the newspaper under his arms.

'Move your butt,' he ordered casually – but Holly was aware of the wall between them. 'We might as well make up the bed and be comfortable.'

Al began the hated process of transforming the sofa into night duty while Holly went into the bathroom, changed into a nightie, went through the usual bedtime routine. When she returned to the living room, Al was hunched up on one corner of the sofa bed – concentrating on the Book Review section. He wasn't going to start another battle tonight. Thank God for that.

* * *

Holly awoke with a guilty realization that she had overslept. She was alone in bed. The sections of the *Times* had been gathered together and stacked on the coffee table. For a moment the heavy stillness of the apartment triggered alarm in her – until she saw the note propped against the lamp on the night table at Al's side of the bed.

'Jonny and I had breakfast,' Al had scrawled in his large impatient handwriting. 'Fresh coffee in the percolator. I'm giving you a break – taking Jonny to the park.'

She lay back for a final few moments. Al took Jonny to the park. Knowing that soon he might not be seeing him? Not with three thousand miles between New York and California.

How can Al do this? How can he destroy a marriage that has survived so much?

Restless now, she tossed aside the covers, slid bare feet to the floor, pattered out to the kitchenette. The percolator was just warm to her fingertips. Al and Jonny must have been out for quite a while. She *always* heard Jonny, she thought self-consciously – Al must have picked him up at the first squeal of wakefulness.

While she moved about the kitchenette in breakfast preparation, her mind hurtled from one segment of last evening to another. Ron's last-minute withdrawal from the dinner party could have been legitimate, yet she found this difficult to accept. Claire and Al had both been blunt about Ron's using people. Nobody at last night's dinner was of current value to Ron Andrews.

340

Mitch. Poor Mitch. They had seen the signs of trouble – without understanding. She sighed, sat down to breakfast with the taste of defeat in her mouth. Don't blame this crisis in their marriage on Ron, though. Like Mitch's breakdown, it had been mounting all along. She'd refused to face it.

The ringing of the phone was harsh in the silent apartment. She crossed into the living room to pick up. How would she live here without Al? Financially, she could manage – if she budgeted carefully. But what about the emotional needs?

'Hello—'

'Hi, honey,' Wendy's voice came to her with an undertone of urgency. 'How're you surviving after last night?'

'Al let me sleep late. He scooped up Jonny and carted him off to the park. Did you have to wait forever for a train last night?'

'You know me,' Wendy said with a touch of humor. 'I sit down to read and forget about the crowd. That late I got a seat. Jerry met me at the station. Holly, something crazy came up. You know about the kids and that gang battle yesterday. Well, last night, Dottie slept over with Carol. She was all upset because her mother insists on taking her to the family doctor tomorrow for a complete check-up. Holly,' Wendy said tiredly, 'the kid's four and a half months pregnant!'

Holly was shocked. 'How old is she?'

'Fourteen and a half. The mother isn't anything to brag about,' Wendy said drily. 'There are four or five kids, all from different fathers. It's too late to do anything about the baby when Dottie's this far along. I figure – before we tackle the mother – we ought to have some kind of plan to offer for the kid's future. Claire and Bernie run into these situations, don't they? They ought to know about homes—'

'I'll phone right away,' Holly promised. 'And call you back—'

'Will you, sweetie?' Wendy said with relief. 'I'm ready to flip my lid with all this.'

'I'll get right back to you,' Holly said. These crazy little kids!

She put down the phone, cut the connection with Wendy, dialed Claire. Bernie would have answers. The phone rang several times before anyone responded. When it was picked up, Holly heard Claire yelling at Cindy before speaking to her.

'Hello,' Claire said, an edge to her voice.

'I didn't wake you, did I?'

'Are you kidding?' Claire jibed.

'I just spoke with Wendy,' Holly began, and launched into a full recital of the problem.

'Sure, there are agencies,' Claire conceded, a trickle of exasperation lacing her voice. 'Tell her to look in the classified directory under Social Services. Holly, I'm neck-high in my own problems right now.'

Shock silenced Holly for painful seconds. This was Claire? She had never refused when Claire sent out an SOS. Up till this moment, she'd expected the same response from Claire. Claire always came through. But now Claire was neck-high in her own problems. The world changed – only she stood still.

'Wait a sec, Holly,' Claire said – ashamed at her initial reaction. 'Talk to Bernie – he'll fill you in.'

Bernie came on the line, listened to the repeated tale, gave her names to call, phone numbers, contacts that would speed Dottie through the red tape. He was realistic, unruffled, interested – despite the matter-of-fact dry humor with which he discussed the pregnant fourteen-year-old.

'Thanks, Bernie,' Holly said gratefully.

She tried to call Wendy right back. The line was busy. She tried again – every five minutes for over half an hour. Each time meeting a busy signal. In desperation, she asked the operator to check Wendy's phone. The phone was in use, the operator reported.

Holly focused on returning the living room to its daytime status. Now, she thought, and dialed Wendy again. This time there was no busy signal.

'Hello.'

'I talked to Bernie,' Holly reported. 'Get a pencil and paper. I have the whole routine for you.'

'Go ahead,' Wendy urged. 'I think the kid's cried out by now. We'll go over to their apartment with this stuff.'

'I tried to call you a dozen times,' Holly reproached when all the information had been relayed. 'Don't those kids ever get off the phone?' It was always that way when she tried to call Wendy, of course. Wendy swore that if she could afford it, she'd put in a second phone for Carol.

'It was Jerry and me on the phone this time,' Wendy said with an unexpected lilt in her voice. 'With Mom. Holly, that's what I've been dying to tell you. Jerry couldn't take it any more – last night he phoned Mom and told her about Tim getting married. She practically went into hysterics for a while. She swears she'll never talk to Tim's wife. But in the meantime—' Wendy's voice was rich with excitement, 'she was so upset about what happened to Carol in the playground – and I suppose Tim's getting married triggered the thing,' Wendy acknowledged, 'that she's offered to put up the downpayment on a house for us out on the Island. She realizes it'll take us years to pay it back, but she doesn't care!'

'I'm so glad for you!' Holly spilled over with pleasure. Then caution moved in. She was conscious of her own distaste for suburbia, of Claire's and Bernie's rejection last night. 'Wendy, you're sure that's what you want?'

'Holly, I can't wait. You know how I feel about getting Carol into a good element. She's at the age when that's so important. Jerry's about ready to pop his cork, he's so excited. He wouldn't budge if we had to sweat out the down-payment – but now there's no excuse for us not to go ahead. We're picking up Mom this afternoon and driving out to look at this development she's been reading about. I'll call you when we get back.'

Holly went into the bedroom, pulled down a

pair of slacks, a blouse, from the closet pole, moved into the cozy warmth of the bathroom to dress. Ever conscious of the stillness of the apartment – the absence of Al and Jonny.

Dressed, she went back into the living room. At loose ends now. The apartment felt so empty. She missed the sounds of Jonny and Al. But Al would come back in a little while – and that confrontation she had been avoiding would come about. He said he was giving two weeks' notice on Monday. A coldness closed in about her. How could she even think about a life without Al? But he gave her no alternative.

Had Al put a warm enough sweater on Jonny? She crossed to the window, gazed out at the autumn-tinted saplings in their patches of dirt below. A grayness now, a harbinger of winter about everything. Seasons changed with relentless regularity. Why was she so reluctant to admit that life – *people* – change?

Plagued by restlessness, she went into the kitchenette, poured herself another mug of coffee, settled in the living room. Should she try the hospital, inquire about Mitch? No, call Mitch's sister later in the afternoon. What was there to learn – except that Mitch had a long, rough road ahead? At least, now they were aware – and would be standing by.

She should channel this bonanza of quiet into work, she chided herself. Instead, she picked up the theater section of the Sunday *Times*. A brief article snared her attention.

One of Sandra's clients – a girl who had made the show-business rounds with stubborn resolu-

345

tion – all these years later was breaking through with something more substantial than walk-ons on television and small parts Off-Broadway. A major role in a play receiving great out-of-town notices.

Others *did* make it. Not just this girl. Others in the theater and in Hollywood, who had been round-makers when she worked for Sandra all those years ago.

In a fashion she and Al had made it for a while with the Trio – though not in the area closest to their hearts. She sat at the edge of the sofa while doubt took possession of her. Where were Al and she going with their lives? For a while they had been caught up in the need for survival – but there must be more than physical survival. The *soul* must survive.

A coldness closed in about her. That was what Al was talking about, wasn't it? He refused to compromise with life. He would never admit, *'This is the way things are – we must accept that.'* Al was fighting for the survival of the soul – and she had been lost in physical survival.

She'd tried to stifle the dreams in Al. Dreams were for eighteen. *But that was wrong.* The human race moved ahead through its dreamers. In science, medicine, the arts. For all Al's ranting about the blackness of today, he clung tenaciously to the belief that tomorrow doesn't have to be black.

How had she allowed herself to be so blind? Trembling now with discovery – her mind sharpened into awareness – she struggled to cope with reality. She believed in Al's abilities.

She believed in her own – despite the facade of being content with the monthly check that kept them above water. Al refused to bury his dreams. So must she.

Let Al have time to finish his novel. Not one year, she decreed. Five years. He talked about rewriting the plays as novels – he was excited about the prospect. This was his time. Hers would come later. Other women saw their husbands through medical school and law school. Would this be any different?

In five years she would be forty. Many writers were never published until they were past forty. She knew – Al knew – she should be hitting a better market. Let her dare to dream – because only then would she be fully alive.

She started at the sounds of Al and Jonny in the corridor. Al fumbling with the key. A poignant love for her small family surging through her, she hurried to the door, reached for the knob, pulled the door wide.

'Hi.' She bent to scoop up Jonny. 'What kind of a day do we have out there?'

'Miserable,' Al reported. 'Until a few minutes ago, when the sun suddenly broke through.' As truth had broken through to her.

'Al,' she said after a sticky kiss from Jonny, 'I've been thinking about us—' She strived to sound casual, though her heart pounded. 'Was McHenry serious about that crazy mortgage arrangement on the house?'

'What's the difference?' Al's eyes were wary. He was protecting himself against disappointment.

347

'Tell him we'll take it,' Holly said. 'No down-payment, no amortization for five years, the way he said. We'll take it, sight unseen.'

'You're out of your mind,' Al said – but she felt the excitement charging through him.

'Haven't we always been?' she challenged.

'I thought you weren't buying that jazz any more,' Al countered. 'Little "Rock of Gibraltar" Holly.'

'So he may get the house back at the end of a year or two,' she shrugged. 'No, five years,' she stipulated. 'We'll give ourselves five years. Call McHenry right now,' she prodded. This was turning back the calendar, finding their younger selves again.

'You're sure?' Al asked. But he knew.

'If my market dries up, I'll flush out another,' she said calmly. 'I can work anywhere. You have priority with your novel. It's bursting at the seams – isn't that what you said?'

'It'll mean a lot of sex books – much hack writing,' Al warned.

'We've never gained anything the easy way,' Holly reminded. 'Why should we expect things to change now?'

She owed this to Al and herself – and to Jonny. The ambition that had faltered, gone underground in her had emerged with a lion's strength.

'The old boy will be pleased.' Al radiated a new confidence. 'He wants this deal.'

'Balzac was wrong,' Holly said softly.

Al lifted an eyebrow. 'Wrong in what?'

'He said, "Hope is the only sin." ' Holly's face was luminous. 'How wrong he was! Hope is the

348

gift that makes life worth living.'

She remembered Robert Browning's poem – 'God's in his heaven – All's right with the world!'

All's right with our world.